Each day the basket was replenished in a small way—a root, a piece of dried deer meat or salmon, some nuts. Meribah continued to look for her own food sources. She did not feel it right to take everything from the basket or to become reliant solely on her secret benefactor. The notion of total reliance on anyone except herself was becoming an alien one to Meribah. But she did continue to visit the tree hollow almost daily—never, however, catching a glimpse of the basket's replenisher. Between the basket and Meribah's own successes in finding nuts, food was not the problem that it had been several weeks before.

There were, however, two other problems. The first was that of making fire. Meribah had fifteen matches left for starting her fire. She tried hard to keep the coals going, but when she was out gathering, they often died. Meribah knew no other way to start a fire than by striking a match. She had heard that Indians rubbed sticks together until they smoked or sparks flew, but to Meribah this seemed like a magic reserved for Indians alone.

The second problem was loneliness. As Meribah's hunger diminished, her sense of loneliness increased. Questions of survival had occupied most of Meribah's time. As she grew more proficient at the tasks of survival and more a master of her cave-forest world, she had more time to think about things other than keeping her stomach full, her body warm, and the cave safe from predators. Meribah came to realize that simply to survive was not enough for her. There were periods of loneliness, of need for human conversation, that were as acute as hunger pangs. She missed her father, and she missed Goodnough. Their conversations had blazed as warmly as any fire. She yearned to share a thought, a word, a sunset, with another person, not just any person, but one who could respond in kind.

KATHRYN LASKY has written several books for young readers. She lives in Cambridge, Massachusetts.

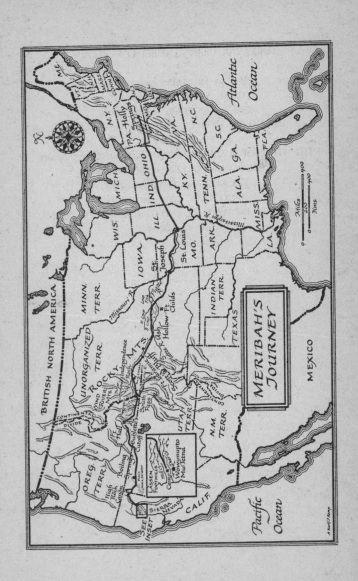

BEYOND
THE
DIVIDE

Kathryn Lasky

LAUREL-LEAF
BOOKS

LAUREL-LEAF BOOKS bring together under a single imprint outstanding works of fiction and nonfiction particularly suitable for young adult readers, both in and out of the classroom. Charles F. Reasoner, Professor Emeritus of Children's Literature and Reading, New York University, is consultant to this series.

Published by
Dell Publishing Co., Inc.
1 Dag Hammarskjold Plaza
New York, New York 10017

Laurel-Leaf Library ® TM 766734, Dell Publishing Co., Inc.

ISBN: 0-440-91021-8

RL: 6.8

Reprinted by arrangement with Macmillan Publishing Company
Printed in the United States of America
First Laurel-Leaf printing– April 1986

10 9 8 7 6 5 4 3 2 1

WFH

In memory of Susan Hurwitz Sorkin
(1946–1981)

Contents

BEYOND THE
DIVIDE

PROLOGUE

The doe's carcass was between them. Meribah stood near the head. Across from her by the hindquarters, two enormous vultures had lighted in the snow, their gaze coming at her like fierce black needle points. She stared back, her own eyes growing large.

A half-hour before, she had spotted the birds circling in flight, jagged wings printed blackly against the dull winter sky. She knew that if she could scare them off from whatever was on the ground below them, she could have herself a meal. The emptiness in her stomach had grown into a craving, and she started toward the birds, half running, half hopping, through the snow toward the circle of flight. When the circle had disappeared as the birds descended into the trees, she moved toward the memory of it. The cold air hurt to breathe, but she continued across the field, jackknifing her knees up through the snow. She picked her way across a creek and finally clawed up a short wall ragged with granite out-croppings. At the top of the wall she found the two birds presiding over a deer's carcass like high priests at some familiar mountain ritual.

As she stood challenging them in the half-light of the snowy forest, there was an echo of something past that for a split second almost distracted her. Then with a shrill scream as savage as anything ever heard in those mountains, Meribah charged the birds, jabbing at them wildly with her rifle and twisting her face into awful masks as the cries ripped from her throat. The birds squawked and spread their wings

1

menacingly but stood their ground. Outraged, Meribah cried, "Mine!" and with a powerful swing of the rifle's butt slashed at one of the bird's spreading wings. Black feathers flew up in swirls. The bird seemed stunned for a second. The wing bent at an awkward angle. The other bird had flown off. "Fly! Fly!" she hissed. Painfully, with one wing brushing the snow, the bird began to lift. For several yards it skimmed close to the ground while Meribah prayed, cursed, and willed it into flight.

The black form rose and vanished over the ridge where the other bird had already flown. Meribah watched as they disappeared. Even with a broken wing, she thought, that bird can make it to the gold-mining camps in the valley, to life, to food. Why did they come up here at all? She cut off the thought because she knew the answer too well. Then pulling out her knife, she walked over to the doe's carcass and hoped that between the wolves and the vultures something had been left for her, Meribah Simon, who was fourteen years old, alone and starving in the Sierra Nevada.

I

THE SAFE VALLEY

She heard her parents' voices in the other room. The sounds were low and unclear, so she tiptoed down the back stairs a little closer and waited in the shadows.

"I can't work this farm any more, Constance."

Had she heard him right? Meribah lowered herself down two more steps, pressing herself close to the wall. Now she could see them but they could not see her. She had imagined them to be facing each other, but her mother's back was turned, and instead she was staring straight ahead at a blank white wall.

"No, thou cannot," she said, still facing the wall, "not if thou continues in thy ways."

This was the part that Meribah could never understand— "his way." When her cousin John Stoltzfus had taken to "his way," or "worldly ways," it had been so clear. He had begun to wear fancy clothes and even to talk to girls who were not Amish. But when her father had gone his way against the church elders, he had only attended the funeral of a man who was not a strict Amish. What could be less fancy than a funeral? Less worldly? Meribah studied him carefully, as he stood there in the small room in his broadbrim hat, black trousers with suspenders, and sackcloth coat without lapels. He had not changed at all as far as she could tell. The only thing that seemed different were his hands which hung lifeless and odd-looking from his sleeves. Looking at them, Meribah could remember their powerful and lively movements as they carved beautiful wooden things, like the birthday dolls.

3

She leaned away from the wall to see a little more, and her cheek left a sweaty mark on the white plaster. The room appeared much smaller than she had ever noticed. The beams seemed to press down and take a scrape at her father's head, and she thought that he had to hunch over a bit while standing there.

"Well, the farm needs all of us together," he said. "The winter damage is too much, and if I'm not permitted to manage these affairs . . . ."

"Thou knows . . . ." Her mother's voice was taut but level.

"I know! I know!" He spoke insistently, repeating the words as if trying not to say more. "I know," he said again. "But, Constance, we must!"

"Must what?" She finally turned around. "I shouldn't even be speaking to thee."

"But spring is here. The harrow is broken. Planting time is coming. We can't afford another year like last year. It'll wipe us out. I'm not permitted to live in this house or speak to my own family. Now the bishops tell me, thy own brothers tell me, I cannot manage the farm or borrow the money we need for seed. Thou understands what this means? I cannot even provide for my own—our own—children!"

Meribah shrank back into the shadows and concentrated on making herself small and flat against the wall and on not thinking, for what was happening in her house was beyond understanding. Work, family, God—as specified by the Amish community, the relationships among these were rigid and unquestionable, enforced by the bishops and reinforced by group pressure. There was no room for error. To err meant to be shunned, to be punished by being isolated from society, starting with that of the violator's own family. This was the Amish way of justice, ensuring security but little freedom. And Meribah suddenly felt as if the beams were now pressing down from above on her, that the walls were leaning in and narrowing the living space until there was nowhere to turn, no place to think, to dream. There were only shadows for eavesdropping and low-ceilinged rooms for hoarsely whispered exchanges.

This was the closest Meribah had ever seen her parents come to an argument. They rarely showed anger, at least not in words. She remembered a time long before when her father had criticized the church bishops, two of whom were her mother's brothers, and her parents did not speak to each other, except for necessities, for a few days. It had been uncomfortable, but then it passed and life went on just as it always had. However, for the past three months, since the shunning began, everything had been different. Nothing seemed quite right. And now even the room where her parents stood seemed wrong. The size, the proportions, seemed unnaturally close in spite of the bareness and the simple furnishing.

For the first time it occurred to Meribah that the rest of her life would continue in rooms just like these. And whether the walls were there or not, whether the proportions varied or not, there were the unseen walls, the unvarying measurements, the inflexible proportions that were always there in the community, being taught, upheld, ingrained. The ones that ensured order, godliness, and life for the Amish people. The ones that people lived for, died for, were punished and shunned for. This was her life—defined not by herself but by others. She did not think that it was unfair. She just suddenly felt it to be terribly odd, peculiar. Her family, her ancestors, had been Amish for hundreds of years. So why did their ways now seem peculiar to her? It was scary to think this way, and deep inside her something stirred—she was not sure whether it was dread or excitement.

"Sunday is coming. Thou could repent." As her mother spoke, she saw her father shift his weight uneasily from one foot to the other. "Thou could, but thou won't!" There was a new harshness in her voice.

Meribah had tried to follow the pattern of this conversation as best she could, but it jumped about. It seemed that her

5

father always talked about the farm and her mother always talked about God.

"I have been thinking, Constance, about leaving here." In the shadows, Meribah clenched her fists and strained even harder to hear.

"And," her father continued, "I . . . well . . . know of a place for sale where we could all go and. . . ." He hesitated. "It's Bird-in-Hand."

"Why, Willis, really! What does thou think my parents and brothers would say?"

"I know. I know." He moved his hands slightly to indicate she need not say more. "It's just a notion. I mean, the land is good and . . . and . . . ." His voice tightened. "We could be a family again. I mean, they are Amish there. It's just that they don't . . . don't . . . ."

"Shun!" she interrupted. "They don't shun because they've become so worldly that if they did shun there would be no community left at all. Willis, we must end this conversation. I fear to think if my parents and brothers saw us now. Thou knows exactly what thou must do."

There was a long pause. Will fingered the edge of his coat. Meribah waited, scrutinizing her mother. Meribah could tell that she was showing signs of baldness. The hair at her temples and on her forehead where the cap did not cover had grown thin and patchy from being pulled back so tightly. Everything seemed taut and pulled in her mother's face these days. The cords of her neck always stood out in bold relief; and there was a muscle just below her jaw line that seemed to clench at odd moments. Her mother had never been given to smiles, but there had been a time when the contours of her face had easier curves, the mouth settled into a softer line, and the brow was clear and unmarked by the deep vertical lines that now creased a furrow above her nose and between her eyebrows. It was the "Stoltzfus brow"; Meribah's grandfather and uncles all had it. She never would have believed it could mark her mother so indelibly. It would never happen to her. Never! She pressed the heel of her hand hard against her brow.

She suddenly remembered the piece of paper in her pocket, which her father had given her that morning. It had been his first words to her in three months. During those months all of his children, following the orders of the shunning, had grown strangely skillful in avoiding him, as one learned to avoid the sharp corner of a table or duck for a low beam. All, that is, except for Meribah. She had found herself going by way of the barn, where her father now ate and slept, for chores that were nowhere near there. Lately she had grown more daring, and catching her father alone, she might run up to him and touch his hand, then under her breath whisper an almost inaudible "Oh, Pa!" or just "Hello!" She had dreams too, dreams of being with her father. She dreamed of March thaws and walking in the raw wetness through the maple grove with her father at tapping time, their breaths misting as they exchanged a few words while stopping at a tree to collect the sap. She dreamed of reading with him and holding the book with him. She dreamed of sitting beside him and watching him carve the dolls. And in her dreams she could see the ropy muscles in his hands that stretched down from his fingers over his knuckles. She could see them stand out and begin to move back and forth with their own rhythm as they explored the wood. It all came back to her in the dreams, and then she would wake up again and everything would be wrong.

In the past week Meribah had become desperate with worry over her father, for it appeared that he had almost entirely ceased to work. She would find him with a tool in his unmoving hands, his eyes staring out into nothingness. One night she had had a really terrifying dream. In it her father had started to fall, and he just kept falling and falling into gray empty space. She woke up feeling afraid and alone, as if only she realized how terrifying life was for her isolated father.

The day after the dream, Meribah began to write him notes. On her circuitous routes for daily chores, she would catch him when no one was in sight and flash by, stuffing a crumpled piece of paper into his hand. The notes were silly little things, but they were all she could think of. One said: I HAVE GROWN ONE INCH SINCE DECEMBER. Another read: TAYLOR HAS A NEW TOOTH, and there was a drawing of Taylor slobbering food all over. There were several notes about Taylor, for he was a special favorite of Meribah's and her father's. Yesterday she had written: THE MOUSE IN THE PANTRY HAS LEFT FOR SPRING. This morning as she raced by him to deliver another note, he had caught her hand and pressed into it a piece of paper. On it was a nonsense verse:

> Some mice think twice about pantry spice
> And silky heads in cozy beds.

It had been nonsense until this moment on the back stairs.

"Well," said Will, still fingering his coat, "nothing more to say?"

Meribah bit her lip and kept her eyes fastened on her mother's thinning patches of hair.

"Nothing," her mother replied. It was as if crockery had shattered when the word was uttered. Meribah never heard the cracking. She simply knew there was nothing left but broken pieces, shards of what had been.

Meribah did not hear what her father said, for the creaks of the floorboards as he turned to leave drowned his voice. But the conversation—their first in three months—was finished, and yet nothing, absolutely nothing, had happened to make things right. Now, she knew, her father would be leaving the farm. Meribah pressed each hand hard against a wall of the staircase. For a moment her feet lifted from the step and only her arms braced her, supporting her entire weight.

"Thee is going to make thyself sick with all this worry!"

Meribah jerked up from the floor chest, bumping her head on the sloping eave of the attic bedroom.

"Oh, Jeanette, I didn't know thee was there," she said to the handsome girl leaning in the doorway.

"And thee didn't know the eave was there either." Her

8

older sister laughed. "Meribah, thee has grown up a bit this winter, and thee—"

"One inch since December," she interrupted.

"Well, thee can no longer clear that eave. I think thee bumps thy head every time."

"Yes, I do." Meribah laughed self-consciously. "Maybe the room is too small. I've outgrown it."

"What is thee doing anyway?"

"Nothing."

"Well, what's that thing in thy hand?"

Meribah looked down at the roughly carved figure, more hacked at than actually carved, that she held. "Thee is right to say thing," she said.

"Well, what is it?"

"It's Malcolm's attempt to do what Pa does by carving a birthday doll for Liesel." Meribah made a face as she looked again at the grotesque wooden figure, which was barely sanded. It looked weird and unborn. "I'm supposed to paint it a face. But I can't. I just can't. I mean, look at this thing compared with Indian Betsy." Meribah held up an exquisite doll her father had made for her seventh birthday. "Or Fancy Lady."

"Better we not have another Fancy Lady!" Jeanette laughed.

"The lace battle!" Meribah whispered with delight. Meribah's father had bought an eighth of a yard of beautiful lace for the doll's outfit, but her mother had instead sewn the plainest, severest iron-gray dress and matching cap imaginable. Yet there had been something in the way her father had carved the doll's face that absolutely defied severity and made it dance with a wild fanciness that seemed to be coaxed right out of the grain of the wood. "Flirting with wood" Pa had called this kind of carving, and when her mother had finished the dark gray dress and put it on the doll, she had exclaimed in horror, "Good heavens! She still looks as if she's wearing lace!" Then muttering something about "wicked as the day he carved her," she had thrown the doll into a corner.

Meribah looked from Fancy Lady, with her exquisitely crafted elegance, to what was in her other hand. "Jeanette, how can I paint a face on this mess? It almost gives me splinters just holding it."

"Meribah!" Jeanette sighed. Meribah looked into her sister's serene blue eyes, the eyes of a true optimist. They did not reflect and never twinkled. Instead, they filtered everything they saw through their blissful, impenetrable blueness. "Dear old thing," Jeanette said.

"I feel a hundred and eight." Meribah sat down with a thump on the lid of the chest.

"Thee really is going to make thyself sick over Mother and Pa."

"Well, Jeanette, doesn't thee ever think about Pa and how he must feel? To be out there alone all the time and never—Well, thee knows what I mean."

With genuine puzzlement, Jeanette leaned toward her sister and said, "I can't think about what I can't imagine. I'm me. I'm sixteen. I'm not a fifty-year-old man. Besides, it will all work out. Things do, as thee knows."

Meribah was incredulous. "Jeanette, he is thy father and thee is his daughter. I mean, can't thee imagine—"

"No." Jeanette said flatly.

"Well, I think about him all the time . . . him out there alone."

"Thee must stop it."

"How in the world does one stop thinking about something?" Meribah asked.

"Thee does. Thee just does."

"It's impossible. If I tell thee not to think about a cloud, can thee not think about a cloud?"

"Of course," Jeanette said calmly.

"How?" demanded Meribah.

"I just think about Paul Stoggsmeyer." She burst into giggles, and Meribah groaned. Then suddenly Jeanette turned serious. "I hope he gets no ideas about Californie and that gold rush," she said. Her mouth was pursed, but her eyes remained cloudless and blue.

"Now why would thee ever think that? An Amish boy going to California—never!" Meribah almost laughed.

"But they all talk about it and the gold. Why would they want to leave this safe valley and go chasing after gold?"

"Maybe it's not the gold. Maybe it's something else."

"Something else? What does thee mean, Meribah?"

Something quivered deep within Meribah. She suddenly felt astir and confused, a little frightened, as if she were on some brink and her known boundaries were slipping away. "I don't know," she said, then changed the subject quickly. "What else does thee think about, Jeanette?"

"Oh, let's see." She paused. "I think about Lindner's cheese and how at market this time tomorrow I'll be eating a thick slice of it."

"Thee will get fat. Come, now, really, what does thee think about?" pressed Meribah.

"Well, hmm . . . I think . . . I think . . . Oh, I don't know, a hundred things. What does thee think about—besides Pa?"

"I think right now it's just nice to be with thee and not feel odd saying his name."

"What else?" Jeanette said sharply, as if steering her back onto a narrow path.

"Oh, like what it would feel like to wear a colorful dress."

"Oh, me too! Me too!" Jeanette exclaimed. "I really think that I would look wonderful in green—pale, pale green . . . with some yellow trim. I used to think I would look nice in blue, but then I decided that it really didn't—"

"And leaving."

"Leaving? Leaving what?" Jeanette asked.

"Home." The minute Meribah said it, she knew it would happen. And yet how strange it was that she had never really thought about it until that very moment.

"What in the world is thee talking about, Meribah?" Jeanette looked at her in alarm.

Meribah sprang for the door and shut it. Then she walked

straight to her sister and tightly gripped her shoulder. Their two light heads were just inches apart.

"Jeanette," Meribah said urgently, "listen to me."

Jeanette nodded her head, her mouth half open.

"Pa's leaving, I know it. In his own way he's told me." Meribah thought of the scribbled verse. "And I have to go with him."

Jeanette appeared so stunned that for a moment Meribah thought that she might have stopped breathing. "Is he going to Californie for gold?" she whispered.

"I don't know where he's going, Jeanette, but it's not for gold."

"For the something else?" she said, still whispering.

"Yes, and this evening I realized that I have to go too. Nobody can stop me." The firmness in her voice surprised her. "And thee must swear not to tell a soul. Does thee?"

Jeanette blinked.

"Well, does thee, Jeanette?"

Jeanette pulled away, rubbing her shoulder.

"Swear it, Jeanette. Swear it."

"I swear it . . . but, Meribah, I don't understand thee."

"Thee needn't try to understand. This, this is the way it has to be."

"But, Meribah, what will happen to thee?"

"Something already has happened."

"What is thee talking about?"

"Never mind."

"Meribah, nothing's for sure out there. It's strange. People are different from us. I . . . I mean . . . ." The blue eyes filled with tears.

"Jeanette," Meribah said quietly, "for thee it is safe here, but not for me and not for Pa." She thought of the beams, the tight low-ceilinged rooms. "I'm going, and thee has sworn to me not to tell. I *have* to go. Does thee understand? I just have to!"

Jeanette nodded. Her eyes looked down. Meribah knew there would be no protest.

"Meribah?"

"Yes?"

"Is it forever?"

Forever? Meribah had shrugged her shoulders in response. Now as she lay in bed next to Jeanette, waiting for the house to fall asleep, the word haunted her and dug into the far corners of her imagination. Forever? She knew what she had to do, but what would it all mean? Would it mean never seeing any of them again, forever being the daughter who chose the father over the family? Would it mean never hearing Taylor call her name or seeing him grow beyond his baby years? She shut her eyes tightly and buried her face in the pillow. Would it mean forever feeling cut off and disconnected from first things, those things she had known from birth, those things most natural? She stopped. Nothing was natural any more. If she stayed or left, it was all strange and unnatural.

Jeanette was sound asleep now but still held Meribah's hand tightly with both of hers. Meribah had to lift off Jeanette's hands with her own free one to unlock herself from the sleeping girl's clasp. Carefully she slipped out of bed. To save time she had not taken off her stockings, and she had left her dress hanging over the chair so that the creak of the closet door would not awaken her sister. Within half a minute she had thrown her dress over her nightgown, put on her cap and heavier shoes, and thrown a thick shawl around her shoulders, but as she stood there in the plain room, she suddenly felt quite peculiar. Was she really to leave forever just like this? It did not seem right. She must need something more. But what? She held nothing in her hands except the corners of her shawl. Was this how a person left?

Meribah looked around for something to take. Then she remembered the chest under the eaves where she kept her drawing and painting things. She would take them even if it meant a big creak as she opened the lid. She lifted it slowly. Miraculously, it did not creak. Her paper and paint box were

13

on top, but as she reached for them, her hand brushed the head of one of the carved dolls. The dolls? She could not take them, but she could not leave them to molder away, uncared for. In the darkness of the room, Meribah traced the specialness of each wooden face. Then making a basket with her shawl, she carefully dropped in the seven dolls. Her paint box pressed between her arm and rib cage, she tiptoed out of the bedroom with her cargo.

Liesel's door was open, as she had expected. Her younger sister was a sound sleeper, so there was little danger of waking her up. Meribah walked to the end of Liesel's bed and let go of the edges of the shawl. The dolls tumbled softly onto the quilt. She lined them up, all seven of them. Her eyes had grown accustomed to the dark, and she could see them quite plainly now. There was China Girl, Fancy Lady, Indian Betsy, Amish Girl, Dutch Girl, Moon Fairy, and the Queen of England. Each face seemed incredibly alive with its own individuality, even though all except Indian Betsy were dressed almost identically in plain dresses and caps. Indian Betsy wore a hide dress, as her mother thought it would be insulting to put a savage in civilized clothes. The Queen of England, though clothed in gray, had been permitted a crown.

But Meribah was barely conscious of the carved dolls in front of her. They had suddenly become unimportant as the little sputtering snores from the crib filled the room. She could not leave without one more look at Taylor. She did not make a sound as she leaned over the crib to gaze at him. He slept safe and oblivious in his little cocoon of soft snores, tiny hiccups, and baby sweat. In the warm night air of the room, his silky hair had curled into a lather of damp ringlets. His fat fist was squashed into his mouth. She would not let herself touch him because if she did she might not let go.

She was in that bedroom and then she was out, outside the house. For a moment she stood still in the wet grass and felt some deadly weight roll away. Then she turned and looked back. Everything was different now. She could picture them all—her mother, her older brothers, Jeanette, Liesel, the baby. But they were all across some indefinable space. Separate. As she had known she would, Meribah heard the creak of wheels from the barn.

"Pa!" she cried, tearing across the farmyard down to the barn. "Pa! Pa! I'm here! I'm here! I'm going with thee."

Her father turned around. "Oh, Meribah!" he said, about to protest.

"Pa, there's no other choice. It's not that I don't love them. I just can't stand the hating any more."

He reached out his hand to help her up on the seat beside him.

"Pa," Meribah said, "where we're going, it's farther than Bird-in-Hand, isn't it?"

"It certainly is." He smiled.

"Well, where exactly are we going?"

"California," he replied.

She looked overhead. The black sky was chinked with a million stars. The same stars are over California, she thought. Then she sat a little straighter and tried to look brave and clever, but all Meribah could think about were the silky heads in their cozy beds. Her father slapped the reins on the horse's back, and they left.

2

THE EAST BANK OF THE RIVER

"Pa, it says here, in this book, 'Such is the ar-i-dye-ty....'"

"Aridity." Her father looked up from the wagon rim where he was fastening the stout drop curtain to the frame.

"Aridity, then," Meribah corrected. "What does it mean?"

"Dryness—no moisture in the air."

"Well, it says here," she continued reading from her perch on the wagon seat, "'Such is the aridity of the climate, that ordinary wheels, that will do very well in the states, fall to pieces by the time of reaching Fort Laramie. Therefore no person should start with wheels about which there is a ...'"—she hesitated as she tried to sound out the word—"'par-tickle of doubt, or'"—here Meribah's voice rose slightly with dramatic intensity—"'they are sure to meet with trouble and vexation.' Does thou have any par-tickles of doubt, Pa?"

"No. I do not have a particle of doubt."

"Well, if thou does have any par-tickles—or particles, rather—there is a certain Mr. Murphy of St. Louis whom the book recommends as a fine wheelwright."

"Too late for that, unless thee would like to return to St. Louis."

"Oh, dear, no!" Meribah looked up from the book. As far as she could see, the bank of the river, the hills beyond, the valley between, the entire countryside, was speckled with the white tents and covered wagons of the emigrants. Meribah and her father's wagon was among the seven thousand or more waiting to cross the river. They had been waiting with their

16

group of nine other wagons for three days and had a good chance of making it by afternoon. There were just two scows to ferry the wagons across, and these were being worked from four-thirty in the morning until midnight.

The waiting was tedious. Even the violent eruptions among the people over position in line were so commonplace that they had become tedious. Just last evening two men not more than three hundred yards ahead of them in line had killed each other in a fight. Although she was horrified, Meribah knew she did not feel as shocked as she might have a month ago, and this realization in itself shocked her more than the event.

"Didn't like St. Louis, did thee?"

"No," Meribah said firmly. "I was made to feel strange." She remembered walking through the streets and the people staring openly at her gray gown and cap. It was in St. Louis, right in front of the big hotel on the main street, that a little boy had stopped, pointed directly at her, and said, "What's that, Mama?" The mother, as if to confirm that Meribah was nothing resembling a human being, stared right at her and explained to him with great patience, "Oh, it's one of those pee-culiar sorts with the weird religion and funny talk." No, it was much better here in St. Jo, waiting a thousand deep to cross the river. Everybody was "pee-culiar" and had weird ways. Nobody noticed particularly that she and her pa talked "funny." Differences did not really stand out but made them all the more similar.

Meribah went back to reading her book, which was actually a pamphlet called an accompaniment to the map of the emigrant road. Her father had bought it for three dollars months ago, but had shown it to her for the first time only when they arrived in St. Jo. She pored over it, fascinated by every detail, and had already read it several times. The only book she had ever read other than the Bible, it seemed to her much more practical. The author had among other things a particular knowledge of bread, which he was intent on discussing throughout the book. It was all excellent advice, especially when compared, Meribah thought, with the bread talk in the Bible.

Meribah reread some of the bread sections: "Take plenty of bread stuff: This is the staff of life when everything else runs short. A diet exclusively of fine flour bread has a bad effect on the bowels and is unwholesome. Take a portion of unbolted wheat flour and Indian corn meal. Upon these you can subsist and enjoy good health." Meribah looked into the back of the wagon at their bags of wheat and meal. "Good bread," the author continued in another section, "is the most important and best food to be had upon the journey—how few know how to make it!" This part Meribah had read at least fifty times. "That made by most of the emigrants is a vile compound"—I am not one of those emigrants, Meribah thought—"of bad flour, hog grease, and salerates. Such bread with the free use of bacon and the neglect of the bath produces camp fever." She was never sure in this sentence whether the author was talking about bathing the bacon or the person, but it did not matter, for she would not use bacon in her bread. "Every person who starts upon this journey should know how to make good bread." The author is inclined to repeat himself, Meribah thought. "It should not contain a particle of grease—it should be mixed with its own leaven and well kneaded. It is"—and this was new even for an experienced bread maker like Meribah—"quickly baked in thin loaves, or in the form of biscuit, in a portable sheet-iron pan." Meribah put down the accompaniment and let her eyes rest on a stack of sheet bread she had baked that morning.

"Pa, I'm not sure we have enough sacks for the bread."

"We can use the number-one cotton."

"Is that as good as skin?"

"Equal."

"Because the author says, 'Keep bread in goatskin or bladders,' and he swears that if it falls in the river, 'when recovered immediately, it will not spoil.' Isn't that practical advice—a practical miracle: to pull bread out of water and have it still whole!"

"A practical miracle," Will agreed, chuckling.

"All that palavering about bread in the Bible, and they never—" Meribah cut herself short, biting her tongue.

"How much Bible has thee been reading these days—palaver or not?"

"Oh, Pa!" Meribah cried. "I did not truly mean palaver. "Did I blaspheme?"

Will gently patted her hand. "No," he said softly, "thee did not blaspheme. But thee should know the difference between practical advice and miracles, and reading the Bible as well as the accompaniment is a good way to learn."

Meribah looked down. She had hardly read the Bible at all since leaving Holly Springs. "We're still Amish, aren't we, Pa?" she asked suddenly.

"Of course we're still Amish," Will said with genuine shock. "What did thee think we were?"

"I don't know."

"Thee need not have, as the accompaniment says, a particle of doubt about that."

Will turned back to his work on the wagon.

"Particle of doubt," Meribah thought. She did believe in God, and she did believe in the Bible. So why did her father's use of the phrase disturb her? Perhaps any girl who could use "palaver" and "Bible" in the same sentence was in some sort of imminent danger. Was her soul like one of these wheels that did very well in the states but in the aridity of the climate fell to pieces before Fort Laramie? She did not know what to do. Possibly, she thought with sour humor, she should go to see Mr. Murphy.

Meribah looked out over the banks of the river, covered with its thousands of people, oxen, tents, and wagons. When she squinted her eyes in the noonday sun, the thousands became a squirming white mass—like creek foam—a white festering on a hillside. She touched her cap lightly. She looked Amish, that was certain. But in the shops she had addressed clerks as "you," and although it sounded funny to her ear, it felt good to say the strange new word. She enjoyed it—she loved it, as a matter of fact. It was so much more comfortable not having people stop short and open their eyes as if caught by surprise when they heard themselves addressed as "thou." She was such a weakling she could not bear giving up "you." Meribah sighed. Perhaps she could make a deal with herself. She would alternate "thou" and "you." If she addressed one person as "you," the next she would call "thou." And she would alternate reading the Bible and the accompaniment too. Yes, that was what she would do.

Meribah felt relieved. She would sort out all these things, these particles of herself, and alternate her language and her reading. It was very practical, this plan. She saw it in almost diagrammatic detail—a precise drawing for her soul, with straight lines and right angles that indicated compartments for this and that, a tracing similar to the one Pa had drawn a few years earlier when he was planning to build the new barn. He had drawn hair-thin, precise lines that had shown storage eaves, watering troughs, feeding bins, stalls, equipment rooms, and so on. The tracing had a beautiful clarity. These, of course, were just the kinds of lines that Meribah was the worst at making in her own drawings.

Will Simon looked up from his work again. "What is thee thinking, Meribah, that has fixed thy face as tight as a locked box?"

"Oh, nothing, Pa! Nothing at all."

"Well, would thee go and ask the McSwats if they have a length of three-eighths-inch tallowed cord? Give them these spare spokes. Tell them they should fit in a pinch, specially if soaked in water."

Meribah took the spokes and ran off toward the McSwats' wagon, nimbly threading her way through the crowded terrain.

"Hello, Miss Meribah!" It was Mr. Wickham. Meribah, flushing, waved at the pale young Englishman with his beautifully curled hair and waxed mustache. Mr. Moxley, their scout, had used the word "dandy" to describe Mr. Wickham, and although she had never heard the word before, it seemed to fit. He was busying himself around the Gentlemen's Wagons, as the two wagons belonging to Mr. Wickham, his friend Mr. James, and Mr. James's uncle, Dr. Forkert, had come to be called by the rest of the company.

"Those spokes, Meribah?" Dr. Forkert asked, striding out from behind one of the wagons.

"Yes, sir. Spares my pa pared for the McSwats."

"Fine idea. Think I'll do some myself." Dr. Forkert smiled at Meribah, and she smiled back, reflecting that he seemed a good sort of man. He was an ecstatic envisioner of the West, referring to it as "that shimmering vision," "that ultimate glory of our continent." Indeed, he had as many names for his western dream as medicines in his bag. Twice as old as his nephew and Mr. Wickham, he outstripped them both in his enthusiasm and energy. Meribah lingered for a moment, answering a few questions about her father's preparations of the wagon, and then she hurried on.

Not far from the Gentlemen's Wagons was that of the Billingses. Mr. Billings, no less a gentleman—not by a hair— was reclining as much as one could on the driver's seat.

"Off to town, Miss Simon, no doubt to escape the tedium of waiting? Serena and Mrs. Billings could not tolerate another minute. And for women I think nothing relieves boredom like shopping. Would you agree?"

How could anyone not agree with Mr. Billings? Meribah thought. There was something so easy and agreeable about him.

"Yes, I guess thou is right," she said shyly. "I must be on now. Doing an errand for my pa."

Breaking into a trot, she swept close to the Billingses' huge wagon, hoping to steal a glimpse inside, for it was a trove of unforgettable articles of beauty and luxury the likes of which Meribah had never seen—sumptuous quilts and tasseled cushions, a miniature silver tea service, elegant leather chests, and a beautiful needlepoint sewing basket that stood almost two feet high. The Billingses were from Philadelphia, where they had lived in a fine mansion, and it looked to Meribah as if they had brought half of it with them. Where others used tin camp mugs, the Billingses were often seen drinking from fine bone china cups. And where most women wore the same dress every day, Serena Billings and her mother had worn three different dresses in the space of one week! Meribah could see something lovely and peach colored hanging in the dim light of the wagon now.

The Whitings' wagon came next. It was empty, but Simon Whiting, the cow her father and the Whitings had bought in common, was tethered to the back end.

"They went to buy udder balm." An enormous woman came round from behind a neighboring wagon. It was Mrs. McSwat and she held her baby girl in her arms. All the McSwats were huge. Even the baby, whom Meribah, remembering Taylor, tried hard to ignore, was so fat at eight months that she probably outweighed Liesel, back in Holly Springs, who was eight years old.

"They are the worryingest folks I've ever seen!" Mrs. McSwat said. "Lucky they don't have children—they'd grease 'em to death. This is their second jar of udder balm in a week."

Meribah knew exactly what Mrs. McSwat meant. There was no better way to learn about folks than to own a cow with them.

"What you got there, Meribah?" Mrs. McSwat asked, nodding toward the spokes.

"Oh, for thee. Extra spokes my pa pared down. He says to tell Mr. McSwat to soak them if they don't quite fit, and he would like to know if thou has a length of three-eighths-inch tallowed cord?"

22

"Come round back with me. I'll take a look. I'm sortin' through a box now."

Mrs. McSwat's size and strength were truly amazing. With one arm brimful of the biggest baby imaginable, she reached into the back of the wagon with the other and lifted out a small trunk that would have required two strong arms for most men and that would have been a backbreaker for women. Mrs. McSwat's arms, however, could probably encircle an ox's midsection and hoist it.

"Where's that cord?" she said, rummaging through the trunk's contents. "I saw it yesterday." Then her eyes slid sideways toward the big Conestoga a few yards away, and she muttered to Meribah under her breath, "Barkers don't seem shy on it." A second, smaller wagon stood near the Conestoga, and in and out of both of them, quicker than a hummingbird gathering nectar, darted Mrs. Barker, carrying an endless stream of goods—bolts of linsey cloth, oilcloth, canvas, and calicoes, bags of goose down, crockery and tinware ample for a small army, nails and bolts of every size, enough to build a town, let alone a house, nests of buckets, crates of Castile soap—brown with rosin, pale brown without—boxes of sperm candles, piles of Mackinaw blankets, and stacks of hats—palm leaf and stout white felt. And then there was the cordage—rope and twine in all thicknesses, tallowed and untallowed.

All this came from their store in Franklin, Indiana, which Mrs. Barker described as being the "largest emporium of life's necessities in the three-town region."

"Here it is!" Mrs. McSwat exclaimed triumphantly, and she held up a coiled length of rope. At that instant Mrs. Barker looked up. "Got more over here if you need it, six cents a yard. Two cents cheaper than that cheat store in St. Jo."

"No, this will do," Meribah called to her. "Thank thee anyway." Mrs. Barker never traded. Some of her vast repository of dry goods she sold, and often she sent little gifts to the Grays. Mrs. Gray and Mrs. Barker had become best of friends. The Grays had been in commerce, too. They had owned an

23

apothecary shop. But it had burned to the ground, lock, stock, and barrel—"Not even a pokeberry leaf left!"

Meribah thanked Mrs. McSwat for the length of cord and started back toward her own wagon. She took the long way, threading through the surge of animals and wagons and people that covered the hillsides, waiting to cross the river. Inch by inch the crowd moved closer to the bank where the scows transported them to the other side. There was the constant wrangling and fighting for place in line, bickering over the price of goods sold or traded for the journey to come. Away from the river where the crowds were less dense, campfires for cooking and forging new wagon parts were numerous, but closer to the river, people and wagons were so thick that there was hardly elbow room to strike a match, let alone start a fire. Even here, a half-mile from the bank, people and animals pressed so closely around Meribah that she felt crushed by their single-minded, blind desire to get across, to get on with it! To start the great trek to the gold fields and to new farmlands—that single notion obsessed every living soul there and was nearly touchable in its presence. For a moment Meribah felt as if she might suffocate. A short breath of panic lodged shallowly in her throat when she thought that she had lost her way in this pressing maze of emigrants. Just then there was a jerk under Meribah's arm, and she felt her feet leave the ground.

"You're going to get yourself crushed, Meribah!"

It was Mr. Moxley, and she was soon sitting in front of him on his saddle. Traveling with only a horse and a pack mule, he was to ride in advance as scout and report back to the rest of the company on the whereabouts of good water, campsites, and Indians.

"Lost and crushed," added Meribah. "Thank thee." She looked around from her new vantage point as Mr. Moxley guided his horse through the throng. "I had no notion I'd wandered so far off," Meribah said. "How long does thou think our wait is now?"

"I was down to the river early this morning and, provided

that second scow keeps going, maybe this afternoon late."

"Thou has been all the way down to the banks! How did thou ever pass through?"

"Believe me, Meribah, once you've cleared granite from wheatfields in New Hampshire, moving through this crowd is like spooning out Indian pudding."

Meribah giggled. Mr. Moxley had the oddest way of putting things. He was about the same age as her father, and the two men had become good friends in the few days since they had joined the company here in St. Jo. Mr. Moxley had told them he had done everything from reading law to farming to schoolteaching. He had an opinion on everything, too. It often differed from Will's, but that did not interfere with their enjoyment of each other's company.

"Well, I'll be!" Mr. Moxley said, slowly turning his horse for a better view. "Look who's edged themselves right down to the bank there."

Meribah craned her neck but still could not see where Mr. Moxley was pointing.

"If it isn't the good brothers Timm," he said, his voice tinged with sarcasm.

Meribah finally spotted them. Sullen and narrow-faced men, they had threaded their way through the line on horseback, trailing their pack mule, and had managed to arrive at a very good spot.

"I thought they were with our company!" Meribah exclaimed.

"In name only. Those two keep their own company—of, by, and for themselves, no one else."

Suddenly, from the rumbling din there emerged distinct voices crying, "Fight! Fight!" There was a roar, a flash of knives from exactly where the Timm brothers stood.

"Uh-oh!" Mr. Moxley said. "Here it goes."

The crowd had pulled back from two men and formed a small circle. Everything happened so quickly that Meribah was aware only of a woman bending over a fallen man. When the woman backed away to let the others help him up, her bodice bloomed with a bright red stain as big as a poppy.

"Oh, no!" Meribah whispered. "I hope they won't be coming with us, Mr. Moxley."

"If they get across the river soon, maybe they'll not wait up for us," he replied, turning his horse. They rode off at a brisk trot toward the Simons' wagon. Children scattered, dogs ran, but Mr. Moxley expertly guided the horse through it all.

When they arrived at the Simons' wagon, Captain Griffith, their company leader, was there talking with Will. Watching him, Meribah thought that the captain was an odd blend—his body was heavyset, but he had the quick movements of a much lighter man. He had a clouded left eye with a perpetual squint, as if it were always high noon in a glaring sun. He looked up at Mr. Moxley now, his left eye clenched tighter. "Second scow's broke," he was saying. "Just talking with Mr. Simon here, and I've come to the conclusion that it is in our better interests to go up the river to cross. From your reports, the cholera here and on the other side is spreading. Also, directly on the other side the going is very marshy for some distance, lots of streams to cross." Captain Griffith would know this. Will had told Meribah that their leader had crossed the country to California no less than twenty times, sometimes following the emigrant trail, sometimes exploring new ones. His condition was movement. The act of getting someplace was far more important than actual arrival. He never spoke about places in the sense of being in them, just of passing through. He is like a shuttle, Meribah thought, weaving in and out of the land's warp. But Meribah wondered what it was he was weaving—what was the piece? It had astounded her to learn that Griffith had been to California so many times and had never seen San Francisco. "He's a puzzle of a man," her father had said, "but I trust his knowledge."

"Well, Captain Griffith, when does thou propose leaving for upriver?"

"A couple of hours. Still time to go into St. Jo and get fleeced if you want. But be here by one-thirty and be ready."

26

Griffith touched his hat and lurched off toward the other wagons.

"Meribah, would thee like to be fleeced for some colored drawing chalks?"

"Oh, Pa! Thou is not joking me?"

"Certainly not! Here, take this." He drew a coin from his pocket and placed it in her hand. "We've bought food to sustain the body, but nothing for the mind. That's artist's work."

"Oh, Pa!" Meribah was thrilled. She had seen the chalks in the general store the day before and had not dared to ask. But she had craved them from the moment she first spotted them. Although she had never used chalks before, she knew they were her kind of drawing tool. They were for representing the nuances, the shadows and smudges that suggest depth, mass, and volume, rather than the hard, sharp edges and perimeters of things.

When she reached the store, it was deep with people lined up to buy cooking pans, kettles, flour sacks, grain, wrought nails, dried fruit, candles, tin lanterns—everything imaginable to keep body and wagon together.

"Hello, dearie." The pleasant voice flitted through the crowd like a chirping bird. Meribah turned and saw Mrs. Whiting. Mr. Whiting could not be far behind. And there he was, right next to his wife, with his head turned the other way.

"Oh! Mr. and Mrs. Whiting!" They were undoubtedly here on the errand Mrs. McSwat had referred to.

"We're just waiting to buy some beeswax and tallow, child. Makes awful good udder balm in case Simon-Whiting should get a bad patch of soreness. You know the dryness and all."

"Oh, yes, ma'am." It seemed to Meribah that she had heard more and read more and thought more about aridity in the last few days than a person would in a normal life span. Yet they had been waiting to cross a river for days and now were going upriver to avoid miles of marshes and creeks.

"Oh, Mrs. Whiting, that reminds me. Captain Griffith came

by just now and said we're going to move upriver rather than cross here."

This news came like the scent of a fox into a henhouse. The Whitings were instantly in a dither, and the air around the two people was aflutter with their own words of exclamation, fury, and fret. "My word, Henry, we might have been left behind . . . never a warning . . . All this last-minute switching." They twisted and wrung their hands. "Sakes alive . . . no organization, Rietta . . . That Griffith!" Their eyebrows danced up and down in antic slants. A patchwork of creases scored their foreheads. "Really, we have to get that wheel fixed immediately. . . . Now, Rietta, calm yourself. . . ." "*Calm yourself*, Henry! Cholera here? . . . Oh, well, yes, I suppose it does make sense. Yes, but so sudden! When? One-thirty! . . . Oh, mercy! How will we ever?" Henry and Henrietta Whiting clutched each other for mutual support.

"Well, now, there's nothing you should be upset about," Meribah said, thinking that she had never seen two people work up so much confusion and anxiety. They were having a two-person panic. "We don't leave for almost three hours. Pa was working on your wheel this morning. I think it's almost ready. There's plenty of time. Look, I'm here. Pa sent me to buy some colored chalks, so you see there's plenty of time." Meribah silently applauded her fluent use of "you" in this situation.

"Yes! Yes!" they both replied in unison.

"It is important that we get the beeswax and tallow," Mrs. Whiting said.

"Rietta's right. Nothing more painful for a cow than parched udders. Believe me. We've been through it in Illinois. Rietta's right." Mrs. Whiting nodded in agreement.

"Well, child, you run on and get your chalks. You'll have no wait. Look, there's no one at that counter except one man. So don't hold yourself up for us. But for heaven's sake do tell them not to leave without us."

"Of course, Mrs. Whiting." Meribah turned to leave.

Leaning on each other, their shoulders pressed together, the

Whitings spoke softly, almost inaudibly, smooth words of comfort and solace.

Meribah moved to the counter where paper goods and writing and drafting materials were sold. A man was asking for all sorts of special pen nibs, quills, and paper blocks. "How might I keep my compass from rusting?" he was asking. Meribah was perplexed.

"A little rosin and tallow should do it."

"How would thou ever see thy true direction through the grease?" she blurted.

The bluest, liveliest eyes she had ever seen turned to her. "Not that kind of compass, miss." His lean, hawkish face crinkled into a friendly grin, but his mouth was almost hidden under a thick blond mustache. The man was talking to her now, something about compasses for drawing, not for direction, but she was not hearing the words. She had never seen a face more alive than this one before her now.

"Pennsylvania, Holly Springs," she answered mechanically.

"Washington, D.C.," the reply came. Meribah suddenly realized that she must have asked him a question.

"Does thou know the President?"

"Lord, no! I'm just a draftsman for the Bureau of Topographical Engineers."

"What is that—'topographical engineers'?"

"Mapmakers—cartographers."

"Oh, thou must draw very precise lines for that."

As if to confirm her statement, a clerk arrived with a box of thin lead pencils, several quills, and ink. "Here you go, Mr. Goodnough." The clerk handed the supplies over the counter for him to examine. Meribah was impressed.

"Thou draws in ink?" she asked, amazed at her own boldness.

"Quite a bit."

"Oh, then thou must make true lines."

"True lines?" His eyes rested on her with a perplexed interest, as if he were seeing something quite unusual.

Meribah knew it was not the Amish difference that arrested

his attention. Oddly enough, she had never felt less self-conscious about her dress and language than she did now.

"True lines?" he said again.

"Yes. I can't make them. I can draw only wiggly, scratchy ones."

"Can I help you, miss?" The clerk had finished wrapping Goodnough's materials and had turned to Meribah.

She was almost embarrassed to give her order. She took from her pocket the money her father had given her and placed it on the counter. "As many colorful chalks as this will buy, please." Then she turned to the man beside her and said in a low voice, almost apologetically, "They're good for wiggly lines and shadows—the fuzzy, uneven things."

"You don't call those true lines?" His eyes snapped with a blue fierceness, but Meribah felt a gentleness in them too.

She colored. "I . . . I don't know, sir." The clerk came just then with her package.

"All the basic colors, miss."

"That will do fine. Thank you." And she quickly tucked it under her arm. "Good-bye."

"Wait a minute, little . . . ."

"I have to go—my pa's waiting on me." And she turned and left the man with his fine quills and thin lead pencils. She could feel him staring after her cap as she threaded her way through the crowd.

Meribah hurried down the crude main street of St. Jo, her eyes set straight ahead, as if her cap had blinders on either side. The way was clogged with hawkers selling everything from gold-finding devices to barrels full of worthless trinkets and baubles that supposedly could be traded to the Indians. A perfectly lovely face appeared from the crowd and leaned into her narrow line of vision.

"Hello, Miss Meribah."

"Why, Miss Serena!"

"We're here buying an automatic gold-washer"—the young lady paused as if to arrange her face as much as her thoughts for the next part of her speech—"to go with our goldometer." Another pause. "A companion piece, one might say." She closed her tiny valentine mouth firmly and waited for a response, but Meribah was always rendered speechless in front of Serena Billings. There was something about this almost-woman that made the breath lock in Meribah's throat. Serena cocked her head prettily. The fringe of curls around her face shook slightly in a way that made her features even prettier. She smoothed the intricately tucked and pleated bodice of her muslin dress. "Miss Meribah, I do declare, the cat must have your tongue. You are shy, aren't you?"

Meribah recovered. "Why, I was just admiring the nice pleats of your dress."

"French tucks." Then looking down at her midriff, she said, "Yes, they do make the bodice lie superbly. As I was saying, my father decided that we must have a gold-washer. Well, as long as we have the goldometer...." Serena prattled on about the practicalities of a gold-washer, her talk laced with curlicues of speech the likes of which Meribah had never heard: "I daresay," "I fancy this," "I fancy that," and many things that were "charming." Serena's curls bobbed, accenting her speech. The French-tucked bodice heaved slightly as she drew in her breath. "And so, my dear, that is why we have bought the gold-washer."

"Your gold will be as clean as your dress, Miss Serena."

"Oh, how charming!" It was Serena's mother coming up from behind them, laden with packages. "I hope we shall find as many gold nuggets as Serena has dresses. I really feel that this gold-washer is *de trop*—too much," she said, swiveling her head in translation for those within earshot, "but Wrentham insists." It was hard for Meribah to imagine Wrentham Billings insisting on anything. "And what, may I ask, might you be carrying in your package? Our shopping lists for such a journey seem endless."

"Some colored chalk. My pa gave me money to buy some." And then she paused. She was about to say that they were a companion piece for her paper but decided not to. "I like to draw."

"Oh, how charming. Not a necessity, mind you, but enchanting. Serena of course draws elegantly. Why, in Philadelphia her teacher claimed that she was one of her premier pupils, and to think she is also so accomplished musically."

"I'm not very good," Meribah felt compelled to announce.

"That I cannot believe," Mrs. Billings said kindly. "Serena's work is superb of course." She turned to her daughter, her smile fading. "And how lovely you looked at the pianoforte in the music room, or by the French windows of the big room upstairs, your sketch pad in hand. I could just. . . ."

Serena's brow knotted and for a split second a dark light seemed to pass over her face. "Now, Mama." She spoke with a kind of stern sympathy. Then in a brighter voice: "I'll tell you what I propose: I shall give our dear little friend here drawing lessons on our route west."

"How splendid of you, Serena," her mother exclaimed.

Serena's face twinkled at the notion, and her curls shimmied in a golden agitation as she began to speak rapidly. "The prairie shall be our studio, the campsite our salon. We shall have soirées, and I shall inform you of the great artistic traditions!"

"I must go," said Meribah. "You know we are to leave at one-thirty to head upriver to cross? Captain Griffith told you that?"

"Yes. Yes. So stalwart! Such a colorful, robust man."

Meribah could not wait to be off. She made her farewells as politely as possible and raced down the street, bits and fragments of their conversations buzzing through her brain with a waspish fury. Suddenly she stopped dead in the busy street —drawing lessons with Serena! Shaking her head, Meribah went on, jostled by the crowd and thinking of Jeanette.

3

THE OTHER SIDE OF THE RIVER

Meribah tipped her face up toward the fine drizzle. The rain felt clean and soft and quiet, quiet except for its light rasp on her India rubber hat. It was a pleasant, insistent sound, one that washed away the yammering echoes of the people buying, selling, and fighting in St. Jo, washed away the memory of faces sullen or contorted in the wheelings and dealings of preparation. They were moving at last, and it felt so good to be sitting high and free on the driver's bench next to her pa, both their faces wet and shiny, their eyes looking out over the team's horns and drawing into the thin crosshairs of their imaginary sights a vision of the West, of California! Never mind the thousands of people who had moved with them up the river in all manner of conveyances, from wagon to packhorse to mule. Meribah and Will were alone with their visions.

The manic inventory of provisions that had run through Meribah's mind for days and nights preceding their departure from St. Jo stopped. There was nothing more she could do. The fears, the anxieties, the haunting voices of other people who were taking this and that, would serve no good. Meribah had done all she could with her father to make them fit and safe for the journey. So she sternly ordered the gnawing demons to rest. Let the soft drizzle rinse clean the petty devils of the provisioning lists. Find a horse's head with mane flying in the clouds above. Follow the tracery of a hawk's flight.

They had finally crossed the river at Andrew's Ferry. For Meribah, crossing the river had meant the real start of the journey. It was where the vision of the West would become one with the reality of the West. It was the significant, tangible starting line, a kind of vertical equator that divided the continent into two hemispheres: that of the States and that of the Frontier. On one side there were people; on the other side the people became Argonauts and shared an identity with the mythical seekers of the Golden Fleece, which her father had told her about.

Maps of the routes for the Argonauts to California were as poor as they were plentiful. For three dollars or more, an emigrant could buy a map "to start upon the journey and pilot himself through." The one that Will had bought with the accompaniment, Map of The Emigrant Road, was one of the best. But no matter how hard Meribah studied it, she could not grasp it. At some point, all the names for forts and trails, all the lines and the dashes for rivers and mountains, collapsed into meaningless squiggles in front of her eyes. She soon realized that these maps were hopeless for her own understanding and that she would do better to make her own map—a sketch perhaps, rather than a map—that suggested the shape of the journey rather than the direction. She would fill it in as they went. The important places she would mark in advance, but the little creeks, the smaller rivers, those would all be set down when they were crossed or forded or passed.

So from Pennsylvania west to St. Jo, Meribah's map was as busy as a crazy quilt with crosshatchings and shadings. There were sinuous lines for the roads and trails and clearly printed place names. But starting at St. Jo, at the near edge of the frontier, Meribah's map was almost blank. She had drawn in the Missouri River because it was so important. The frontier began on the other side, the *real* West. She had sketched in ever so faintly a horizontal line that forked north and south. That was the Platte River. Her father had said that when they crossed the Missouri and turned north into the Nebraska territory, they would pick up the Platte and follow it almost six hundred miles until they joined a lovely sounding river called the Sweetwater. To the south would be the Rocky Mountains, and to the north would be the Wind River Mountains. Meribah especially loved the sound of the Wind River range. That Wind River was the name for mountains and water made it such a beautiful mystery that she dared not even draw a mark to indicate the range for fear of somehow spoiling it all.

But she had taken care when she drew so faintly the two prongs of the Platte. At first she had made the river look like a pitchfork on its side, the tines forming a broad *U*, but it didn't seem right, so she drew a river that branched like a sharp *V* rather than a *U*. It looked just like the kind of branch her father had once told her was used by folks called water witches to find springs for wells.

The first name written on the map was FORT CHILDS, and then about three inches to the left and one inch up on the map—a little under four hundred miles away—Meribah had written FORT LARAMIE. In between the two forts, about a half-inch to the left of Fort Laramie, she had written INDEPENDENCE ROCK because she had started hearing about that rock almost as soon as they had left Pennsylvania. Otherwise, there were blanks that waited to be filled on either side of the thin scratchy lines that suggested the Platte. And there were no states outlined after Missouri because there were none, only territories or areas known as Pawnee or Sioux country. There was no trail marked from St. Jo on, only a line of dots coming out of the direction they had already traveled. Ten inches or more away from the dot where Meribah had written ST. JO was CALIFORNIA, in small block letters. This was Meribah's map. It told only where she had been. Yet somehow, just by making it, she believed that it would "pilot her through."

The geography of the imagination is often more precise than that of the landscape, and Meribah found that crossing the Missouri River was less significant and exciting than she had anticipated. The West did not instantly begin on the far side of the river. The land on one side was just like that on the other. It was not The Beginning, The Grand Start, that she had imagined. Indeed, over the next week, as a kind of anticlimax to crossing the river, there were numerous other creeks and streams that had to be ferried or forded. Meribah began to suspect that every journey had several starting points. Since leaving their farm, she had considered any number of places the true starting point. But when she marked the point on her map, it became insignificant, only one of many dots that formed a line beginning in Holly Springs.

"I am quite certain that there is as much fortune in being a ferryman as a gold digger." Meribah had just finished paying the scowman the fifty-cents fare for the wagon and an additional twenty-five cents apiece for the two oxen. Simon-Whiting had gone with the Whitings on the trip before, and they would settle his fare with Henry and Rietta on the other side of this oversized mud puddle that would end up costing them one dollar and twelve and a half cents.

"Thee was speaking, Meribah?" Standing at the head of his team, Will turned toward his daughter.

"Yes. I was just saying thou should open a ferry if thou really wants to get rich. There are more creeks, streams, and rivers around here than veins in an old lady's hand!" They were almost to the other side, and Meribah hoped some minor disaster did not await them. It seemed as if every time they made a crossing something happened. The day before, Simon-Whiting had got stuck in the mud on a steep bank. Her father, Captain Griffiith, a ferryman, and Henry Whiting had to extricate the poor beast and actually carry her up the last three feet while Meribah and Mrs. Whiting shouted encouragement from the sidelines.

Today as they rolled off the scow, Meribah instantly knew from the twin expressions of disgust on the Whitings' faces that something was amiss.

"Billingses' wagon tongue broke," they announced in unison.

"You know what this means, Will?" Henry said, weary-voiced, while Henrietta sighed in Meribah's direction.

"I know," he said, starting to their wagon.

Meribah looked beyond the Whitings and saw Wrentham and Serena Billings sitting by their wagon in total bewilderment. Henrietta Whiting, although a plumpish woman, negotiated her way down the steep slope quite deftly and stopped by Meribah. "It irks me no end," she rasped in Meribah's ear. "There they are sitting by their wagon like they're in their fancy Philadelphia drawing room, ready to let us do all the work. Who was the only one yesterday who didn't lift a finger when poor old Simon-Whiting got stuck?"

What Mrs. Whiting said was true, but Meribah did not know how to answer. She was not used to participating as an equal in a discussion of this sort about another adult.

"Rietta," Mr. Whiting said as he came down the bank, "we'd better go up there with Will and have a look at the situation."

"S'pose you're right, Henry. Come on, dear," she said, nodding to Meribah. "Let's see how bad it is and pray there will be no hysterics from the ladies."

Mr. Billings, a handsome, smooth-faced man, was busy agreeing with everything that Will was saying about the problem and was affecting an appearance of helpful interest, which was nice enough, but it did strike Meribah that active participation would be more in order.

"Quite right, Mr. Simon. Yes! Yes! Uh huh. Yes. Yes. Certainly . . . a splendid idea . . . Ah, Mr. and Mrs. Whiting, Mr. Simon suggests something called a scarfing joint here to . . . Is that what you call it—scarfing joint?"

"Just scarfing it," replied Will.

"Yes, yes, a scarfing to mend the fracture. Splendid idea, don't you think?"

"We imagine that Will here knows best," Henry replied.

"Yes. We trust Will." Henrietta added, "He's an absolute genius with wood. Whatever he recommends is bound to be the best answer."

"Yes. Well, now!" Wrentham Billings clapped his slender hands together. "How do we go about this scarfing business?"

"Does thou have an adz and a plane?"

"An adz and a plane?" Mr. Billings asked. There was almost a scholarly tone of curiosity in his voice. "Adz and plane? I do not believe that we have those in our tool inventory. No, I am afraid not."

"Well, I have them," Will said patiently. "Meribah, would thee find them, child?"

"Sure, Pa."

Half smiles of utter disdain creased the Whitings' faces. "We'll get our files," Henry said, "to smooth off those rough spots for the joinery work."

There was a blizzard of yeses from Mr. Billings, accompanied by nods and other expressions of agreement. After delivering the tools there was nothing more for Meribah to do, so passing by Mrs. Barker, who, like a mother with a sick child, was hovering over an unrolled bolt of linsey and various other damp articles from the largest emporium of the three towns, she joined the Billings ladies on their grassy resting spot.

The worried expressions had evaporated from Serena's and Mrs. Billings' faces when they saw that the situation was now under control. They were engaged in an animated conversation regarding a certain Miss Phoebe Van der Vere and Miss Van der Vere's shocking décolleté gown at a Philadelphia ball. Meribah certainly had never been to a ball, but the entire conversation fascinated her. Where the Billings might be condescending toward others in the company, they seemed not to be able to place Will and Meribah onto any particular level in their social scheme of things. They treated the Simons as a special case. "Your way" was the manner in which Mrs. Billings described and justified Meribah's odd drawing of the creek they had followed and crisscrossed for three days. The drawing was a sinuous dark line that darted in and out of patches of sunlight and shadow. Serena and her mother had stared as if it was one of the most confounding things they had ever seen, and then with all the graciousness she could muster, Mrs. Billings said, "You say it's a creek, dear? Well,

I suppose it could be . . . although it does lack some detail. But I suppose that's your way."

There had been no further discussion of drawing lessons since that day. Meribah knew exactly what "your way" meant in their minds: the Amish way. They would treat her drawing style in the same way they did her speech and manner of dress, as something different and therefore excused from the normal standards. So the Billingses were warm toward Meribah and her father and respected their differences. Meribah treated them somewhat similarly and once she had overcome her initial apprehension of them, she no longer became so flustered in their presence and indeed found them curious and engaging. It was so easy to listen to the Billingses. They made her feel comfortable even though she did not participate much in the conversation. They seemed to enjoy her as a listener to their opinions, their amusing observations, their asides and exclamations, which for Meribah glittered like ornaments in their conversation. She adored their decorative descriptions of everything from food to balls to clothes. She had learned so much about "couture." For Amish women there were either shawls or cloaks, but for Serena and her mother and the rest of the Philadelphia ladies there were not only shawls and cloaks but pelerines and pelisses and pardessuses and capes and crispins and mantles. Meribah had known of three materials for clothes—cotton for summer, and wool and flannel for winter—but from the Billings women she heard about grenadines and satins, Chantilly and velvet, tulle and crepe. She learned about bishop's sleeves and bavolet hat draperies and brandenbourg tasseling and babet bonnets. And then there was ruching and shirring and ruffling and tucking. These were words that she had never heard before, but they were delightful to whisper in one's head even if one would never have a use for them. It seemed to Meribah that she and her father talked mostly about adzes and planes, tallow and beeswax, grain and meal, the wagon's condition and Simon-Whiting's condition.

In spite of his lack of desire or inability at any really laborious task, Francis Wrentham Billings had an easy manner and amiability that made Meribah in turn feel relaxed and comfortable. He had drifted over to join the women and now stretched out on the grass beside them. Meribah thought that he probably would not have a wrinkle or speck of dirt on him when he got up again. He was that kind of man.

"Your father is an absolute wizard, my child, and between his wizardry and the Whitings' industry, the problem will be solved, the wagon tongue mended, and it will be Westward Ho! once again. Why, even McSwat and son have lent a hand."

Meribah looked over to where her father and the three other men were straining and sweating. Mr. Billings was as cool and crisp as the new morning. She was convinced that he never sweated, no matter what. But there was Mrs. Whiting, who even on this relatively cool morning was breaking out with beads of sympathetic perspiration as she watched her husband and Mr. McSwat drag a heavy timber to act as a support under the wagon tongue.

"Those McSwats," sighed Mrs. Billings, "are beyond belief!"

"Beyond the pale, perhaps?" Mr. Billings laughed gently. "But hard workers, my dear."

"But so slovenly, so greasy!" Serena's little valentine mouth curled in disgust.

There might have been some vague stirring within Meribah to move away, to ask her father if there was anything she might do. But it seemed so harmless sitting here just listening, and as if to confirm the truly harmless nature of the conversation, Mr. Billings broke in, "Now! My dear Serena, let us not be too critical or quick in our judgments. The McSwats are different, just as our friend Meribah here is different."

"Not just as!" boomed Mrs. Billings. "Meribah is a dear, charming, lovely child," and then in a whisper, "as delicate as the McSwats are coarse. You cannot speak of them in the same breath, Wrentham. You owe an apology to our dear Meribah!"

"Of course I did not mean to compare you with them, Meribah. And I am sure that you, my child, understand what positive value I put on your differences."

Meribah was not the least offended. She had never heard herself discussed by others for more than five consecutive seconds, and never had she received such a string of compliments. She was charming, lovely, dear, and delicate. She could listen to these people all day long.

"The McSwats!" huffed Serena. "Look at them, Father. They're so . . . so piggy!"

"Somewhat porcine. I would agree." Mr. Billings nodded. "Yes. Yes, that they are."

Meribah looked over at Mrs. McSwat, rolling about on the grass, tussling with her immensely chubby baby girl. She found herself enjoying their jumbo grace when suddenly her eyes filled. Don't let go! she sternly ordered herself.

"I dare say"—Serena's fringe of curls bobbed—"you're an absolute lamb in comparison!"

I'm a lamb, Meribah thought absently, a charming, lovely, delicate lamb.

In the next two days Meribah lost count of the number of creeks, rivers, and streams they crossed, either by ferry or fording. Some were swollen with heavy flows from spring floods, and their banks were steep and slippery. When it was a fast-moving current they were fording, Will insisted that she remain in the wagon for fear of her being swept away. Then it took two men to guide the oxen across, one on the left side of the wagon, holding the reins, and one at the oxen's heads. It was slow and tense work. Will and Henry Whiting would help each other and then alternate helping the Billingses. The Barkers and the Grays exchanged men at the fords. The McSwats and the Gentlemen's Wagons had enough men to work their own way across. The Timms, with no wagon, were usually first across. In the beginning, Meribah was perplexed, but she gradually became irritated with what seemed a seething impatience on the part of the Timms as they stood high and almost dry on the far side while watching the other folk skid, break down, stumble, and strain through the mud with their heavy wagons.

Meribah and Will had crossed a lot of rivers between Pennsylvania and St. Jo, but these west of the Missouri began to wear her down. The innumerable breaks of axles and wagon tongues, the wheels stuck in mud, had slowed their pace considerably. One day they covered only three miles between morning and dusk.

"Why don't they go on? They could, thou knows. They could ride scout like Mr. Moxley." Meribah spoke in a harsh whisper and glared at the Timm brothers on the other side of the stream. "Why do they always wait for everyone on the opposite bank with all their . . . their anger!"

"They wouldn't have any place to put it if they left us."

Meribah looked at her father with surprise. "What does thou mean?"

"Some folks are born angry. I reckon those two were. But don't waste thy time thinking on them. There are a lot more streams to cross, so those two are just going to be there with the mud on the banks. Get used to it or thee will wear thyself down for no good reason."

Meribah already felt worn. By the end of the day she was usually soaked and mud-splattered. And the end of a day was not really the end. Muddy things had to be washed, damp bedding had to be dried as much as possible, Simon-Whiting had to be milked and her udders "balmed" according to the Whitings' instructions. Mrs. Whiting also insisted that they make "a good square meal for the menfolk." Meribah would have been very happy to send everybody to bed with a hunk of bread and some jerked beef.

Not only was it tiring to make such a meal at the end of the day, but Meribah resented Mrs. Whiting's always saying "for the menfolk," as if the women did not work. She worked as hard as her father. Maybe she didn't get into the fast streams,

42

but then again he didn't build the cooking fires or do the washing. Besides, they all—menfolk and womenfolk—ate the food, so why say it was for the men? There was a tiresome cycle to Meribah's thinking just before sleep. She thought about not having had dry stockings in almost a week. She thought about the vexing "square meals." She thought about "menfolk" and "womenfolk." She thought about Mrs. Barker hovering over her storehouse of goods like an indulgent mother over a spoiled brat, and about the Timms on the opposite bank. Then damp, tired, and frustrated over things she could not change, she would fall asleep.

The stream, mud thick and slow moving, was shallow. So Meribah, whose dress was already soiled, said that she would lead the team and that there was no need for Mr. Whiting to slog back across to help. Theirs was the third wagon to cross. Meribah took hold of the yoke bow and led the team into the stream. The Timms should be happy, she thought—I'm saving the group time. So should Mr. Billings, for he too had become a bit touchy over the slow progress of late. The water was cold, and the mud sucked softly beneath her feet. They were past the halfway point when she felt a huge bubble of mud burst underfoot. She heard a loud muddy gulp, and suddenly everything was brown and swirling. She clamped shut her eyes and mouth. There was a roar of water and a horrible wet furry thing all over her face. Then she felt herself being pulled up by some incredible strength. She broke through the surface gasping and choking and black with mud. She felt herself being lifted high, clear above the ox horns, by a big ham of an arm.

"She's all right! She's all right!" Mr. McSwat shouted, and gave her a little shake in the air, as if to dry her off, before setting her down on the opposite bank.

"Meribah! Thee is a sight to behold, my mud lass!" Will's mouth was a trembly smile.

May 20, 1849
On the prairie: moving from
Kansas Territory northwest into
Nebraska Territory

4

THE EVERYWHERE SKY

The land suddenly flattened, and the sky seemed everywhere. There was an occasional tree, perhaps a single house on an otherwise unmarked horizon, but mostly there was immensity and aloneness. When they stopped one day—perhaps the second or third since crossing the last creek—for lunch, there was not a tree for shade, a stump for a table, or even a rock to sit on. So Meribah and her father used the ground for both table and seat, with the tall thick prairie grass shielding the two of them from the hugeness of it all.

In a crush of grass beneath a great blue plank of western sky, Meribah lay flat on her back and, eating her sandwich, thought of other rooms, other tables, other ceilings. "That wind, Pa, it comes right from the edge, doesn't it?"

"The edge of what, Meribah?"

"The edge of the continent, I guess."

Will laughed softly. "Thee perhaps feels in need of edges and fences in this hugeness?"

"Sometimes. Yes, just now I suppose I do, but I like not having edges too. There is a loveliness to an endless wind and an everywhere sky."

Meribah stood up and stretched. Her muscles felt kinked and knotted, and there was an ache deep in her bones from the days of lurching and jolting in the wagon along the roughest road she had ever seen. If blood were milk, she thought, she would have butter in her veins by now, for there was no easier way to churn a bucket of Simon-Whiting's milk

44

than to hang it from the rear of the wagon on this fractious road. She lifted her arms higher and stretched skyward with all her strength, fanning her fingers until she thought that the skin between them might split. She marveled at the wedges of blue sky that they held—six blue V's and then two deep curves between thumbs and forefingers. As striking a design as was ever quilted back in Holly Springs, Meribah thought.

Just as she dropped her arms, Meribah caught sight of the Whitings. They were not more than fifty yards away, but they could have been dots on the horizon. Meribah walked toward them, and even though she knew they should become bigger as she closed the distance, they seemed to become smaller, and she felt herself grow smaller, too. There was something appalling about this immensity and the way it dwarfed people. The Whitings had found an old wagon wheel in the grass and were now perched on its rim, arm in arm, shoulder to shoulder. Mrs. Whiting's apron billowed out over Mr. Whiting's knees. When she spoke, her voice was a small scratch in the wind.

"Meribah, child, Henry and I have been discussing the trail dust—"

"Yes," Henry broke in. "We think it's mighty hard on old Simon-Whiting to be tethered behind all the time in the dust kicked up by the wagon."

"So," Henrietta continued, "we think it more healthful if we should take turns leading Simon-Whiting in front, where the air is a little clearer."

"We certainly don't want her lungs going bad. She'd be dead before Fort Childs."

"Oh, you're absolutely right, Mr. and Mrs. Whiting. I'd be much pleased to walk a ways. I'll take the first spell now. I don't mind the sun."

"Well, that's mighty kind of you, dear," said Mrs. Whiting. "Wear your larger bonnet now, and we'll spell you whenever you get tired."

A sudden sharp crack split the prairie air like a dry log consumed in flames.

45

"The Timms!" Mr. and Mrs. Whiting said at once.

"Those durn brothers!" Mrs. Whiting seethed, "and their durn pistol practice."

The sound tore the air again.

"I can't stand it!" Meribah whispered. "I just can't. Why do they do this?"

"The space is too big for them." Will had come to join Meribah and the Whitings. "They need to fill it up with their own noise."

"With their own savagery. They're going to make the Pawnee look like something out of Mrs. Billings's Philadelphia drawing room!"

The four of them watched the thin black curls of smoke rise in the low sky and blow away. The shots stopped suddenly. Meribah saw the lurching swiftness of Captain Griffith slice through the prairie grass. Fifty yards or more ahead of him, where the grass grew much taller, she watched it rustle, part, and come together again in a thin winding line, as if something were gliding through it very close to the earth. She turned quickly and walked back with her father and the Whitings toward the wagons. Nobody spoke.

Meribah took the first spell of walking in front of the wagon with Simon-Whiting. As she walked across the prairie, her head was full of valley thoughts. She looked for robins where there were only hawks, land dips where there was only flatness. She imagined a river where a wind current chased through the feathery grass. A white puff came blowing toward her.

"Serena!"

"I came to take a turn with you on this prairie promenade." She spoke out from under the layers of gauze swathed about her straw bonnet. Around her shoulders was wrapped a thin cream-colored pelerine that fell in two points near her knees. Her hands were gloved, and she carried a white parasol.

"Serena, I thought you were an old dandelion blow tumbling down the road."

"How charming! An old dandelion blow! You are a funny dear, Meribah. I thought I resembled at least a meringue glacée!"

"What is that you're wearing?"

"A sun costume, my dear. One shouldn't venture into the noonday without it. Your skin will turn as tough as an old hide, Meribah."

"Well, I don't have such a costume."

"Here! Take one of these." Serena daintily untied a gossamer layer from her hat and draped it around Meribah's bonnet so it hung down across her face. "Now how's that?"

"Very nice. I feel as if I'm in a nest peeking out. Do I look like a what does th—you—call it? A meringue glacée?"

"No. You look like the charming Amish girl you are, with a veil on your bonnet." Serena paused. "I have noticed, Meribah, that you have altered your speech a bit. You started to say 'thou' and then said 'you.' "

"Yes, it's easier. With Pa, of course, I speak Amish, but it's easier with you to say 'you.' " Meribah spoke cheerfully.

"Yes, I suppose, but these little differences are nice. They can . . . they can. . . ."—it was one of the few times Meribah had ever heard Serena falter for a word—"make us special in spite of all this." She gestured toward the sky. "Why, my mother and I have a cup of tea and read some poetry every night before retiring."

"Poetry!" a voice exclaimed from behind.

"Mr. Wickham!" Serena cried with delight.

" 'Keen, fitful gusts are whisp'ring here and there,' " he began, and then paused, looking about. " 'Among the bushes half leafless, and dry.' "

This must be poetry, Meribah thought excitedly.

> "The stars look very cold about the sky,
> And I have many miles on foot to fare.
> Yet feel I little of the cold bleak air."

The rhythm began to move her feet along. Even Simon-Whiting seemed to feel the cadences in her gait.

> "Or of the dead leaves rustling drearily,
> Or of those silver lamps that burn on high,
> Or of the distance from home's pleasant lair."

Meribah felt as if she could listen always to this poet's words delivered in Mr. Wickham's shimmering English accent.

> "For I am brimful of the friendliness
> That in a little cottage I have found;
> Of fair-hair'd Milton's eloquent distress,
> And all his love for gentle Lycid drown'd;
> Of lovely Laura in her light green dress,
> And faithful Petrarch gloriously crown'd."

"Oh, Mr. Wickham!" Serena's face was beaming—Meribah thought "brimful"—with admiration. "An elegant recitation. Such sensibility! Such lilt! Such perfection!"

Mr. Wickham obviously found Serena's rhapsody as pleasing as the poet's.

Serena turned quickly to Meribah. "Was that not superb?"

Meribah was quite at a loss for words after the stylish praise Serena offered. She paused to search for the phrases to match her feelings. Serena and Mr. Wickham both looked at her. "It...." she began, and then stopped. "It...it...."—Serena's and Mr. Wickham's faces were set with anticipation—"it moved my feet right across this prairie, Mr. Wickham. It truly did!"

Mr. Wickham's face brightened. "How charming, Meribah! How enchantingly plain! How plainly enchanting!"

She felt a warm rush in her face, and bit her lower lip. Why couldn't she answer poetry with poetry, as Serena did? How undeserving she felt to hear such poetry. Mr. Wickham was now discoursing on the man who had written the poem, and Serena, her face tilted in pretty attention, was listening to every word with an interest that Mr. Wickham must have found extremely flattering. The two of them seemed quite oblivious of Meribah, and she began to feel uncomfortable.

"Meribah! Did you hear what Mr. Wickham said?"

"Yes. I mean no. I'm sorry."

"Mr. Wickham says that by this time tomorrow we shall be seeing Indians!"

"Pawnee," added Mr. Wickham.

"Are you not frightened, Meribah? Why, we shan't be walking about like this if we value our lives. I understand that they think nothing of abducting white women."

"Yes, we shall have to set guards about. Captain Griffith has already spoken to several of us about that. They're a terrible thieving lot, these Pawnee."

"Murderous, I've heard," said Meribah, entering the conversation.

"Er . . . yes. I have heard that adjective used too. However" —he turned toward Serena—"there is no need for alarm as long as we are prepared, and I can assure you that Captain Griffith is prepared and quite proficient in dealing with these savages."

Meribah was not alarmed in the least. She had seen a painting somewhere, in either St. Jo or St. Louis, of a Pawnee chief and two warriors, with shaved heads and painted bodies, festooned in all kinds of feathers and draped in scarlet and blue blankets. She found them spectacular and actually looked forward to seeing them. If the day ever came when she put aside her cap and gray dress, she would be hard-pressed deciding whether to wear in their place a blue satin hoop gown with ruching and Chantilly lace or a scarlet blanket with a gorgeous turkey-feather headdress and thin stripes of white paint on her cheekbones. She almost laughed out loud just thinking about this unimaginable choice, or about what Serena and her mother would think if she actually did appear in a blanket and feathers, or about what her own mother would think if she appeared in either costume.

"Did you. . . ." She began to giggle, "Did you . . . ." She could not stifle the giggle.

"Meribah, what is so humorous?"

"Indeed," Mr. Wickham said, "does our friend find the prospect of the thieving Pawnee entertaining? You look absolutely mirthful, child."

"Pray tell us, Meribah, what is the cause of all this mirth?"

Meribah stopped giggling and was possessed with the old feelings of awkwardness in their company. "Did you happen to see the painting of the Pawnee chief and warriors? It was in St. Louis, I believe."

"In the hotel?" asked Mr. Wickham. "The one by George Goodnough?"

"Yes, that one in the hotel, and the artist's name was Goodnough. Goodnough," Meribah repeated. The name sounded very familiar.

"Yes, Goodnough, quite a chap with the brush and palette. He has done some of the best portraiture of Indians about."

Meribah searched her memory. Goodnough! It suddenly came to her, the man at the counter in St. Jo buying quills and ink and paper! The clerk had called him Mr. Goodnough. "I met a man named Goodnough in St. Jo, but he said he was a mapmaker."

"Well, it's a very common name. I doubt if this mapmaker is the same Goodnough, although there's always the possibility."

"There are so many subjects for the painter's palette out here," Serena exclaimed. "Tonight I plan to do a still life of prairie flowers I have been gathering."

"Oh, how splendid!" Mr. Wickham exclaimed.

Serena described to Mr. Wickham exactly how she would arrange the bouquet in the adorable Wedgwood bone china vase against the setting sun. Meribah silently thanked God and mentally tapped wood that the subject of drawing lessons had not been raised again since the Billings women had seen her drawing of the creek. There was some discussion about the hour of sunset, and it was decided that Mr. Wickham would like nothing better than to join Serena while she sketched. "So I shall see you at six, Miss Serena, and help you with the arrangement of your still life."

"I shall await you in my atelier, Mr. Wickham," Serena said, and gestured at the sky.

Will Simon took the next turn with Simon-Whiting, and Meribah drove the team. From the high seat she could see the entire procession of wagons and pack animals. If she squinted into the westing sun, this line seemed to ooze in slow undulations across the prairie like a ribbon of molasses, languid but destined.

Henry Whiting then spelled Will. Although Henry walked and Henrietta, some one hundred feet behind him, drove their team, it was as if they could not let go of each other. Constant instructions on driving the wagon and leading Simon-Whiting were called back and forth. And in Meribah's ear the two voices became one, echoey but without resonance. Next to Henry, as Meribah watched him walk, there grew an empty space that kept apace, until a mirage of a skirted, bonneted woman walked alongside him, and gradually, as the minutes slipped by, Meribah watched the mirage figure move closer and closer to the real walking figure. Then the two began to overlap and melt into an indistinguishable solitary form that was neither man nor woman, Henry or Henrietta. Meribah felt oddly unnerved. She looked away to find Will watching her.

"Did thee ever notice," he asked, "how much Mr. and Mrs. Whiting walk alike? Put a skirt and a bonnet on Henry Whiting and thee would think him to be Henrietta."

"Oh, Pa! Thou is a thought-reader."

"So thee noticed the same?"

"So much so that my eyes could barely sort them out. They have a oneness that is perfectly odd, but makes for a true marriage." As soon as the words were out, Meribah was overcome with shame. "Oh, Pa! I did not mean . . . thou should . . . Oh, how foolish I . . . Oh, Pa! I am so shameful!"

"Meribah, there is nothing to be sorry about. Thee spoke what thee believes to be true. There is no shame in that. If there is shame, it is not thine."

51

For what seemed like an endless hour, the wagon lurched and jolted its way across the prairie, and Meribah watched as Henry Whiting led in front. When the time came for Henrietta to spell her husband, Meribah quickly jumped down from her seat and said she would be most pleased to stretch her legs. Henrietta protested, but Meribah insisted, saying this was her favorite time of day to walk, and she quickly conjured up a number of reasons why it would be sheer delight for her to lead a cow across this infinite flatness. Henrietta Whiting finally gave in, calling Meribah a blessed little saint.

A blessed little saint. As she walked along now, kicking up slight explosions of dust, Meribah suddenly thought about those "particles of doubt," the ones that had bedeviled her in St. Jo. In spite of her grand plan, the precise drawing of salvation, with its straight lines and right angles, Meribah had not really given an hour's attention to it since that day. She had ceased alternating "thou" and "you" and, as Serena had pointed out, had slipped into addressing everyone except her father as "you." She had read the Bible only when her father had brought it out, but never on her own initiative. The rest of the time she had spent reading the accompaniment and some other guides that Mr. Billings had lent her, one in particular about gold-panning techniques.

The dark feelings, the inadmissible feelings, crept back. Crept back across the flatness of the prairie, slithered through the oceans of grass. There was no distraction, only immensity swept with fear. And then there was loneliness, a terrible loneliness that waited for her patiently.

"What is thou here for?" Meribah looked up, startled to see her father walking beside her. "Who is minding the team?"

"They know to follow," Will said. "I thought thee needed some company."

"Oh, I am fine, Pa. I am."

"Oh, yes, I know. Perhaps I need thy company."

The wagons pulled into a square formation for the night camp. The Whitings and the Simons usually had supper together, and this evening Henrietta insisted that she would get the baking underway and that Meribah should go and have herself some fun. Henry and Will set out with Captain Griffith in hopes of shooting a prairie hen for supper. Pushing thoughts of cheerless tasks like mending from her mind, Meribah decided to watch the last flash of the setting sun. On her way to do just that, she came upon Serena and Mr. Wickham arranging the bouquet of flowers in the Wedgwood vase atop an old wagon hub they had found in the grass. Her instincts were to turn away, but Serena called out to her to come join them.

"Do stay, Meribah. Mr. Wickham proposes the most marvelous setting for this still life. Oh, pray explain it, Mr. Wickham. He really describes it much better than I shall ever be able to sketch it."

"Nonsense! It is merely a matter of setting this simple prairie offering"—he gestured toward the bunch of flowers— "so selectively gathered and composed by Miss Billings in this exquisite vase, against the vast and triumphant western sky. Miss Billings's use of this wheel hub as a pedestal for her arrangement was an absolute coup, a stroke of true artistry— the contrasting of the fine porcelain against the harsh textures of this hub, roughened and dessicated by the aridity of the climate." Mr. Wickham was becoming quite carried away by his own speechmaking. Serena seemed so limp from his praise that Meribah wondered if she would even be able to grip her pencil. Mr. Wickham, noting the effect of his words, forged on with new vigor. "Indeed, the entire pastiche: the harshness of the hub, the delicacy of the bouquet, the splendor of the vase"—he inhaled deeply and continued—"bring together the grandeur of the West"—he gestured broadly toward the horizon as if to summon it to his side—"and the elegance of the East." He spoke in a quieter voice now. "Why, it is as if Miss Billings in her infinite hospitality has brought a little corner of her Philadelphia parlor right out here to the Nebraska prairie and made it a more charming and intimate place to be."

"Oh, not the parlor, Mr. Wickham, but more likely the winter garden of my grandmama's house."

"Ah, yes!" Mr. Wickham's eyes seemed to dance at the prospect of Grandmama's winter garden.

Meribah felt the old awkwardness returning. Serena had not yet drawn one thing on the paper, but even if she was a premier pupil back in Philadelphia, it was hard to believe that a vase with a bunch of foxglove and wild roses on an old wagon hub was going to make the prairie any different, any more "charming" or "intimate." Nonetheless she told them that the drawing *sounded* beautiful. The sun was sinking fast, and Serena sat down on a small stool to begin drawing. Mr. Wickham stood behind her, holding a parasol over her head to shade her eyes and the paper from the glare of the low-angle sun. The flash would come soon. Meribah watched the flat and coppery sun slide down like a coin behind the horizon. There it was! The vanishing flash of light. All their eyes flinched as the white blindness for a slit in time erased all—the horizon, the ocean of waving grass, Serena's arrangement. At the same moment, the air split with the fire of a hunting rifle. Prairie hen for supper, Meribah thought abstractedly. The vase with the flowers quivered, and she thought she saw a hairline crack begin at the base just beneath a painted rosette.

There was a real chill in the air now, and Meribah, with neither shawl nor fringed pardessus, as Serena was wearing, became cold. "I have to go, Serena. I'm chilled to the marrow, but I can't wait to see your lovely drawing. Will it be finished tomorrow?"

"I hope so," Serena answered. "Oh, my, it is chilly, and you have no wrap. Do run along, dear. Adieu!"

"Cheerio," Mr. Wickham said gaily.

"Good night."

Meribah started toward the wagon square. In a gathering of shadows not fifty feet away from where she had been, Meribah stopped dead in her tracks and inhaled so sharply as to make a small cry. The Timm brothers stood in front of her.

"Dint mean to disturb you, ma'am." They were looking beyond Meribah, but just beyond.

"Skeer you a little?" asked one brother. Their gaze was still fixed on something just beyond her.

"No. Not at all. I just didn't know you were here. That's all."

"Jist watching the sunset like the rest of you fine folks." Still they stared beyond her, and the taller brother seemed to raise his chin a bit as if to point with it toward Serena and Mr. Wickham.

"Well, the sun has set and I'm going back to my father."

"Evenin', miss."

Meribah rushed off thinking that there was something equally dreadful about the Timms' sunset watching and their shooting up the prairie with their pistols. She sped by Mrs. Barker, who had spread out an India rubber cloth and was on her hands and knees sorting out dry goods, laying them out as if she were doing a window display back in Franklin. She raced by Johnny McSwat, who was carving something in the skinny trunk of the encampment's lone tree, a sapling, the single survivor of a grove emigrants had probably tried to plant a few years earlier. People are always trying to fill up this place, Meribah thought. Johnny was most likely carving the same thing he had three days ago when they saw the last sapling: JOHNNY MC SWAT HERE JUNE 1, 1849.

Meribah tried to push the Timms out of her mind as she ran back. It was not a bad idea—leaving your mark in an otherwise markless place. She wondered if the letters in Johnny McSwat's name would grow bigger with the tree— if the tree survived, that is. Maybe she should try carving her name in the next tree she saw. Then all the time she was traveling to California, she could think about her name growing bigger back on the prairie.

"Aha! You're here and hungry as an Illinois farm hand at haying time," Mrs. Whiting greeted Meribah.

"What is thee running so hard for or from, Meribah?"

"Nothing, Pa. Well, no, I did smell Mrs. Whiting's rolls baking and just got so hungry from the smell that I ran all the way back." But her voice had a giddiness that was not due entirely to hard running.

"Get a wrap, child. You'll freeze to death even by the fire."

Later, there was roasted prairie hen and hot rolls, dried fruit that had been stewed, and fine coffee with a little sugar. Henrietta Whiting, who considered herself quite a cook, sat next to Meribah sharing her kitchen secrets. "We always lard the breast a little bit. Keeps the juices in . . . A touch of vinegar in the stewed fruit will help preserve it if there are leftovers . . . And, dear, your suggestions about the rolls, really!"

"Oh, yes, Meribah," Henry interrupted. "These rolls are light as goose down."

"They are very tasty, Mrs. Whiting. Thou has baked them just right." Meribah took a bite. "What is a pastiche?" she asked suddenly.

"A what?" the Whitings said in unison.

"A pastiche."

"Confounds me," Will said. "Where did thee ever hear of it?"

"From Mr. Wickham when he was helping Serena Billings with her drawing this evening."

"Oh, no!" snorted Mrs. Whiting. "It must be one of those king's English words. How's the romance coming?"

"Fine, I guess," Meribah said, licking her fingers from the prairie hen wing she had just eaten.

"Sounds very romantic," Will chuckled, "talking about pastiches."

"It sounds like a fancy roll or cruller twist just like the ones Zoellners made, Pa."

"Now what's a cruller?" Henrietta Whiting asked.

"Oh, the best-tasting thing thou ever ate."

"Can we make them here?"

"Oh, never. They're small cakes of sweet dough twisted or braided into rings and then deep-fried. It takes so much fat that we'd use up all our lard for one batch."

"Imagine that," Henry said. "Talking about fancy cakes out here on the prairie with a pretty girl."

"No, it wasn't cakes, Mr. Whiting. I just meant that the word reminded me of cakes. It has something else to do with great artistry."

"Great artistry?" Will lifted his brow. "Is that what they talk about out here?"

"Oh, thou would be surprised at what they talk about out here."

"What?" said Henrietta Whiting, suddenly curious.

"Oh, all sorts of stuff—poetry, ball dancing, fashion—coo-ture." Meribah screwed up her mouth to say the word.

"Coo-what?" Mrs. Whiting said.

"Coo-ture—fancy clothes and such."

"I'll be," Henry said. "What did we talk about when we were courting, Henrietta?"

"Now, how do you expect me to remember that? Really! We certainly didn't talk about coo-ture."

"We might have talked about dancing, though." Henry's eyes twinkled. "Remember those dances at Lester Creek?"

"Thou danced?" asked Will, suddenly interested.

"Sure we did—quadrilles."

"And reels," added Henrietta.

"And polkas."

"That must be fun, to dance," Will said. Meribah was completely taken aback. Dancing had always been forbidden for Amish people as frivolous and ungodly. Here was Will almost sounding as if he would like to try it. Fun, he had said, it must be fun. Meribah did not think she had ever heard her father say that word before. It was not a word common to the grown-up vocabulary in the Amish community.

"Could thou show us a dance?"

Meribah's eyes flew wide open. She stared at her father in utter amazement. The man must be touched!

"There's no music," said Henry Whiting.

"You need music." Henrietta spoke with a hint of regret.

"Well, could thou sing a little something?" Will urged.

The man has lost his mind, Meribah thought, not so much with apprehension as confusion.

"Well, I don't know," demurred Mr. Whiting, but there was something giving in his voice.

"You know, it's been so long," added Mrs. Whiting. "I doubt if Henry could rightly remember. Could you, dear?"

"Well, now, Rietta, I'm not so sure of that. I might remember a few steps of that one reel we always did down at Clawson's."

"Oh, you mean the one where you do a quarter turn and tap your partner's shoulder with your own?"

"That's the one, Rietta!"

"Do it!" Will said excitedly. "Go on, do it. Meribah and I will sing 'Oh, Susanna'!"

"Pa!" whispered Meribah with astonishment, but he didn't seem to hear her.

" 'Susanna' is the only song we know. Will it work?"

"Oh, it'll work fine," Henrietta said with a giggle. "All right then, Henry, come on."

Will leaned over to Meribah. "Don't worry. If St. Peter really takes offense at this, which I doubt, ask him to speak to thy father." Then in a louder voice, "Ready, folks, here we go!

"I came from Alabama with a tin pan on my knee,
I'm going to California, my true love for to see.
It rained all night the day I left,
The weather it was dry.

The sun's so hot I froze to death,
Susanna, don't you cry."

Meribah could do nothing but stare at her father as he sang the first lines of the song. The Whitings had faced each other, bowed stiffly, and begun to move their feet tentatively. Will picked up the tempo, and Meribah saw that his face glowed, not just from the reflected orange light of the campfire, but from a deeper source, another kindling. She opened her mouth to sing, but no song came out. There was only the shape of a word left on her lips. She took a deeper breath and pushed the air through her windpipe a little harder. A word came out, then another and another. It became easier. It was exciting. It was such a strange new feeling—sounds together like this in your throat and the feel of them on your tongue like a ribbon of honey. To sing! It feels like a miracle, Meribah thought.

They were into the second verse. The Whitings quickened their steps. Their bodies moved with a jerky precision, but also with a spirit and lightness. A fiddle began to play. It was Captain Griffith, who had walked over and picked up the music midsong. The fiddle music helped smooth out the jerkiness in their steps. For most of the reel the Whitings never touched each other, just grazed each other's shoulder in the quarter turns. They faced each other, turned their backs, and jigged out toward the just-rising stars and then back again. They circled while looking over their shoulders at each other. They looked young—young and flirtatious and romantic and . . . and daring, Meribah thought suddenly. Daring. She would never have thought of the Whitings as daring.

Griffith was playing another tune and calling instructions:

"Turn your back and dosey do . . .
Whirl your partner by the hand,
Throw a kiss to the promised land."

Henry whirled Henrietta around, and they swirled off

separately, throwing kisses toward California, laughing and whooping and winking at each other. They looked so different to Meribah. In the dance each had a very distinct rhythm and style. Henry Whiting had a loping loose-jointed gait, and Henrietta moved with a bouncy roundness. They had lost that odd oneness and now seemed separate but still partners, single yet whole.

The dance ended. They both flopped down on the two stools by the fire, breathlessly declaring themselves spent, tuckered, finished off.

"Your turn," said Henrietta Whiting, nodding toward Meribah and Will.

"Yes. Rietta's right. Your turn."

"Oh, no! No!" Will shook his head, laughing. "It wore me out just watching." Meribah looked expectantly toward her father. "Another day perhaps, but not tonight."

"Spoilers," said Captain Griffith with a mock scowl.

"Captain Griffith, it is mighty pleasing to know that you carry with you something more than just that sleeping tarp of yours." Henrietta Whiting pointed toward the fiddle.

"Oh, it's my sleeping pillow, ma'am. Wrap it in a dirty shirt and it's perfect."

"And I suppose thou carries thy cooking gear inside it?" kidded Will. Jokes about the lightness of gear with which Griffith traveled were a favorite topic for Will and the Whitings. His equipment for the entire trip consisted of little more than his horse, rifle, compass, and tarp. He carried no tent but slept on top or under his India rubber tarp with a fragment of buffalo hide for warmth.

"No. But it's not a bad idea."

The party broke up with promises of more dancing another night. In the campfire's light, their long shadows crisscrossed the ground as they walked back to their wagons.

Meribah lay on her pallet in the wagon. Through a small tear in the wagon cover she watched the stars move across the sky. She had meant to patch it but never seemed to get around to it. She liked this little slice of night suspended above her, a piece of the bigger design, and although she could never imagine sleeping out under the vast sweep of it, as Griffith did, at this moment the vastness did not seem so threatening. She thought of the Whitings happily whirling and swirling under the starry blackness, of her father's face tilted skyward and akindle as he sang. Nothing presses down here, she thought, to take a scrape at one's head. Like a faded tracing on worn paper, she had a fleeting image of ceiling beams and other rooms. No, she thought sleepily, this space seems right for him. Holly Springs was tiny and cramped. In an odd way they were both growing accustomed to such breadth of sky and land. She was not sure what kind of drawing she could make of the prairie. Would it have people or not? She watched the few stars that shone through the canvas tear, isolated now in a black wedge from the rest of night's design. I am a tiny speck, Meribah thought, sometimes lost, sometimes a particle of something else. "Particle." She whispered the word and fell asleep.

The next morning before first light, Meribah was sitting at the rear opening of the wagon. She still wore her nightdress and had two wool shawls wrapped around her shoulders. In her lap was her sketchbook. She held one pencil and had another clamped in her teeth. Her chalks were neatly arranged beside her. She would be ready when dawn spilled. The sky lightened in the east almost indiscernibly. She had whittled her pencil to a slant to give its mark a width and softness. Meribah began to move it lightly back and forth, applying a little more pressure to make the paper appear darker toward the top. A cold pink began to steal over the horizon. She worked quickly now and used three or four different chalks, sometimes broadside to the paper, sometimes point on. She rubbed with her thumb to soften certain areas into a thin diffuse color. Wind blew her hair across her face. She looked up. The prairie was a strange sea now, liquid and flowing with waves of grass. A stretch of grass caught by an odd wind current would suddenly turn deeper in color and swim away like a school of trout in a clear river. Meribah drew it all—the wind like a river current, the cold pink of the half-lit world, the thin, fragile-looking double-track trail. Then she drew another picture. It was shapes of blue, wedges and *V*'s and deep curves against the white of the paper.

"How did thee make such a blue?" Will asked later. "It is exactly the blue of high noon, and here it is barely past dawn, yet thee remembered it."

"Well, I *have* seen it every day for almost two weeks, Pa."

"This is the other drawing?" Will said, picking up the first one.

"Yes. I had to make it quite fast while it was still happening."

"Yes. I see." Will paused. "I see the dawn happening."

June 12, 1849
Following the Platte River near
Loup Fork in central Nebraska Territory

5

ENCIRCLED, ENCLOSED

One-Who-Strikes-Chiefs, Fine-Horse-Running, Buffalo Head, Thunder-Coming, Rattlesnake, Sudden-Heart-Jumping, Raging Buffalo. The names, blood-coursing names that were stories of muscle and spirit, of challenge and triumph, filled Meribah's head. They stood before her now—the great warriors, the "terror of the plains," filthy, ragtag, and starving, begging for bread, opening their robes to show their bony rib cages. How would this Goodnough draw them now? With feathers and war paint, she wondered, as she watched a bug crawl out from the leggings of one Indian and up toward his knee. Captain Griffith was talking with one of the chiefs. It was another language. It sounded fast and bumpy to her ear. Gradually as she listened she was able to pick out one word that seemed to be repeated again and again: *Ogalasoo*. She heard it again and again with increasing clarity. The one speaking to Captain Griffith unfolded a cloth and spread it on the ground. Captain Griffith nodded and walked toward the Simons' wagon.

"They want food and tobacco." He spoke to Will softly. "Poor buggers. Been cleaned out by the Sioux." He paused. "And cholera."

"Meribah, get out half a middling of bacon and those loaves thee baked this morning."

"Best thing," Captain Griffith said with a nod. "Give 'em what we can. They'd just steal it if we don't give it to them."

"I say!" Mr. Billings had rushed over and was listening to

Captain Griffith. "These fellows receive a large annuity from the national treasury."

"A large annuity won't stop cholera."

"Well, yes, I suppose you're right. But they're really robbing! Effective measures should be taken by our government. Either give them more or punish them to discourage such acts of savagery."

"They have been punished enough." Just as Will spoke, Meribah had been thinking that Mr. Billings's proposal of more money or more punishment was quite odd.

"Yes! Yes! Poor souls," said Mr. Billings. "You're so right, Mr. Simon. They have been punished enough." He glanced at the loaves of bread that Meribah was handing to Captain Griffith. "Well, I shall go back and discuss with Mrs. Billings what we can spare."

Whatever the discussion was in the Billingses' wagon, it seemed lengthy to Meribah. Johnny McSwat had come and left a bundle on the cloth, and Mr. Wickham's traveling companions had brought two bundles, a contribution from each of their two wagons. Even the Barkers brought some cloth, flour, and chewing tobacco. Finally Mr. Billings emerged. His lips were pressed into a tight grim line that seemed to Meribah totally out of keeping with his usual ease. A small muscle in his jaw seemed to clench into a hard knot just below his ear. He set down a hatful of tobacco. His face broke into an open easy smile. "Well, now here's a hatful of Trefry and Leavitt's best!"

"Him and his la-di-da tobacco," Meribah overheard Mrs. Barker whisper to Eliza Gray.

"Father!" Serena was running toward the group. Meribah started and Will put a hand on her knee to stop her. "Father, here's something else for them. Some tea biscuits and jam."

"But Ser—" She had already turned to run back to the wagon. Mr. Billings looked after her, his mouth hanging open halfway between a smile and a grimace. "Well." He turned with a new jauntiness toward Meribah and Will. "So much for civilization." He chuckled. "So much for tea and smokes in the starlight. These women!"

Meribah wondered what Mr. Billings meant by "civilization." She thought—at least according to her mother—civilized meant being neat and clean and godly and having good table manners.

"Chain up! Chain up!" Captain Griffith's command broke Meribah's reverie. She jumped down from the seat to help her father yoke up the team. The usual noon dinner hour had stretched to two with the Pawnee encounter. She was anxious to get under way. Their route now followed the Platte River. Broad and glittering, it wound like a silver braid across the land. There was much to look at and look for. On one side of the river to the north the plains extended in an expanse until they reached the dim blue mountains. Meribah could see some buffalo, which even at the distance of a half-mile appeared huge and ponderous. Their heavy heads bent low in grazing were as big as the boulders in the creek back in Holly Springs where she and Jeanette had picnicked.

"Wood's scarcer here," Will said to no one in particular.

"Yes, but we have islands." Will smiled at his daughter. "Look at those green lumps popping out of the river silver." Meribah pointed to a string of grassy islets they were now passing.

" 'River silver.' I like that, Meribah. It'll keep me warm as wood on a cold night."

"I'll look for some buffalo chips for thee, just in case." She laughed and started to climb down from her seat.

"Take this stick, Meribah, and turn them first. There can be rattlers underneath."

"All right." She took the stick her father handed her and sprang down from the wagon.

In a short time she had enough chips for a good fire. Meribah actually preferred them to wood, for they kindled much more quickly and kept the heat longer. Baking was a good deal easier with buffalo chips. She had a private laugh when she imagined Mrs. Whiting revealing to the womenfolk back home the secret ingredient for her perfectly baked rolls: "Buffalo chips, my dear. For perfect lightness and even baking, a few chips in the fire!" She saw some wild tulips starting out of the ground, and there were larkspur too and stars of periwinkle scattered everywhere. She would bring a bouquet tonight to the Billingses' tent, for she had been invited to tea, or whatever it was they would serve now that "so-much-for-civilization" had deprived them of tea and smokes.

The outlying lodges came up very suddenly. One moment the river had been to their left, and to their right there had been mounds of earth rising from the sand in various shapes. Then the shapes began to have a sudden regularity, and in the same moment, Meribah and her father realized what they were seeing.

"Earth lodges!"

"A Pawnee village. But it looks deserted."

Will's and Meribah's eyes scanned the lodges as their wagon rolled slowly by. Horizontal poles stuck out of the earthen mounds over the tunnellike entryways. The doorways were dark and silent. As they passed by, only the creaking of their wagon wheels could be heard. Meribah tried to peer into the lodges, but their openings stared back sightless and void. In between the mounds were circular pits filled with rubbish and debris: bones of animals, bleached and cracked, worn-out moccasins, wooden implements, woven mats. Captain Griffith had halted the train, and people were now climbing down from wagons and horses to wander through the village.

Holding her father's hand, Meribah walked through the black portico that led into an earth house. Will struck a match just in time to avoid stumbling, for the floor pitched upon entering, leading one down several feet below the earth's surface. In the flickering light of his match, Meribah could see that they stood in a circular room with a radiating design of rafter poles running out from a high central roof post and joining with horizontal ridgepoles and upright crotches. In this manner the conical roof was braced and framed. The ceiling was covered with rushes and straws. Around the walls were tiers of bunks. Will lit three more matches. He examined the joinery work, pondering the system by which vertical crotches and radials interlocked to support tons of earth. "This is ingenious! Absolutely ingenious!" Meribah knew what her father meant. There was an integrity to the dwelling. She smelled the deep earth smells that blended with the pungency of the rush and straw sheathing. In the perfectly proportioned circular space, Meribah suddenly felt at rest. The effect was extraordinary—it was almost as if until this moment she had spent her life grinding through the hours that made a day, but now it had all stopped in repose and balance.

She began to have feelings about the people who had lived here, who had sat on the mats, ground seeds with mortar and pestle, chewed hide for moccasins, and spoken the names. She found herself trying to move as they might have in this space, and then she sat down on a mat. Crossing her legs, she looked up at the conical ceiling sloped into the walls that met the floor. She felt encircled but not enclosed. There was a feeling in her tailbone and back and shoulders that was unknown to her, that must have come from the earth—the feeling of it underneath and overhead, supporting her and embracing her but never pressing her. Certain inexpressible things were now being expressed to Meribah—certain fears and desires, certain sensations of lightness and darkness, shadow and fire, warmth and cold, hunger and fullness. And, like the sounds of a river flowing underground, there was a profound sadness, sometimes powerful, other times faint, but always insistent.

She came up into a world above that was glaring and fierce with dust and noise. Dr. Forkert was discoursing at length on the perils to the human constitution of living underground. Mr. Billings was nodding in vigorous agreement, suggesting that maybe it was not cholera so much as fetid air that had weakened the Pawnee. "Possibly. Possibly," Dr. Forkert was saying. Mr. Wickham was absolutely exuberant about a load of potsherds and other "archaeological finds" that he planned on taking back to England for a famous museum there. But Meribah was still thinking about the cool dome of darkness and earth. It was hard for her to imagine the exact moment of the Indians' departure. Had they left over a period of time—first the alarmists and the impulsive, then the older and weaker people? Or had they been driven out all at once? Had they had to pack up and go with only an hour's notice, leaving pots bubbling, buffalo skins still wet with blood, children hungry, mortars with unground seeds? Did it really matter how they left? A life of simple rhythms and order had been interrupted when it should have continued; of this, Meribah was sure.

At twilight, just after setting up camp, Meribah made new marks on her map and printed the first words to occur between St. Jo and Fort Childs. She sketched a deep bend in the river and indicated some gently rising mounds. Carefully she printed in the words PAWNEE VILLAGE (DESERTED). To the north of the river, using stippling and shadowing and a smudge of blue chalk, she suggested the expanse of plains into the low mountain ranges.

As Meribah approached the Billingses' tent that night, it was aglow with lamplight and printed with large sliding shadows of teacups and reclining figures. Inside the tent everything seemed soft and plush and shades of rose. Mrs. Billings and Serena, propped up on jumbles of pillows, drank their tea daintily while Mr. Billings prepared a cup for Meribah.

"We have not unpacked all of our good china," Mrs. Billings explained. "Only three cups, but we insist, Meribah, that you be served in this lovely chinoiserie Crown Staffordshire. Mr. Billings will drink his from his tin cup."

"Oh, no!" Meribah protested.

"We shall hear no refusals, Meribah," said Mr. Billings. He was immersing a tea ball in a pot painted with gorgeous birds, funny-shaped houses, and tiny arching bridges. "You are our guest."

The entire tent seemed rather stuffed to Meribah. There were throw rugs and fringed pillows, odd bits of china, and embossed canisters with tea and tobacco. Apparently, Mr. Billings's supply had not been completely exhausted. Indeed, there was an assortment of delicious things to eat. There were more tea biscuits in spite of Serena's sudden impulsiveness to give away the very best, and there was quince jam imported from England and gooseberry jam made by their own dear cook, Louisa, who had cried and cried when they left Philadelphia. Meribah did wonder how they carried it all in their wagon, even one as large as theirs. But she was beginning to realize that beneath the tiers of lace Mrs. Billings was a woman as determined as she was organized. In the mornings, long before Captain Griffith shouted, "Chain up," Mrs. Billings was already directing their own packing with swift efficiency. Mr. Billings, it seemed, could not remember how to put up the tent, but with his wife's instructions night after night, he soon was taking it down speedily. She did all this with a cheery perseverance. And although she loved to tell stories of Louisa's "exquisite cuisine" and how she herself had never cooked a thing until now, she was doing so with great proficiency.

"Mrs. Billings . . ." Meribah paused as she took the elegant teacup and saucer, trying to balance it without rattling it excessively. She never would have started to speak if she had known that Mr. Billings would be handing her the tea so soon.

"Yes, my dear?" Mrs. Billings leaned forward toward Meribah, her own teacup and saucer remaining balanced and noiseless.

"Mrs. Billings, I hope that you won't think this is forward or rude on my part."

"Oh, Meribah, my angel, you could never be that way. Now what is it?"

"Well, I was just wondering, what are those things that you and Serena have wrapped around your necks?"

"Oh, goodness!" They all broke into peals of warm laugher but Meribah was still aware of a certain tension that had been in the tent when she entered it.

"That's what we love about you, dear Meribah!" exclaimed

Mr. Billings. "You just come right out and ask. You are curious because you are quick, and quick because you are curious!" He raised one finger to punctuate his remark. It was a turn of phrase that pleased him, Meribah thought, as much as it did her—although with his finger held high and the tassel dancing from his little embroidered smoking cap, she thought he did look just slightly silly.

"These are jabots," Serena said, pulling softly at the frothy cascade of lace that tumbled from her neck to her waist.

"What do they do?" Meribah asked.

"Now, there is a sensible girl with a sensible question," Mr. Billings said. Then holding the simple tin cup so elegantly that it lost its natural crudeness and could just as easily have been a porcelain cup and saucer, Mr. Billings stood back and studied Meribah with an almost embarrassing thoroughness. "I submit that if all the Amish girls are as sensible and as pretty as you are, Holly Springs must be a lovely community."

Meribah felt her cheeks burn and her stomach tighten.

"Well, she left it, Wrentham! So perhaps it wasn't all that lovely!" The air snapped like dry wood as Mrs. Billings spoke. She turned her head toward Meribah. Her eyes widened and there was a spot of unnatural color on her brow. "As for your question: jabots don't do anything, my dear. They're just there for decoration. . . ." She was facing Meribah, but it was as if she were addressing someone else. "Like some people of our acquaintance!" These last words she spoke with undisguised vehemence.

Serena appeared flustered to the point of panic. The little knot worked furiously above her brow, her pale face caught in the cross shadows of the dark light. The valentine mouth quivered slightly. "And modesty, Mother!" she said with sudden inspiration. "This little fireside jacket does not quite close over my sleeping gown, so I just stuff in this jabot."

"Yes, some I can imagine," Mrs. Billings' voice was cold and tired, the vehemence gone, "wear the *coin-de-feu* open. *Coin-de-feu*, that means fireside jacket." She spoke emotionlessly now. "That's the French name for what Serena is wearing. But some do not have the delicate sensibilities of Serena, I suppose, and wear them open. Quite revealing! Is that not so, Wrentham?" She turned to look at her husband. Meribah felt the tension in the tent closing in like the vise on her father's workbench. Mr. Billings stood so still that his tassel seemed frozen. His eyes, although opened wide, appeared veiled to this scene. His thin, finely molded nose was lifted high as if seeking better air. "I wouldn't know, my dear," he said, clipping his words. "As for delicate sensibilities, those are usually bred or acquired over long periods of time through association with cultivated society." There was a tinny cheeriness to his voice as if to mask a deeper feeling. "But I think it's time for some poetry. After all, that is what Meribah came for! Don't you agree, Serena?"

"Yes! Yes, Father! I am absolutely voracious for some poetry after all that creaking and groaning of wagon wheels. Let the music of the poets balm our ears!"

Meribah was greatly relieved that the interest was at last turning to poetry. She felt the tension begin to recede. It seemed literally to slip back into the shadowy corners of the tent.

"Well, Meribah, Mother and I have our favorites, and Father has his."

"And they occasionally permit me to read one," Mr. Billings added good-naturedly.

"Well, it is the ladies' poetry hour. We thought it up, Wrentham," Mrs. Billings said.

"Then begin, my dear. I trust you want your Angélique?"

"Please. It will be an appropriate introduction for Meribah."

"Angélique Buckham is our favorite poet. Grandmama knew her before she moved to Paris. Paris, France," Serena told Meribah.

"But that's not why we love her," Mrs. Billings interjected quickly. "She has exquisite sentiments. You will see."

Mrs. Billings took the leather-and-gilt book in her hands.

The lace swags at her wrists hung prettily over the pages.
She began to read:

> "Oh! Sweet confection of the spring
> On this visitation I should bring
> A flowerlet for thine hair
> A diamond circlet beyond compare.
> And yet I know in my flaming heart
> That thou art of nature's part
> And as the rose's sweet perfection
> Thy beauty needs no decoration!"

Was that it? Meribah wondered. She had hoped the poem
would be a little longer to give it room to improve. It certainly did not compare with the poem Mr. Wickham had
recited about the Keen Fitful Gusts. Indeed, all Meribah felt
was the still warm air of the tent, thick with perfume and
tobacco. Serena and her mother seemed profoundly moved,
however. There were even tears in Serena's eyes.

"Mother, explain to Meribah about Angélique's daughter.
Oh, it's so tragic."

"Well," Mrs. Billings began, "she had a daughter. Her name
was Rose, and she was the most exquisite beauty imaginable.
It is said that dukes and barons and marquises and even
kings...."

"Don't exaggerate, my dear!"

"Honestly, Wrentham, they did say that King George had
an eye for her! Well, in any case, there was one suitor, a young
painter, completely penniless, but he had background, if you
know what I mean." Meribah did not know what she meant,
but the poem was becoming slightly more interesting. "And,"
Mrs. Billings continued, "he did not have the wherewithal to
compete with the richer suitors. He could not bring her
diamonds, or rubies—the usual, you know. Well, no, I guess
you don't, dear, but anyway, he had nothing, but he would
always say to Angélique, 'Your daughter's beauty is like the
rose she is named for—perfect! It needs nothing more.'"

72

"And then," Serena sobbed, "she died!"

Everybody in the tent, even Mr. Billings, looked terribly sad, but Meribah felt only uncomfortable. "So her mother wrote the poem?" she asked trying to sound appropriately somber.

"Yes," both Serena and Mrs. Billings answered with a sigh.

Three poems later, Meribah was thinking to herself how lucky for Angélique Buckham to have a daughter named Rose and how unlucky she, Meribah, was to have to be listening to the results of her having a daughter by that name. Perhaps after one more poem she could politely excuse herself, as it was getting late and her head ached fiercely. She was trying to look attentive as Mrs. Billings explained something called a doobly on ton dur, which was some sort of word trick that Mrs. Buckham had used in this poem.

"Sheer genius—and to think that she wrote this in the depths of her grief. You see, Meribah, in French the word *blessé* means wounded. So you will understand when I come to the twice-blessed part." She cleared her throat and began to read:

> *"Beyond the portals of my heart*
> *Where none had ere trespassed*
> *Thy sweet visage has made its mark*
> *A blessing, O twice blessed!*
> *At first there was the perfect Rose,*
> *Love's sacred amulet.*
> *And then again when you rose, my Rose*
> *And bid adieu, sans regret!"*

"You look pale, Meribah! Oh, Mother, you read so beautifully. Meribah must feel faint from the sentiments. Don't cry, Meribah! I know one never gets used to the power of Angélique's feelings."

"I think I'd better go." She felt smothered and longed to be out of this tent, with its cushions and sweet smells, its words and smoke. She felt her heart racing. A pulse tinketted in her temple, and she wanted to be outside desperately. She declined Mr. Billings's offer to escort her back to her wagon. There were some words exchanged—thank-you's and evening greetings.

So this is civilization, Meribah thought. And then she was outside, twenty paces or more from the tent. She stood perfectly still. She did not turn when the kerosene lamp in the tent was extinguished and the voluptuous shadow dance on the canvas stilled. She had no desire to move. The crazy beating in her chest slowed, the tiny hammer in her temple stopped. She breathed in the chill black air. Slowly she pivoted to face squarely into the endless wind. Then she took off her cap and shook out her hair. She wanted to feel it all—the starry coldness of the sky, the hardness of the earth. She walked back to the wagon slowly.

Meribah heard a rustling in the brush and turned. She thought she saw two hats in the darkness, but whoever it was, they were going away from her, back toward the Billingses' tent. Things with hats were not a problem. It was the hatless creatures, the rattlers, that she must keep a sharp eye for. She had left her stick back at the Billingses'. No matter, there was the wagon fifteen yards ahead.

"How was the poetry?" Will asked from his pallet when Meribah returned.

"Fine." But it wasn't all poetry, Meribah thought to herself.

"Thee doesn't appear so enthusiastic."

"Poetry is just that—poetry."

"Well, some must be better and some must be worse."

"I suppose thou is right."

"How was this poetry?"

"In between, I guess." Meribah paused. "But, Pa, why does thou think the Billingses left Philadelphia?"

"Financial reversals, I would imagine."

"Hmm."

"Why? Does thee think something else? Know something more?"

"No, I was just wondering." Meribah yawned and turned over on her pallet. She did not go to sleep immediately. She thought about the Billingses, each one—Mr. Billings, Mrs. Billings, Serena. She thought about why they had left Philadelphia and how they came to be here as a family. She thought about the strange tensions in the tent and hairline cracks in porcelain.

June 21, 1849
At the split of the north and
south forks of the Platte River, in
western Nebraska

6

NO BIGGER THAN A CAKE PLATE

"I don't think they are decent people. Not civilized at all."

There was that word again, Meribah thought. It was beginning to grate.

"They should make themselves scarcer."

"Heavens! Serena, who are you two talking about?" she asked.

"The Timms. They're just always there, every time I turn around."

"Oh, I thought you were talking about the Mormons."

"We were, but the subject has been changed." Serena and Mr. Wickham had joined Meribah for a spell as she led Simon-Whiting, and she had been only half listening to the conversation. "We're talking about the Timms now. Every time I turn around they seem to be there, just far enough so as not to be considered an intrusion, but near enough to put me on edge."

"Well, I shall be happy to speak to them about it," Mr. Wickham offered.

"That's very gallant of you, Mr. Wickham, but you see, it is not a precise enough situation to be called an affront. I really don't think you can say anything to them. It would be . . . well, inappropriate, possibly provoking."

"But their behavior is inappropriate and provoking."

"Oh, who knows. Perhaps it is just my imagination."

"Maybe, Serena," Meribah said. "But I too feel as if they are always lurking and slinking about. It is almost as if this is their natural posture—that they simply do not or cannot walk a straight line, just as a sidewinder rattler cannot move in a straight line."

"Oh!" shivered Serena.

Meribah realized immediately that this was an unfortunate comparison. "Well, I didn't mean it that way. I just meant that they always seem to be about—looping and slinking in the grass. It's not only you who feels that way about them."

"Well, the Mormons will be a delight after the Timms!" sniffed Serena. "Let's change the subject."

"I myself must be off," Mr. Wickham said.

> *"To gather ye buffalo chips as ye may,*
> *Old time is still aflying*
> *And this same chip that smiles today*
> *Tomorrow will be frying!"*

"Oh, Mr. Wickham!" Serena's face was a bouquet of blushes. "Shame on you!"

"I love it!" Meribah giggled. "Did you compose it yourself?"

"With a little help from a poet named Herrick, who sang of rosebuds rather than buffalo chips. Well, adieu, ladies."

"Oh!" sighed Serena as she watched him walk off toward the river. "Isn't he the most charming, wittiest man, Meribah?"

"Yes, he is, and I think he finds you equally charming, Serena."

"Oh, do you? Do you?" She grabbed Meribah's hand and gave it a squeeze.

Serena is truly a good-hearted soul, Meribah thought. You can like somebody and still not enjoy having tea and poetry with her family, she reasoned. "Yes, I really do. I shouldn't be surprised if he . . . No, I shall not say it for fear of jinxing it."

"Oh, no, Meribah, say it! Say it! Come, what were you going to say? Please!"

"I can't."

"Come now. I saw it there on the tip of your tongue!"

There was no use resisting Serena's entreaties. "Well, all right, but if I say it, it does not mean it will come true."

"Or won't come true."

"But we must say that to cover the jinx."

"So say it!" Serena was fairly near exploding.

Meribah sighed. "I was just going to say that I shouldn't be at all surprised if Mr. Wickham proposes marriage."

"Oh, Meribah! Do you think it could be so?"

"Well, I only say I would not be *surprised*, that's all. But he does seem so attracted to you. And he is so . . . so. . . ." Meribah searched for a word.

"So what?" Serena pressed.

"So nice."

"Nice?" Serena said, taken aback by the mildness of Meribah's description.

"Well, more than nice . . . so finished, I guess. There is nothing rough about him. He's very graceful, you know."

"Yes, I know." Serena beamed.

"The way he talks, and moves, so easy and friendly. Never shy, never too forward. A lot like your father, Serena! I never thought of it before."

"Oh, no! Never!" Serena blurted. "He's not a bit like Father. Not one iota!"

"Well, not really in physical appearance, but in manner, I mean."

"No. No."

"Well, I think so. What do you imagine being married is like, Serena, being married to Mr. Wickham?" she suggested slyly.

"Now you will jinx it," Serena giggled. "But . . . ."

In fact, Meribah perceived there was no subject that Serena would rather talk about than Mr. Wickham. Each opportunity presented was like a nugget of gold, when she could rattle on nonstop and let her imagination take flight. "Although you may think that he is like my father, our marriage would be nothing like my parents'." She suddenly looked quite agitated by her own words. "Well, I don't mean anything. I just mean that Alec and I—Mr. Wickham and I are individuals, just as Mother and Father are. And as individuals we are quite different from them, so naturally our marriage would be different. You understand?"

"Yes, of course." But Meribah felt a bit uneasy that she had ever brought up the subject.

"But as you were asking me what kind of marriage, well, ours would have certain practical aspects, yes, just like my parents'." Serena spoke with an almost calculated lightness in her voice. " I mean, there are certain things—for example, my father—it took him forever, how to put up that foolish tent, but my mother's mind is such that she can grasp the workings of it, the connections, the order of the parts. She is always able to execute a task of that nature. Although she might lack the physical strength to do it, she can direct my father, and in that sense it is a perfect marriage." Serena then added quickly, "Well, of course not only in that sense, in many others too! But the example shows a true partnership of mind and body, and this is what I mean by practical."

"Yes, I see." Meribah nodded her head almost vigorously. It seemed important to agree with Serena.

"Now, with Mr. Wickham and me, I feel that the partnership is more romantic than practical. Or perhaps I should say more spiritual. Oh, the practical is there. I mean, you have witnessed his ingenious arrangements of objects for my sketching. Yet he himself confesses to me that he cannot draw a straight line." Serena laughed lightly. "And yet he does have a superbly artistic eye. Poor dear, his hand is locked where his eye is open. Where as my hand"—Serena waved her hand prettily in the air—"is absolutely fluid when it takes to a drawing tool, but my eye is not always clear to perceive. Hence this too is a partnership in the practical sense."

Each time Meribah thought Serena was about to stop, she

ran on with renewed energy. Like a bird catching a new wind current, she would soar. "However, I do not think of our union so much as a partnership as a linking," she said dreamily.

"A linking?" Meribah asked cautiously. "You mean like a coupling?"

"Coupling! How coarse!" The valentine mouth pursed in disgust. And then Serena laughed, her dimples winking merrily. "Oh, farm girl! I forgot!"

"I didn't mean it that way!" Meribah spoke with more than a trace of exasperation.

Serena was taken aback. "Of course you didn't. Oh, dear, I myself have been coarse in regard to your feelings and have hurt you. Forgive me, Meribah. I was an absolute boor, swine!"

Meribah stood back and looked at Serena. She was flushed, her eyes shiny with genuine regret. Her cream-colored pelerine, elegantly limp around her shoulders, dropped into points against the front of her white cotton dress.

"Never!" laughed Meribah. "You shall never be swine. No matter how hard you try!"

Serena took Meribah's arm and pressed it close to her side. "You're a dear girl, Meribah."

Meribah had been thinking the exact same thing about Serena. Yet looking at her, Meribah suddenly wondered how this friendship had happened. They were so different in every way. She could not imagine what tiny piece of common ground they had that gave the friendship a footing. If this prairie were an ocean, Meribah thought, then their affection for each other was like an airborne seed trying to find a speck of an island to light upon to germinate. It did not actually need much soil to grow, just a tiny plot no bigger than, say, a cake plate. But something had rooted and a friendship had begun.

"Now, Miss Meribah," Serena said with sudden perkiness, "I have shared my view of marriage with you. You must share yours with me. What do you seek or envision of a union between a man and woman?"

80

Meribah paused for a long time. "I myself seek no union and envision nothing of one with a man."

Serena inhaled sharply. "Surely you plan to marry?"

"Not me," Meribah said firmly.

"Is it not the custom for Amish people to marry?"

"Of course it is. How do you think people have children?" As soon as the words were out, Meribah colored deeply. "I take it back! I take it back! I know there are ways. I just mean that how do families . . . Well, you know what I mean!"

"Yes, of course I do." Under Serena's voice there was a tinkle of a laugh being suppressed. "But tell me, Meribah, if the Amish do marry, why are you so set against it?"

"I'm not set against it. I just realize it is not for me. I'm not really sure why. I mean, I just cannot imagine being a married person any more than I can imagine being a . . . a . . . a horse."

"How strange. I have always imagined being married. There is great joy in such a union, in such a linking."

"Well, there is a joy in singleness too, I think. When one finally grows up enough to enjoy it, to be able to do something all by oneself, with nobody saying how one should or should not—"

"But it is so lonely."

"Single doesn't always mean alone, and alone doesn't always mean single. And there are ways of linking without marriage."

"Meribah!" Serena was absolutely astounded. If Meribah had turned into a tree or even a horse in front of her very eyes, Serena would not have been more shocked—perhaps even less.

"Well, I just feel this way, and if I feel this way, wouldn't I make a husband miserable?"

"I suppose so," said Serena wanly. "But you might change, mightn't you?"

"Yes, I might." Meribah smiled.

"I could never stand to live life alone. To be alone!" Serena spoke fiercely.

They walked on in silence. Serena seemed lost in thoughts of Meribah's unmarried life, and Meribah pondered the similarities between Mr. Wickham and Wrentham Billings and Serena's notions of linkings, connections, and unions.

"Meribah," Serena said suddenly, "are Amish weddings different?"

"Different from what?"

"Different from our weddings, other peoples'?"

"I don't know what your are like. Ours always take place in November."

"That's different. Why in November?"

"Because it's after the harvest is in and before there's too much snow on the ground." Meribah spoke so sensibly that Serena did not dare question this matrimonial calendar, even though she failed to see the logic.

"Are there that many churches in Holly Springs to accommodate all the November brides?"

"Oh, they have to double up, quadruple up. Several couples at a time."

"In one church on the same day?"

"Yes. It's sort of a group ceremony."

"Oh, dear."

"It's quite efficient for the community. A quarter or more of the eligible girls and boys are married off in one month in a single year, starting their families— The first babies usually arrive in August."

"It sounds so . . . so . . . so orderly."

"Yes, it is. But most important, it helps the community work, go forth—you know, survive as a group."

"Do the brides wear wedding dresses?"

"No, usually just a new dress, but it looks the same as the dresses we always wear."

"You mean no lace? No seed pearls? No veils?"

"Heavens, no!"

"Are there flowers?"

"No."

"No flowers!" Serena exclaimed with genuine horror.

"No. At the wedding dinner the tables are decorated with huge bunches of celery. It's very pretty, really. It's my favorite part of the wedding. Sometimes if it is a clear day, that thin, pale November light fills the room and touches the celery leaves in a way that is so beautiful and fragile." Meribah's voice trailed off. Beautiful and fragile—the two words linked in her mind. Was this marriage? It frightened her.

"Your parents, Meribah," Serena said softly, "did your mother die?"

"No." Meribah looked at the ground and shook her head. They were both silent for a minute or more. Then Meribah spoke. "My mother is there, in Holly Springs, and we are here."

June 28, 1849
Following the north fork
of the Platte River

7

THE STONE NEST

The country began to grind on them like a giant millstone. But instead of granite, Meribah thought, this millstone is made of bad water, foul air, and leached earth that gives way under foot and wheel. In the end, however, it ground wood and metal and wheels and oxen like so much wheat. One Tuesday, as they were moving through Apache territory, one of the Barkers' bigger oxen, used for the Conestoga, died. They had extra oxen, but none was so big as the huge one that went down on its knees in the middle of a dried-out section of the Platte and refused to get up. It was dead within an hour. Whether a smaller ox could be used in the Conestoga team was questionable. They had certainly not counted on losing a big one, and their backups were for the smaller wagon. Mr. Billings had two extra oxen for his Conestoga, but he was adamant in his refusal to lend one or even rent one, as his wife had suggested.

"Absolutely not, Barbara! They are fine people. No question about it." Meribah overheard them talking with her father. Mrs. Billings and Will were both urging him to lend the Barkers an ox, while Serena stood nearby, silent. "They should have planned for this contingency. To have all your extra ox power suited for only one of your two wagons is not good thinking."

"But, Wrentham—"

"Look, Barbara, you talked me into giving away my tobacco to those filthy Pawnee, and then Serena pitched in our best biscuits and jam. You women would give away the whole lot, wouldn't you? Biscuits and jam are not life's essentials, but those extra oxen are, my dearest wife, and we shall be in a fine pickle if our team up and dies on us. Then whose shall we borrow?" His voice never rose, but the tone became sneering, and Meribah was glad that she was inside the wagon and not visible. "Or should we," continued Mr. Billings, "set up housekeeping in the middle of some desert? That would suit you fine, I suppose. Aren't you the one who turns sows' ears into silk purses? Isn't that your *spécialité*, Barbara Weiss Billings? Yes, the shabby little apartment above the butcher's shop that you made so adorable, so charming, for your adorable and charming family. Tell me, what can you do with oxen carcasses, Madame Billings? I mean, after all, coming from a long line of wurstmakers, your background, now!"

The way Wrentham Billings said "background" sent absolute shivers up Meribah's spine. Meribah could see the figure of her father already one hundred yards or more away. He must have left in the middle of this diatribe. But the wind carried Mr. Billings's voice directly into the wagon. "What do they call women butchers, Barbara? Butcheresses! Ha!" His laugh sounded like a slap on water.

"Wrentham, please!"

"Please what? I was just thinking how your background—to call it experience is too coarse for a fine lady like you—anyway, how your background could come in handy for our little desert abode. Oxen upholstered love seats, horn sconces, et cetera. You perceive my meaning, my dear!"

"Father, stop it!"

Meribah prayed that Serena did not know she was in the wagon.

Mr. Billings's tone softened suddenly. "Well, your mother was about to give away our oxen, our only hope for surviving this God-awful journey."

"Giving away to strangers is better than . . ."

But Meribah could not understand the end of Mrs. Billings's sentence. It was better than something "from family."

Meribah was not supposed to have overheard the exchange,

and that made it worse. She actually began to wonder if she had heard Mr. Billings correctly. It was hard to believe him capable of that sneering whine that put a razor's edge on words like "background" and even "my dearest." Meribah had always thought him to be a man so pleasant and full of good cheer and grace. He had even managed to explain to the Barkers in the most gently reasonable and friendly way why it was impossible for them to lend their spare oxen. Will told Mr. Moxley that he wouldn't have been surprised to hear the Barkers thank Mr. Billings after his fancy speech. He had never heard anything so smooth. But Mrs. Barker did not thank him. She burst into tears and sobbed that if their backup team didn't work well together, her husband said they would have to cut their Conestoga in half, reduce it to a two-wheel cart so it could be drawn, and dump half its contents—the contents from the "largest emporium of life's necessities"— into the "gol durn Platte."

The day after the Barkers' ox died, the Billingses' left rear wheel broke—not just the wheel but the hub too. Repairing it was an enormous job. A forging fire had to be built to make new bands for the hub. The spokes had all worked loose. The rimwood had shrunk in the expanding rim and was beyond wedging. It would have to be reset, which meant it would have to be heated, hammered, and fitted over the rebuilt rim while red hot and then left to cool and set itself to the wood. It took an entire day and four men: Will to do the forging and rebuilding, Henry Whiting to do the holding work, bracing parts with tongs and blocks while Will hammered, and the McSwats to keep the fires going. Wrentham Billings helped as best he could but fumed as the rest of the company went on, agreeing to wait up at a point some miles ahead.

At first Meribah thought Mr. Billings's anger was due to the ill fortune of his wheel and to the fact that the others were not waiting but "getting ahead," as he put it. She had long realized that Mr. Billings had viewed the journey west as some sort of race. He absolutely bristled when other wagon trains passed them. He was especially envious of horse-drawn wagons, which traveled much faster. His only solace was his conviction that the horses would die in the desert stretches where the oxen would lumber on. But it became apparent that something more than others passing him was fueling his anger.

"He's convinced that the Barkers tampered with the wheel, Meribah!" Mrs. Billings said with great exasperation.

"No!"

"I know! I can't dissuade him. It is the most ridiculous idea imaginable. People hardly have energy left to fix a meal, and he thinks they're going to go around tampering with other people's equipment. I don't know what to do. He's a difficult man."

The wheel was finally repaired. They left in the night and caught up by daybreak with the rest of the train. On the way, as Meribah sat next to her father, looking over the oxen's horns to a still-dark horizon, she told Will about Mr. Billings's suspicions regarding the Barkers.

"He really said that?" Will asked incredulously.

"That's what Mrs. Billings said."

Will's face became grim and set. "He's a fool, Meribah, and what's worse, he's a dangerous one."

Meribah wondered about this. Perhaps Mr. Billings was dangerous because his suspicions about the Barkers would fester into anger and cause a senseless explosion. She supposed that this was what Will feared. She wished dawn would come. She wished she could feel its pink warmth on her back. The worst thing about traveling west at this time of the day was that it was all darkness and there wasn't a chance of seeing light or sun ahead. She could only hope and wish to feel it behind her.

There was an explosion. It was not, however, between the Billingses and the Barkers. It was the Timms, and they had sent a bullet clean through an Apache warrior's head and another through the heart of his younger brother.

"It's going to be a goddam miracle if we're not attacked!"

87

Captain Griffith roared at the two brothers. "You've endangered all of us!" The brothers stood in the middle of a ring of people, their eyes staring down at the ground. Dangling obscenely from their belts were the fresh scalps of the two Indians. They kicked the dust of the road softly with their boots. One of the brothers seemed intent on building a little mound of dust with the toe of his boot. They both heard every word. They were the object of everyone's disgust and anger, an anger that was more of a loathing, as one might feel toward some particularly low and vile form of life that was dangerous, without reason. You either killed it or you walked away from it. But you did not get angry at it the way you did at a human being. What amazed Meribah was that the brothers seemed to be enjoying the rest of the company's revulsion. Their lips were pulled back in nearly toothless grins, their eyes cast down but pleased.

Captain Griffith continued, "You've done a fool thing!"

"What had these Indians ever done to you?" Mr. James nearly shouted.

"They ain't human, them Indians," one brother muttered.

"As if you are!" Mrs. Billings whispered a bit too loudly. The others laughed at her remark, and this seemed to bother the Timms more than anything else said. Their heads barely moved, but their eyes slid sideways and focused on Mrs. Billings in a glittering anger. Something way down in the pit of Meribah's stomach clenched.

The man, standing smack in the middle of the dusty riverbed, poured spirits of turpentine over the bag of sugar. He dropped a lighted match. There was a soft explosion and then a brief roar as the flames consumed the sugar. "Got one more bag, folks. Anybody gimme twenty dollars? Twenty dollars! Going once! Going twice!" He held the bag above the fire. Meribah turned her head away. There was a dull thud, and then the air cracked and hissed in a new rage.

"The waste! The ungodly waste!" whispered Will.

She would never get used to it, and yet that was all they had seen from Fort Childs on. The silver braid of the river had split, become shallower, the water thick and yellow as they followed the north fork. The land became drier, the trees smaller, and there was sand instead of grass. There was often no water at all. The river simply ran dry, as in this spot on the north fork where the man now tended his fire of burning sugar. The banks were strewn with dead oxen and the graves of cholera victims, as well as living people's wreckage—a claw-footed table, a ponderous oak desk with a myriad of cubby-holes, crockery, grandfather clocks, coffee mills, and pots, tools, stoves, gridirons, plows, grindstones, harnesses, clothing, boxes and barrels—all of it flung out and most of it intentionally and meticulously destroyed so that it could be of no use or profit to anyone else. Today Meribah watched as the man burned his sugar supply because he could not get his price and it had become too heavy for him to carry on his pack mule. Yesterday she had watched as a German man and his wife took turns with a hatchet smashing a coffee mill to smithereens.

Meribah kept a handkerchief doused with spirits of camphor to cut through the stench of dead oxen mingled with foul water that assaulted her throughout the day. She had not seen Serena for two days. Mr. Billings told them that she was doing poorly from the dust and bad air. The business of walking Simon-Whiting was now a gruesome one that brought her closer to the rotting flesh of dead animals and the hastily dug graves of the cholera victims. In a peculiar sort of vanity, living people had inscribed their names and dates of passage on the bleached bones of oxen, and for the dead there was sometimes a flat white shoulder bone from a horse or ox that would be used as a grave marker, or two bones lashed together to form a cross. Wood was scarce. There were no coffins, and occasionally she could see a boot tip emerging from a shallow grave. Everything appeared scorched, parched, and bleached. And it seemed as if something more than water had

89

been sucked from the earth. There was an odd perversity to the landscape as things grew more twisted and desiccated in a strange defiance.

Sometimes the trail paralleled the north fork, and sometimes it wound right through the dried riverbed. The sands shifted, and the earth crumbled beneath wheels, hooves, and feet, making the pace excruciatingly slow. Meribah could read every grave marker several times in passing.

JOHN HOOVER, JUNE 18, 1849
AGED 12 YRS. REST IN PEACE,
SWEET BOY, FOR THY TRAVELS ARE OVER

RACHEL E. PATTISON
AGED 18, JUNE 19, 1849

IN MEMORY OF DANIEL MALOY,
GALLITIN CO., ILL.
DIED JUNE 18, 1849, CHOLERA, AGE 48

It seemed to Meribah that every ugly detail could be studied for an eternity: the flies on the rotting face of an ox, their buzzing sound suddenly filling the hollow air; the flattened rattlesnake; the strange powdery traces of salt that limned the ground until the land stood out in eerie skeletal detail. Peculiar alkali smells began to seep out of the earth, and Meribah noticed that the chalky traces were beginning to accumulate in heavy encrustations on rocks and in the gouged veins of the riverbed. She saw pits of the white powder like giant saucers brimful with salt.

Captain Griffith had warned them that there would be no good water until evening or the next day. She knew about alkaline water. She had seen the bloated bodies of cattle that had drunk from the sparse contaminated springs, but she had not expected the poison to ooze out of the earth and harden like white scabs in the sun. The poison salts covered everything, bleaching out the world before her eyes. A dead rattle-snake lay sheathed in a salty white casing, its rattles encrusted with the white stuff. The riverbed was striped with petrified veins of white.

To see green! Meribah thought. To hear the river run silver again! To find the astonishing yellow of a squash blossom! In her mind Meribah began to search for other images, for other sounds—wading in the bone-aching cold water of Briar's Creek with Jeanette, the rows of filled jam jars like prisms of purple and red light in the cool north window of the pantry. There was a crystalline gray color in her memory too. Not the gray of a cloudy day, but a beautiful, clear, early-morning gray, the gray of the world as it appears just before dawn, just before lighting, when the sun is trusted but the minute has not yet come. What was this gray? It was not the gray of day or of her dress. It was not the gray of anything she had ever painted. It seemed as if it were earlier than anything she knew, and yet she knew it. She reached far back in her memory, but each time she was close, the image would vanish. As she walked through the whitening landscape, it was this crystalline gray that possessed her. The harder she thought about the gray, the more elusive it became. She could not connect it with things, only with a myriad of sensations—warmth and fullness, holding and calming, trust and light. To try to imagine anything more simply made the gray disappear. But it was tantalizing, this gray memory. It beckoned and vanished. It washed away like the cheapest watercolor or slipped slowly below the horizon like a setting moon. Though Meribah could not name it, she knew it. And she knew that it was real.

Mr. and Mrs. Whiting appeared suddenly. "Wheel's about to go, Meribah."

"Not as bad as the Billingses'," added Mrs. Whiting.

"But we don't want to push our luck."

"And the McSwats' is nearly as bad, so we're fixin' to stop. Ounce of prevention's worth a pound of cure."

" 'Fraid it will take more than an ounce, Rietta. Gotta stop before Ash Hollow. Griffith says the going gets steep there and we'll have to double-hitch in one place."

Meribah watched them talk. She bent her head in polite attention, but inside she felt panic spread, slowly at first, oozing like the poisonous white salts. The two people before her appeared like bleached figures. It was as if the Whitings had in some odd process absorbed the powdery dust of the land. Now they stood there chalk white, like a single statue carved out of, but not yet released from, the larger mass. She feared for them. She feared for herself.

"You lead Simon-Whiting," Meribah said suddenly, handing Henrietta the tether. "I'll run and get Mr. Wickham or Dr. Forkert to ride up and tell Captain Griffith to stop."

"Bless your young legs, child."

Meribah streaked up the trail, swiftly sidestepping animal carcasses and castoff gear. She swerved sharply to avoid a rattler dozing in the shade of a torn bonnet.

"Dr. Forkert! Dr. Forkert! Could you ride up and ask Captain Griffith to stop? The Whitings' and the McSwats' wheels are about to go. Could you please?"

"Just thinking the same myself. Ours needs to be checked, too, before the double-hitch stretch. I imagine Griffith was planning to stop before then, but I'll tell him now. You run back, child, and tell the other folks to halt within the next quarter-mile."

Meribah ran back, past the same carcasses, the same once-cherished relics, the rattler still dozing under the bonnet. She told the McSwats, who began passing the word. Meribah herself doubled back to the Billingses.

Mr. Billings was still grumbling about the intended stop when Meribah returned to their wagon.

"I certainly don't see why we should stop now," he said to his wife. "They should have checked their wheels yesterday when we were fixing ours. To stop here at this hour with the hardest part to come seems absurd to me."

Meribah had no answer for his complaints. All she wanted to do was see Serena. "Mrs. Billings, can I see Serena for just a minute? I won't disturb her. I promise."

"Certainly, child. It will cheer her immeasurably, I'm sure."

Meribah circled around to the rear of the wagon and scrambled up through the back opening. "Serena!" Inside the wagon the air was suffocating and still.

"Meribah!" The voice sounded frail, almost old. "You came to see me!" Serena propped herself up on one elbow. In her thin gauzy dress, with her blond hair loose and streaming like brook foam, she looked absolutely spectral. Hers was the whiteness not of chalk but of vapor and mist. Meribah wanted to hold on to her but felt it would be like trying to catch a piece of cloud.

"Are you any better, Serena?"

"Yes, yes, dear. I really am. I think by this evening I might take a turn outside when the sun is down. I'm really much improved."

"It's supposed to get better by tomorrow. Good water and better going. I'm sure the air will improve."

"Oh, lovely, and we shall have our promenades once again."

"I saw Mr. Wickham. He's worried sick about you, Serena."

"Yes, I know. He's sent such lovely notes filled with poems. Meribah," Serena said suddenly, "I was thinking about those Amish weddings you described—all those couples standing up together or one right after the other in the church. It strikes me as so very odd. I suppose it's silly dwelling on it, but I don't know." Serena sat up now against the pillows and crinkled her nose. "It seems that weddings are so special that the bride and groom should have the day just for themselves. I mean, you must admit that they lack individuality—these mass weddings. And they do seem rather austere for something that is supposed to be a celebration."

"Well, they are not exactly mass weddings. It's more like . . . community weddings, yes, community."

"You say that word so much when you speak of your home.

93

It's as if there were no individual people or families, just community."

Meribah laughed softly. "It's hard to tell where one leaves off—oneself or one's family—and the community begins." Meribah hesitated and watched Serena's pale face. "We left, Pa and I, because they were shunning him."

Serena's eyes widened. "Shunned! That has a terrible sound to it, Meribah."

"Yes. Kept him out." Meribah spoke rapidly now. "Nobody was allowed to speak a word to him, look in his direction, eat with him, do business. Not even our own family."

"But that is too cruel." Serena was shaking her head. "I can't bear to think about it."

"He didn't do anything bad. He just disagreed with the community. It was nothing that hurt anybody. He didn't steal, he didn't kill. He criticized the bishops and he went to the funeral of a man who they had said was ungodly. That was his sin—breaking the rules, not the commandments. Can you imagine what it does to a person to be shunned, shunned by his own family?" Meribah looked into Serena's eyes and suddenly regretted her outburst.

"No! No! No! Never! Never!" Serena kept whispering and shaking her head.

Meribah felt that Serena sensed her pain, their pain, and she quickly changed the subject. "I didn't mean to talk about all that. But I do have something else to ask you—a favor."

"Certainly, anything! What is it?"

"May I see in your looking-glass? I just . . . I just . . . ."

"Why, of course. It's right over there in the bandbox. I declare, Meribah, you would have thought you were asking for my soul the way you carry on about a simple mirror. And don't worry, I won't breathe a word to the bishops!" She winked, her spirits recovered.

Meribah got out the glass. She had looked at her reflection many times in Serena's mirror, but this time, before holding it up, she felt a dark flutter deep in her stomach. "Will I

94

be...." She did not complete the thought. In the half-light of the covered wagon, her image jiggled on the glass. The wagon halted, the image stilled. There was a band of bronze freckles across her nose, and her cheekbones and forehead were a rich rose-brown.

"I kept telling you, Meribah, to wear the big bonnet. Those Amish caps can't shade a mouse. Now you're just as brown as an Indian." There were a few of the chalky traces in the corners of her mouth and along her lower lip and nostrils. She quickly wiped them away. "Now, when we get to California, Meribah, we're going to be stricter with your beauty regimen."

"What is that?" Mrs. Billings had come under the cover. "See," she patted Meribah's hand, "I knew you would cheer up Serena. Now, what are you two chattering about?"

"Look at Meribah's complexion, Mother. I've warned her and warned her!"

Mrs. Billings held Meribah's chin lightly in her hand and studied her face. "Oh, dear! Oh, dear! We're going to have to bleach you out."

Meribah shuddered. "I'll wear the bonnet."

"Oh, it will take more than a bonnet."

"That's what I said, Mother. Milk baths when we get to California."

"And cucumbers, if we can get them." Mrs. Billings was still holding Meribah's chin, turning it gently this way and that, clicking her tongue and sighing in a medley of disapproving sounds. "Oh, dear! My word!" She smacked her lips and made another clicking noise. "*Quel dommage!* What a pity. Well, you're still young. But Meribah, listen to me." She dropped her hand from Meribah's chin. "If I may give a word of advice. A fair complexion is not a vanity, Amish or not! A fair complexion for a young lady is proper. It simply is not civilized to be dark and mottled. This is something that Amish, as well as high Episcopalians, would agree upon, I am sure."

Meribah, too, was sure that this would be a point of agreement and could imagine her mother nodding in accord with Mrs. Billings on this subject. But she was greatly confounded by that word "civilization." The truth was that she quite liked the freckles stippling a band of bronze across her cheekbones.

When Meribah climbed out of the Billingses' wagon, which had stopped on a rise, she had a clear view of the flat valley ahead. The marks on the horizon that for a day had appeared as vertical squiggles sharpened into dark towers and knotty spirals, jagged and violent against the sky.

"That one over there"—Mr. Billings was pointing—"must be Court House Rock." Meribah supposed he meant the one that appeared slightly squared off at the edges. "And if that is the case, we must be very close to the double-hitch stretch Certainly wish we could get through that by this evening."

"Well, we're here, Wrentham. So just relax. Take a walk, dear, and see what treasures you can find. Maybe you'll turn up that Seth Thomas watch." Mrs. Billings spoke in the bright assuaging tones one might use with a pouting child who has suffered some minor disappointment.

"Splendid idea, my dear." Mr. Billings had a seemingly endless fascination with the discard of others. He raked through it, perused it, mined it with an almost scholarly attention. He would always return with a hatful of bits and pieces and report in vivid detail on the wreckage he had sifted through. The day before, he had found a waist chain that he was sure belonged to a Seth Thomas watch. He felt that he was on the trail of a "substantial household," a "family of stature." He did not seem disturbed by the waste or the purposeful destruction. He viewed the fractured relics as parts of a grand puzzle.

Wheel repair was a tedious, hot, and sticky business. Fires had to be built to boil up the tar, rags had to be soaked in oil.

"What d'ya say, Will? How long a job you think it'll be?" Captain Griffith asked Meribah's father, who had become the acknowledged wheelwright of the company. Dr. Forkert, Mr. James, and Mr. Wickham stood behind Will, looking over his shoulder as he ran his hand around the hub bands.

"Well," he said with optimism, "none of these wagons—Forkert's here, Whitings', or McSwats'—needs band work done. So we won't have to be building any forging fires like yesterday with Billingses'. None of them that bad."

"That's good news." Captain Griffith winked at Meribah with his good eye, the one that was not locked in a squint.

"But," Will said, "they all need a good soaking. It seems to me not to make much sense to soak and tar them just to roll again in this heat. If they set overnight, they'll hold the tar and oil a lot better."

"Better camp here, then." It was not a question but a statement. Captain Griffith believed in Will Simon's judgment on these matters. "I sure don't want these wheels flying apart on us during the double hitch."

Since there was no contribution Meribah could possibly make to the wheel repair, she decided to take her sketchbook and chalks and go someplace away from the fires, away from the wreckage, away from the dead oxen and cattle and white scabs and alkaline pits. She was tired of seeing things close up. She wanted to be able to look far away, to vanishing points where details lost their definition, where lines blurred and shapes melted, someplace where an animal carcass could be a boulder, a wrecked piano a bluff, a smashed snake a furrow from a wheel. She wanted to be where she could set the meaning of things and will a shape, a form, into something else.

Meribah found her place. It was a bluff that thrust out of the ground like a stack of tabletops in diminishing sizes. To climb it was as easy as walking up stairs. The top narrowed to a point, but she had a hunch that on the far side, the side facing the valley, there might be a sitting spot if she could edge around to it. The rock stair steps had become smaller in size toward the top, and there was barely a shoe's width for walking around to the other side of the point. She could almost reach around the top with her arms to try to feel if there was a sitting place, but then again there could just as easily be a rattlesnake's nest. She would inch around. Pressing her cheek against the rock, she moved carefully along the edge. A perfect rock hollow with a smooth surface for sitting faced due west. There was an overhang for shade and even a small stone with a footstool of ledge that cropped out beneath. She untied her cloth sack of drawing equipment, which she had fastened to her waist, and swung it into the hollow, then easily climbed in. The flat valley, blue and placid, spilled before her. Through it the north fork of the Platte, neither wet nor dry from Meribah's vantage, wound in lazy elegance—if rivers can be elegant, Meribah thought. Serena and her mother used the word all the time to describe dresses and fine bone china, but why not rivers? From far off, a thick blue column of smoke curled up from what must have been an Indian campfire. This was Cheyenne country now, and Meribah could imagine them sleek and bronze in white leggings and moccasins, their cheekbones striped vermillion.

From her stone nest in the sky Meribah surveyed it all. She imagined, she invented, the land that stretched before her. The white scabs and veins of salt became a delicate embroidery stitched into the earth. The rock towers lost their violence and rose serene and magical, like the spires of fairy castles. Moon Fairy! Meribah suddenly remembered the charming doll. It seemed like a million years ago, but she had once built a castle for Moon Fairy down by the creek with stones and pebbles. Moon Fairy had spent the night there on one of her earthly visits. She wondered if Liesel, a thousand miles or more back, played with the dolls now. It was hard to believe that she herself had once dressed dolls and built castles and destroyed them. She thought east and looked west. Time and distance mingled oddly, and Meribah wondered about who she had been and who she was becoming and the connection between the two persons.

At first, it came to her like a murmuring, hushed and steady.

In the stone nest she felt a dim quiver, then heard a distant thunder. Meribah leaned out from her perch, squinting toward the horizon. A sudden mark appeared against the land to the west of the encampment. The mark grew into a smudge, the smudge became a dark ocean, surging in from the north, heaving and roaring. The entire valley floor began to shake as a thousand buffalo beat across the earth. Meribah stared in disbelief as the stampede moved in front of her, filling the landscape, rolling by now in a single black undulation, one huge blood-pumping muscle. Breathless and high above the smoking land, Meribah felt as if the stone nest would shatter.

Dust rose everywhere, pulled up like fuzzy carded wool and obliterating everything until only the sky was left. Meribah, her sense of boundaries lost, waited in silence for her own world to reappear.

Finally the dust settled. She could see the thrusting stone spires, the wagons, the tarring fires, the figures circling about slowly, randomly, like motes of dust in a column of light. One figure she suddenly recognized. White and puffy, it blew lightly into her view like tumbleweed. Serena! She must be feeling better, Meribah realized. There was another figure beside her, a man, either Mr. Billings or Mr. Wickham. Meribah hoped that it was Mr. Wickham. They seemed to be walking off, away from the trail. She guessed that it was Mr. Wickham and that they were looking for a sketching spot. Besides them, she saw a solitary figure picking his way through the rocky wreckage in the dry part of the river. Probably Mr. Billings on his treasure hunt. It became a game to guess people's identity from her perch. The people around the fire must be her father, the McSwat men, Dr. Forkert, Mr. James, Captain Griffith, the Whitings, and perhaps Mr. Moxley, for there was a man on a packhorse. She saw two other figures standing apart from the wagons. Off in the distance, several river bends away, she saw another wagon train winding toward Chimney Rock.

"Wedding bells!" Mrs. Billings had said. "Perhaps we shall

hear wedding bells by California!" Meribah was thinking of this as she descended the rock bluff, her drawing satchel tied to her waist. She had never heard wedding bells. They were not part of Amish weddings.

She was so busy thinking about wedding bells that at first she did not hear that deceptively ordinary sound, like fine rain on dry leaves, or wet wood burning. But then it was there, right there. A sudden unmistakable hiss—deadly, insistent. Meribah felt her skin grow cold, her breath stop. She was still on the narrow part of the stone stairs with her face pressed against the rock. She could not see behind or ahead or down. She could only see straight up, but the hiss came from below, perhaps a foot away, perhaps a yard. She did not know. Up was the only safe way. And if the rattler were close enough, it could follow her and corner her at the peak in the stone nest. She had no weapons and she had no choice.

She clawed her way straight up. The snake kept hissing, stropping the air with its fury. She was back in the nest. She must be calm. She must think. She must figure things out. If the snake had followed, each second now was gold. She carefully turned around in the nest on her knees and braced herself to lean far out and around the rock so she could see where the snake might be. She could still hear it, but it did not sound any closer. She leaned out and around. She could not see anything, but the hissing was still clear. She had to lean out farther. She quickly untied the drawing satchel. She looped the rope around a rock spur and, holding onto it, leaned out farther and farther toward the hissing. Farther still she leaned; like a rock flower growing against gravity, she arched into the sky. Then she saw it, ugly and spitting in its dumb fury. Coiled on a wide ledge near the base of the bluff, the snake reared its head, striking again and again toward the sky in a blind primeval rage. It was far below her. She knew that she was safe, that she could easily get down to the other side of the bluff, but she was transfixed by the creature, at once repugnant and fascinating.

She shook off her reverie and swung herself out of the nest, then quickly descended to a wide part on the other face of the bluff. When she was on the ground again, she walked around to see it. The snake was still there, coiled and striking. It was a big snake, the biggest she had ever seen. There was a rock nearby at her feet. With a well-aimed throw she could probably injure it, maybe kill it. She picked up the rock and aimed. The snake swung its head around toward her. Meribah's breath locked, and she felt a shudder deep inside. There was something unbelievably shocking in those eyes, filling her with terror. She dropped the rock and ran back toward the wagons.

"Thou cannot eat it or plant it, and it won't keep thee warm at night. Thou can only hoard it or spend it," Will chuckled.

"Spend it!" Mr. Moxley said good-naturedly.

"Better than hoarding it. I agree."

Meribah had arrived in the middle of this conversation. She had composed herself several yards in advance so as not to alarm her father, but he was very much engrossed in this discussion and did not notice her. He enjoyed Mr. Moxley greatly but rarely had opportunity to talk with him, as Mr. Moxley usually rode ahead as a scout for the company. A lively, jolly sort, he loved joking and debating as much as he professed to love gold.

"As a farming man, I like to know that some of what I take out of the ground can be put back to grow again," Will said. Meribah thought of the bag of seed potatoes in the wagon.

"As a spending man, I don't think about tomorrow," Mr. Moxley answered, "and certainly never of sticking gold in the ground or in the bank! Makes a man mean to hoard. Stunts the spirits, throws the humors off balance, not to mention wreaks havoc with the liver, is bad for the bowels, and constipates the soul. Whereas spending," Mr. Moxley said with renewed vigor, "prevents imbecility, increases virility, inhibits softening of the brain."

Meribah could not help laughing out loud.

"Meribah! Where has thee been?" Will turned to his

daughter, slightly embarrassed that she had overheard Mr. Moxley's florid language.

"Forgive my speechifying, Miss Meribah."

"Oh, I enjoyed it!"

"Where has thee been?"

"Up yonder." She indicated with her head.

"Did thee see the buffalo?"

"I could hardly miss them."

"Magnificent!" Mr. Moxley added.

"How's the wheel work coming?"

"All finished for the most part. But we'll not pull out of here for Ash Hollow and the double hitch till tomorrow. Mr. Moxley has already surveyed it."

"Pretty steep," Moxley said with great sobriety. "It'll take at least the day to negotiate those two hundred yards upward. And that's not the most of it. The descent—road hangs a touch past perpendicular. Your pa's absolutely right. Those wheels have to set tonight. A good chill would be perfect to harden them off."

"We'll leave before dawn—cold breakfast. So plan on turning in early tonight, Meribah. I got to go now and check the yokes and harnesses and make sure there are no weak links there."

Meribah had a hundred questions about the double hitch, but she knew her father probably did not know the answers any more than she did, and he seemed in a hurry to get on with his work.

"Well, I'll go and help Mrs. Whiting with supper."

"Yes, we'll want to eat early. Mr. Moxley, will thou join us?"

"Pleased, sir! Much pleased."

There were pork and beans, buffalo meat, rolls, bean soup, stewed dried apples, and pie for supper. Henrietta Whiting insisted that she and Meribah cook up enough to last two days, for Lord knew what cliff they would be hanging from this time tomorrow, hanging and hungry and unable to cook!

102

"Two days. More like two months you cooked for!" Mr. Moxley exclaimed as he helped himself to another piece of pie. "We'll still be eating some of this sumptuous repast by the time we reach California!"

"Well, it won't be so sumptuous by then," Henrietta said wryly.

Despite the good food and the bantering conversation, Meribah felt a tension in the air, a tension not just where they sat but throughout the camp. It was as if people were reinforcing themselves, bracing themselves for the double hitch, in which two teams were hitched to one wagon to pull it up a steep ascent. Despite all the checking and rechecking, there was real fear that a link in the chain might break. A steeple ring or a yoke bow could suddenly split, precipitating a calamitous avalanche of wagon, oxen, and people down a sheer rock face.

While they were cleaning up, Serena came by.

"You're better!"

"Yes, much better. I'm on my way now for a stroll." She had a lively light in her eye. Meribah knew immediately with whom she planned to walk and did not offer to accompany her.

"Well, don't be out late," Mrs. Whiting warned. "Tomorrow is the big day. We're leaving before dawn."

No sooner had Serena walked off than Mrs. Billings arrived, her plump face absolutely crowded with excitement and joy.

"Which direction did they go?" She grabbed Meribah's hand excitedly.

"Serena went that way."

"But we told her not to stay out late," Mrs. Whiting added, "because of the double hitch."

"That's not the only double hitch!" Mrs. Billings trilled, then giggled, delighted with her own cleverness. "Ladies, I cannot contain myself a moment longer, but I think you shall be hearing an important announcement soon!"

"What do you mean?" Meribah asked.

"What do I mean, dear? Why Serena and Mr. Wickham, of course! She received the most charming note from him, just an hour ago, to meet him by the river. And she had just been walking with him earlier. . . ." Mrs. Billings seemed indefatigable in recounting the minutest events and details that were leading up to this announcement. "And after that walk, seeing that she was sufficiently recovered to receive his proposals, he sent her a note asking her to join him for an evening promenade. You see, Mr. Billings—oh, he is so naïve at times —kept running up to them on the last stroll to show them his finds from his silly old treasure hunt."

"Well!" snorted Henrietta Whiting, "they certainly do a lot of promenading about this God-forsaken land just to make proposals."

"You can rest assured that this is the last promenade for this purpose. I have Mr. Billings waiting in the tent to receive Mr. Wickham. Oh, he is such a charming young man!"

The notion of Serena marrying Alec Wickham was a source of such joyous stimulation to Mrs. Billings that she was incapable of checking herself. Mrs. Whiting winced throughout the enumeration of Mr. Wickham's qualities, which was strewn with frequent references to his superior breeding, connections, and background. It would be a "dazzling" union. Mrs. Billings only wished all of Philadelphia could be there. And the vision of Serena settled so stylishly and comfortably just outside of London in the Wickham country house eclipsed the sorrow of the distance. Who knew—after Mr. Billings rid himself of this "gold thing," perhaps they would all settle there! But how lucky they were! To think! She had never imagined this happening that bleak day they had left Philadelphia.

Bleak day, Meribah thought, as she looked out the back opening of the wagon from her sleeping pallet. It was eight o'clock. The sun was just setting. Will was already asleep. She had often wondered why the Billingses had left Philadelphia—the balls, the drawing room, the music room, the City Club, Grandmama's winter garden. Her father had mentioned financial reversals. To Meribah, the term "financial reversals," though serious, also sounded almost mechanical, fixable in the same way a wagon or a piece of farm equipment was fixable. But when Mrs. Billings referred to "that bleak day," Meribah suddenly had an image of something very different. Something irreversible and unfixable that went beyond material loss.

Meribah stared out the back of the wagon. Spreading fingers of red light felt their way through the underside of the low clouds that gathered close to the horizon, and the sky, sucked colorless at noon, bloodied as the sun began to sink. The wild splendor was framed in the *U*-shaped opening of the wagon, and although Meribah could see only this circumscribed piece of it, she felt the whole sky, dark red and powerful, pressing down on the land. It was as if she were on the underside of light, and for a brief second she had a suffocating sensation that made her fight for a breath. Her mind, however, was swirling with thoughts of the double hitch. It would be tricky. A rare interdependence must be forged through combinations of wood and iron, animal muscle, and human brain. She trusted their wagon. She knew their oxen to be in good condition. Their yoke was hewn from hard pine; their bows were of hickory. It was like bone and muscle, Will had said, each unique in its qualities but working together for extraordinary conjunctions of power. But some people had used yellow poplar, which cracked as it seasoned. Black gum was all right if it had been seasoned well. The more Meribah thought, the more worried she became. She could not help but wonder whose team would be hitched with theirs. She thought of Mrs. Billings's little joke about the double hitch. It had taken her a minute to catch the meaning. But this might be as bad as getting married, she thought—hitching up with a team that has yellow poplar for a yoke and sassafras for bows. That was absolutely the most dreadful combination she could imagine! She could almost hear the wood splinter now. She could envision them cascading down the near-perpendicular road, with wood flying and oxen cartwheeling.

"Trust, Meribah!" She nearly jumped from her pallet at her father's voice.

"Is thou awake?"

"Thee is the loudest silent worrier I know!"

"I can't help it."

"That is just the point. Thee can't help it. So trust. We have done all we can."

"What if somebody has a yellow poplar yoke and sassafras bows?"

"That is the most ignorant combination of wood imaginable. Nobody has that!"

"Thou cannot be sure."

"Thee is becoming pert."

"But, Pa!"

"Don't 'but, Pa' me," Will said shortly.

"Well," Meribah said with resignation, "some of those yokes—the McSwats', for instance—are painted and stained so dark, who knows what they are made from?"

"Meribah." Will propped himself up on his elbow and looked across to his daughter. "Thee must have faith!" Meribah felt as if she were caught in a glare of hard bright light that beamed from her father's eyes. She felt a calm steal through her body. She remained very still.

"Thee knows what faith is?"

"Belief?"

"Belief in things thou cannot see!" He called her "thou." It had always been "thee" for fourteen years. "It is faith that separates us from animals." Then in a quieter voice that was warm, almost conspiratorial: "This is the believing that makes us human! Thou must have faith. Now get thy sleep and get thy faith!"

8

NIGHT TORN

She did not know how long she had slept, but it was pitch black when she first heard the muffled voices, taut and quick in the night air. She looked straight up at the tear in the cover overhead. Dark and starless, the sky gaped like the toothless mouth of an old man.

"Pa!"

There was no answer. She sat up and let her eyes adjust. He was not on his pallet. From outside the wagon she caught fragments of speech—a word, a phrase, but nothing whole. Yet under all the conversation was a sharp, familiar trill that swirled and eddied constantly midst the bits and pieces of words and sentences. Meribah strained her ears but lay frozen in her bed. She stared straight up at the black piece of sky torn from the night, her body stiff with dread.

"Which direction did they . . . Follow the river back . . . no sign of either Timm . . . always carried a pistol . . . Send out a party now . . . If not by first light . . . ."

Will's face suddenly appeared in the rear of the wagon, a white mask in the *U*-shaped opening.

"What's happening, Pa?"

"Stay here! Don't move. Mrs. Whiting will be here to stay with thee."

Angry confusion replaced fear. Meribah jumped up and was getting dressed when Henrietta Whiting clambered into the wagon. She had thrown on her skirts and shawls over her night clothes, and she still wore her sleeping bonnet. She

107

looked like a bundle of laundry. Not saying a word to Meribah, she immediately turned her back and leaned out the opening. Meribah could not see Henry at all, just his hands clutching each side of the huge bundle that was his wife and filled up the opening. Their hoarse whispers scored the night. Again, there were only fragments, maddening half-phrases.

"Shouldn't tell . . . No, no need for a child to . . . Yes, I'll be safe . . . Don't be a hero . . . Stick to Will . . . Watch out for rattlers . . . standing guard . . . Will doesn't think so . . . Meribah knows . . . She will know . . . She won't know . . . can't know . . . Mr. Billings does, does he? Is he going? . . . You'll let me know . . . all over by dawn."

There was a sigh and then a thud as the voluminous bundle collapsed on the pallet opposite Meribah.

"The poor thing," Mrs. Whiting exclaimed. "And to think what Mrs. . . . ." She clipped off her words. Her eyes widened and her face turned blank, then she said with stony authority, "I'm here to be with you until the men get back. Don't ask any questions, Meribah!"

"Mrs. Whiting, you must tell me what is happening. Where are the men going? What has happened? You *must* tell."

"I can't tell you."

"You won't tell me!"

"Your father wouldn't want you to know."

"*I* want to know! I'm not a baby. *I* want to know."

"Oh, Meribah!" Henrietta said with deep exasperation. "I don't even know myself yet what's really happened!"

"Well, can you not tell me what you do know?"

Henrietta Whiting pressed her lips together and set her face.

"It's something with Serena, isn't it?"

Mrs. Whiting squeezed her eyes shut tight, as if she were locking up her face.

"It is! It is! Isn't it?" Meribah's voice rose.

Henrietta's face contracted as her eyes squeezed shut tighter and her lips clamped and rolled inward, until there was only a thin line between nose and chin and two short slits for eyes.

Meribah felt wild with frustration. She grabbed the bunchy

shoulders and shook as hard as she could. "If you do not tell me what's happened to Serena, I'll go out there and find out for myself!" She screamed the words.

Henrietta Whiting's eyes flew open. Just at that moment there was a shout from outside. "Is it them?" cried a voice Meribah thought she recognized as Mrs. Billings's, shrill and distraught. She and Mrs. Whiting turned toward the opening and stared into the black socket of night.

"Wickham!" another voice shouted. "It's Wickham! Quick, get him . . . get him the doctor. He's hurt . . . Oh, no! No! No!" The words flew like shards of glass through the air.

"Serena!" It was Billings's voice this time. "Where's Serena?"

"Leave him alone, Billings." That was Dr. Forkert. "Can't you see he's barely conscious?"

Meribah jumped from the wagon and stood back a few feet. Mr. Wickham sat limply on the ground, supported by Mr. James and Dr. Forkert. There was blood on his pant leg and boot.

"Not much of a wound to faint from," Mrs. McSwat whispered.

Mrs. Billings turned to her with huge eyes.

"How does a person get shot in the foot?" Mrs. Barker whispered less than quietly to her husband.

"Running away," a voice in the darkness behind Meribah said.

Mr. Wickham stirred, a strange light in his eyes.

Mrs. Billings wrenched away from her husband's grasp. "In God's name, Mr. Wickham," she cried, "where did you leave our daughter?"

Mr. Wickham groaned. "I did not leave her, madam. She left me, she left me of her own free will."

Mrs. Billings made a violent gesture. "Are you mad?" she cried. "Left you to go where on a night like this?"

"She meant no harm," Mr. Wickham whispered. "I am sure she meant no harm."

A cold hush had fallen upon the small group. There was a

shifting, a change of mood that Meribah could not read.

Mr. Wickham's eyes darted nervously over the people staring down at him. His eyes stopped at Captain Griffith, who stood coldly silent, waiting.

"It was the Timms," Mr. Wickham stammered.

There were gasps and exclamations, and Mrs. Billings covered her mouth with her hands.

"No doubt it began as a jest of sorts on her part to make me jealous. But then the Timms . . . it turned nasty, beyond her control and when I tried to stop them. . . ." Mr. Wickham gestured toward his foot.

"Where is your own pistol, Mr. Wickham?" Captain Griffith asked quietly.

"Out there. I drew to return their fire but dared not shoot because of Serena." Mr. Wickham groaned and fell back on Mr. James's shoulder.

"Liar," Mrs. Billings whispered. "Liar!" she screamed. She turned to Griffith. "We must find her. My God, we must find her now."

Looking around, her own heart pounding, Meribah could see that few in the group had any heart for this. They shifted uneasily, and suddenly Meribah was apart from them, afraid.

Captain Griffith seemed to have made up his mind. "We'll search tomorrow morning," he said with authority, "when it's light. But we can't delay long." And he turned on his heel and walked off.

"Wrentham?" Mrs. Billings turned pleadingly to her husband, her mouth twisted in fear.

He took her arm, and Mr. Barker took the other, and they lead her away, struggling in their grasp.

Meribah still could not be sure of what was happening. She peered with confusion into the faces of the people that she had traveled with for weeks and felt a sucking tide, an undercurrent of terror that threatened to sweep her away.

"Well! The high and mighty have a long way to fall!" Mrs. Whiting said, with almost a hint of triumph in her voice as she looked toward the Billingses' wagon.

110

"Right you are, Henrietta." It was the first time Mrs. Barker had ever called Mrs. Whiting by her first name. "Why don't you join Eliza Gray and me for a cup of tea. I think we all need it."

"Don't mind if I do."

"Mrs. McSwat, want a cup of tea?"

"No, thank you. Gotta git back to my baby girl."

"You'll bring her up right, I know," Mrs. Barker offered.

What was going on? Meribah was stupefied. For all anybody knew, Serena might be dead, yet suddenly Mrs. Barker, who had never said as much as a how-do-you-do to anybody except Mrs. Gray, was inviting not only Mrs. Whiting but Mrs. McSwat for tea. And nobody mentioned the Timms. It was just Serena that occupied them. The air swirled with bits and pieces of talk and exclamations about Serena's behavior—"unimaginable," although they seemed to be imagining it all quite well, and finding it "shocking." Somebody referred to her as a "tart filly from Philly." And there was furtive laughter.

"Lies, Meribah." It was her father, who now stood behind her. "They're lying because they're scared—easier than chasing the Timms. They've found their culprit, had their trial, and sent back their verdict."

Meribah knew her father spoke the truth.

She, Will, and Mr. Moxley stood silently by the wagon.

"We'll search now," Mr. Moxley said suddenly. Without another word, they walked out into the night.

Before dawn, just before the night melted into gray, Meribah spotted her. She saw her being blown across the face of a hill like a random leaf from another season, another place. So light and dry, without direction or velocity, she seemed carried by the wind currents. Meribah started running up the hillside toward her. "Serena! Serena!" But Serena stared vacantly off beyond her. Just as she was within a few yards of her, Will and Mr. Moxley came from behind the hill. "She's here!" Meribah shouted.

The two men rushed to Serena and each took an arm. There

was the most dreadful noise, a low gasp, then "Off! Off! Off!" The word throbbed again and again through the air. Will, Mr. Moxley, and Meribah backed away and looked on in a kind of numb horror. Serena had been transformed before them into a palsied, rasping creature. The word came repeatedly, and it seemed no longer connected with a human voice emanating from a throat, but crashed again and again like waves in a stormy sea.

"Somebody's got to do something," Mr. Moxley whispered.

"She won't let you touch her," Will said. "She's like a wounded animal."

Meribah was too frightened to move. Serena's cheek was bruised, her dress torn. Spasms rippled through her body. Meribah watched and saw everything—the thin thread of foamy spittle starting at the inner corner of her mouth, the hair comb hanging loose, the fingernails torn and grimy, the ripped bodice with a button on a single thread bobbing in some oblivious merriment, the torn hem, the great rent in the front of the dress. Meribah wanted to reach out her hand to Serena, and yet she was appalled by the very thought of touching her.

"Serena!" It was Mrs. Billings, running toward them from the encampment. With great curved arms she wrapped Serena into a tight circle close to her own body. "Move away! Move away!" She began half carrying, half walking Serena down the hillside, her mouth murmuring soft sounds close to her ear. Meribah strained to hear the sounds, to break up the soft blur into intelligible words. She had a deep craving, as if her own ear thirsted for such words, such sounds.

"Well, I'll be...." The voice was like an itch, a sudden tittle around her head, as annoying as a fly buzzing when one tries to sleep. "This is nothing for a child to witness. You come along with me." Mrs. Whiting took Meribah's hand firmly and began walking down the hillside. Meribah felt her body follow.

July 7, 1849
Near Scott's Bluff, on the
north fork of the Platte River
in the Karante Valley of western
Nebraska Territory

9

ACROSS THE HOLLOW SQUARE

Meribah did not know when she first heard the words "blame" and "judge" used. It could have been on that short trip down the hillside, but she would think of them later when she tried to sort things out about what happened to Serena after she had been found, in the days that followed, over the miles between that hillside and the beginning of the Sweetwater River.

Led by Henrietta Whiting, she had walked dumbly down the hillside. She vaguely remembered Mrs. McSwat going down with them and one woman saying to the other, "Hardly a mark on her," and the other replying with a snort, "None you could see." But Meribah recalled that there was a mark. Serena's mouth was no longer the perfect little valentine, but bruised like an old apple blossom.

One hundred yards before the sharpest ascent thus far, on the road that led into Ash Hollow, they had hitched with the Whitings' team. On the double hitch, each team had to make two trips, one for its own wagon and the second for another. Everyone, including the drivers, who walked beside the lead team, got out of their wagons to make them as light as possible. But Serena did not come out. She remained inside, and nobody questioned it. Mrs. Billings walked directly behind the wagon, calling in to her daughter in those low

113

murmuring sounds. Will tried to dissuade her from walking so close behind. If there were an accident, if a yoke split, an ox stumbled, if the wagon backslid suddenly, she could be killed. But there were no disasters on the double hitch. And Meribah, who had once been consumed with worry over this part of the journey, could barely remember a detail about the ascent or descent into Ash Hollow.

A long time before, she had once rubbed a windowpane with sausage grease to show Liesel how pretty the wild buttercups in front of the house looked, all smeary in the sunshine and the thick green grass. This was the way those two days would always seem to her—not pretty, but smeary, with blurs of color and sound.

Court House Rock, Chimney Rock, Cathedral Rock, all appeared wavy and insubstantial, like licks of flame against the land. Once they had been among the bold marking points of the journey in her imagination, punctuation that had indicated the outer limits of her knowledge. Now she perfunctorily printed their names on her map. Unlike the previous points, which had diminished in importance as they were left behind, the spiral rocks with the picture names crumbled before they were seen. She did not even come out of the wagon to see the view of Cathedral Rock. As for Chimney Rock, Mrs. Whiting said it was in "spitting distance," but she could not lure Meribah over to inscribe her name on its base in an evening walk.

"The wonders of the West are passing you by, child!"

"Ask Serena if she'll join us and maybe I'll go."

"Don't be pert with me, young lady!"

That was three days after the incident. Meribah still was not sure what had happened. People in the wagon train referred to the events of that day as "it." The Timms had simply disappeared with their horses and their pack mule and a general feeling of relief prevailed. Mr. Wickham languished for a few days in his wagon but did manage with a crutch and Dr. Forkert's shoulder to make the ascent of the double hitch. Will had said that Mr. Wickham had only a flesh wound, but Meribah had no clue as to what had happened to Serena, what kind of wound she had suffered. Of two things Meribah was certain: Whether one could see it or not, Serena had been wounded in some terrible way, and for Meribah, not knowing made her own self more vulnerable. She felt as if she were walking on a hillside of crumbling rock, that her feet had no secure purchase, that at any moment she might begin a long slide into nowhere.

Meribah's father was so pained by the mere mention of "it" that she dared not press him further. So she continued to wander in this world of part knowledge, a half-lit world of penumbral images and vague shadows of truth, where what had happened was called "it" and the people involved were "she" and "them"—except for Mr. Wickham, who in spite of bearing the only visible wound, retained his wholeness as "Mr. Wickham, the English gentleman."

They had caught up with a New York company, and Mrs. Whiting had found a new friend in a Mrs. Thompson. "It" was often the topic of conversation between the two women as they walked together, shooing the mosquitoes that were nearly as thick as the dust in this region. Of course, every time Meribah approached, they would quickly change the topic, and it was often by the very changes of the topic and the way in which Meribah was addressed that she began to have glimmerings into what had really happened to Serena. The topic was often switched to marriage, and Meribah, who had previously been called "sweet," even "a little mother," was now often hailed by Mrs. Whiting as "our innocent," "our unspoiled little girl." She hovered and became annoyingly inquisitive about things that Meribah considered too personal ever to speak about.

The fragments of conversation that she did hear about the Billings from other people were both revealing and confusing. "Proud people . . . taken down a peg . . . silly flirt . . . a tart filly from Philly." And one night when Meribah had turned in early, she heard her father and Henry Whiting talking about "it." She heard Henry say that he felt sorry for "this tragic comeuppance," which Meribah found to be a most confusing combination of words. Will must have found it equally confusing, for Meribah heard him reply quite curtly, "Henry, there is no such thing as a tragic comeuppance: It's either tragic or a comeuppance. A person either does or doesn't deserve it. No woman deserves that. It's tragic."

And if what had occurred nearly a week before and one hundred miles back was tragic, what was happening now had a tragic familiarity for Meribah and for Will. Serena had been in the wagon or in the tent since that day. No one outside her family had seen her. There had been little exchange between the Billingses and anyone else in the company. Every evening Meribah had watched them make camp. Mr. Billings had actually learned how to set up the tent by himself and no longer needed the running instructions called out by his wife. When night fell, Serena would leave the wagon, where she took her meals, and move quickly to the tent. Every night Meribah would watch to see if Mr. Wickham would leave the whist game with his friends to make his way toward the Billingses' tent to pay a call, as he had been accustomed to do in the past.

On the fifth day, just before sunset, Meribah stood a short distance from the campfire, where Mrs. Whiting, in infinite and tedious detail, was describing to Mrs. Thompson how she made the biscuits so light and fluffy. Meribah, her back to the women, stared across the hollow enclosure of wagons toward the Billingses' wagon, which stood apart and just outside the square. She was thinking about all the fears that people had had on the journey so far: fear of Indians, fear of drought, fear of massacring Mormons, fear of cholera, fear of bad water. Yet no one had spoken of this fear, the nameless one that was within, within the hollow square, within the wagons, within the people.

116

"Go thee to her, Meribah!"

"Pa! What does thou mean?"

"Just that. She needs thee."

"She needs him," Meribah said defiantly.

Will sighed and shook his head sadly. "He won't go."

"Thou is sure?"

"Yes, but I shall go with thee if it will help—although thee is closest to her, and it might be easier for Serena if it were simply thee."

Serena. It was the first time in all these days that Meribah had heard her called by name. Things suddenly came into a keener resolution.

"Pa! How could I have not gone to Serena for all these days? Pa, her loneliness! I am so ashamed!"

"Ashamed!" The air was striped with indignation. "Mr. Simon, I must protest. I do not think it proper at all for little Meribah to visit her since the incident."

"Mrs. Whiting." Meribah turned, feeling herself grow stiff with anger. "I shall not only visit Serena, I shall drop by Mr. Wickham's as well and ask him if he cares to join me."

"My dear little Meribah." Mrs. Whiting sighed and took both her hands gently in her own. "You don't seem to understand." Mrs. Thompson was busily pretending to be kneading dough.

"I am afraid that I am beginning to understand too much," Meribah replied, without a trace of anger now.

"You are a motherless child, and I feel that I should—"

"Thou forgets, Mrs. Whiting, that I am Meribah's father."

"But so much of this is women's business."

"I shall accompany Meribah. I thank thee for thy solicitude."

"Oh, I did not intend any harm, any affront, Mr. Simon. I mean . . . ."

"Of course not. Come along, Meribah."

The arrival of the Thompsons had handily provided an excellent replacement at the whist table for the spot vacated by Wrentham Billings. Mr. Thompson was a much sharper player than Mr. Billings had ever been and, as Mr. Wickham's partner, had advanced their winnings substantially in just a few evening sessions. Wickham said that this was some sort of compensation for the pain and inconveniences he had endured because of his foot wound. The wound, while still smarting, was healing nicely, and Mr. Wickham kept it elevated on a small footstool while he played. Dr. Forkert and Mr. James did not seem to begrudge Mr. Wickham his new-found success at the whist table. Indeed, they admitted to each other that the game had picked up considerably since Mr. Thompson had become the fourth player. Billings was an fine enough fellow but terribly predictable at the card table, and the notion of playing whist with him all the way to the Sierra Nevada was not an exciting one.

They were just finishing a hand as Will and Meribah arrived.

"Ah!" exclaimed Dr. Forkert. "The Simons! A pleasure on this capital evening."

"Is thou winning yet?" Will asked with cheerful ease.

"Not yet, sir. This Thompson fellow is a strategist."

Mr. Thompson chuckled, enjoying the compliment.

"To my benefit," Mr. Wickham added lightly, "for I am hardly a strategist."

"Now, Mr. Wickham, you are one better than that," Mr. Thompson replied. "You have a fifth sense and can follow the strategy on the smallest cues. No sense having strategy if your partner can't catch the drift, if you know what I mean."

"Oh, I know exactly what you mean, sir." Mr. Wickham rolled his eyes skyward in mock horror.

Dr. Forkert and Mr. James laughed heartily at this. Some private joke had just been shared.

Meribah found the hearty, jovial atmosphere disturbing and Mr. Wickham disgusting. She wanted to wreck it, just as a child wants to wreck a row of perfect mud pies or sand castles an older sister has made by the creek.

"We are going to visit Miss Serena." Meribah thought her

voice sounded a bit high but suddenly older. "We were wondering if you, Mr. Wickham, would like to join us. It's a fine evening, you know, and I'm sure . . . ."

Mr. Wickham had suddenly turned quite pale. His lips twitched slightly. "No. No," he finally said, "I don't think so. Thank you."

There was a silence. The other men looked down at their cards. Was that all he was going to say? Meribah wondered.

"Well," she continued, sounding young again, "are you sure?" It was so lame, such a futile thing to say.

"I think she would enjoy a visit from thee," Will said steadily.

The color began to creep up around Mr. Wickham's collar. "I don't think it would be appropriate."

"Why not?" Meribah asked stubbornly.

"Meribah!" Mr. Wickham had suddenly jumped up, flustered and angry. "You're a child and can't understand these things—although your father should. Things are different now with her. So just stop with your notions. Have . . . have . . ."—he began to stammer—"have I made myself clear? You know I nearly got my leg shot off out there. Enough now!"

"Thou had better sit down then, Mr. Wickham," Will said icily.

Will took Meribah's hand, and they began to walk toward the Billingses' wagon on the other side. It was a short distance, shorter than from the house to the barn back in Holly Springs. But it felt longer. It seemed to Meribah like an endless minute, and she could feel every pair of eyes in the company on their backs. She saw Captain Griffith, a perpetually moving man, stop in his tracks and swing slowly around to look at them as they moved across the hollow square. She felt the Whitings and Mrs. Thompson lift their eyes from their dinner preparations to fasten their gaze on them. She felt the stare of the McSwats, and of people in the company whom she hardly knew, like the Grays, and the Barkers. Even the Browns, who had joined the company just that day, stopped to turn their heads and look. She felt their gaze like pinpricks between her shoulder blades. Then they were there.

"Oh!" That was all Mrs. Billings could say, just "Oh!" when they came.

Serena had not yet left the wagon for the tent, and Meribah, now feeling quite sure, asked her question again: "Please, Mrs. Billings, may I see Serena? Please. I . . . I . . . miss her. I really miss her."

Barbara Billings's lips, as if in some spasmodic reaction, were silently repeating the words "miss her." It was as if she could not quite comprehend the meaning. Just as her lips were trying to frame the words for her brain, Serena appeared.

Meribah first noticed her mouth, heart-shaped and perfect again. Serena looked perfect. Her skin was so pale that it was almost milk-blue. Her hair was uncurled but smoothed back neatly in a low knot at the nape of her neck. And it was while Meribah was studying this outward flawlessness that she came to perceive the truth of the real wound. Rape. She'd heard of it, heard it whispered—not in Holly Springs, but along the trail. She felt her throat close and her eyes widen as the meaning flooded through her. Rape. She took a step back and bit her lip. She wanted to shut her eyes, but they were locked open on this creamy sheath of perfection. She suddenly felt her father's hand solidly upon her back, firmly moving her a step closer.

"Serena, Meribah here has missed thee. She would like nothing better than a visit and a friend to talk to."

"Um-hm." Meribah nodded mechanically. What would she ever talk about with Serena? Everything was different now. She felt herself recoil. "There's acres of dwarf sunflowers over there, Serena!" she suddenly blurted out.

"I am different now, Meribah."

"We don't have to paint them."

"I am different."

"Well, sunflowers are still sunflowers, and couldn't we just

120

go look at them together?" Meribah's vision blurred with tears. She blinked her eyes, and everything came into sharper focus. "We haven't seen any colors since I don't know when. Please come." Meribah stepped forward and reached for Serena's hand.

10

SHARING THE LIGHT

They sat on a crest and looked over a wide sweep of land gilded with sunflowers. Will sat a short distance away. Meribah, still holding Serena's hand lightly in her own, talked about the sunflowers. She talked about how the first seeds might have been blown there to make such a field. She talked about their color. She told Serena how she had once smeared the grease on the window to see buttercups blur. She talked about the seeds again and repeated what her father had said: that every kind of flower grew along the trail because the wagons from every state carried with them—embedded in their wheels, in their gear, in their animals—the pollen and seeds from their own barnyards and fields.

There were long stretches when Meribah did not talk and they sat wrapped in the extraordinary clarity of the gold light. Serena, still and luminous, said nothing. When they walked her back, Serena turned to look into Meribah's face and held onto her hand a little longer. Then gently slipping it free, she turned into the tent.

A ritual was established. Each evening Meribah, accompanied by Will, would first go by the whist table, at her insistence, where she would ask Mr. Wickham politely to join them. Equally polite, he would refuse, and they would continue on to Serena's. She would be waiting for them with her shawl and hat, her gloved hands folded in her lap. They would walk for a while, then find a place to sit. Talking grew less important to Meribah. The silences became just as communicative. There seemed to be a special value in just sitting together, holding hands, sharing the light, and saying nothing.

Once when they sat with their heads back against a rock, Meribah took Serena's thin shoulder wrap and covered both their faces. It lay on them like a blossom skin, and they looked through it toward Laramie Peak and watched their own breaths stir the thin veil between them and the snow-crowned mountain. Meribah knew that she would remember that moment for the rest of her life.

"Does he limp?"

"Does who limp?"

"Mr. Wickham."

Meribah was startled. Mr. Wickham's name had not been mentioned since the walks began, and only a minute before they had been talking about celery bouquets. It took Meribah a few seconds to sort out her thoughts. She could answer the first question simply, but what about the others that might follow? She was afraid that Serena might press her for more information, and all she could think of were the bits and pieces of conversation between her father and Mr. Moxley on the oddness of the wound and something about the bullet not being that of a pistol but another kind of revolver.

"Does he?"

"Limp? Well, no, not so much. Of course, I haven't seen him walk that much."

"Oh, dear, he probably can't. This terrain is so rough. I myself fear for twisting my perfectly good ankles when we're out for a walk. The bone was not shattered?"

Meribah looked at Serena with disbelief. "Heavens, no! It was just a flesh wound."

"Oh, no. I'm sure it was more than that. It was as if I could hear the bone splintering."

"Well, I am sure that he will recover."

"Eventually, perhaps, but his bravery had a high price," Serena said in a dreamy voice. "So much blood. *So* much blood." It was almost as if Serena were in a trance. There was no breaking through it. Besides, Meribah thought, what would be the use?

After the first walk, when Meribah and Will returned to

123

their campfire, Mr. and Mrs. Whiting had greeted them with a stony silence, a silence not of anger so much as awkwardness. Mrs. Whiting's mouth had been set in a crooked line halfway between a smile and a grimace. Her eyes had held the question locked behind the crooked lips. Meribah knew the question without hearing it: What did *she* have to say for herself? The burden of proof had clearly been placed on Serena. What had happened was not a *crime committed* but an *incident brought on*. Meribah raged inside and would not give way to their curiosity. Upon returning that evening, and the ones that followed, she immediately began making biscuits or rolls or dumplings. Let them be curious about how a nice little girl could still make such light airy biscuits after having associated with *the likes of her*. While Meribah mixed and kneaded and rolled the dough, she carried on furious internal dialogues in which she told everyone just what she thought. She knew it vexed Mrs. Whiting to be eating the biscuits and hearing enthusiastic praise from the Thompsons.

One evening when Meribah had just come back from walking with Serena and Will had stopped to talk with Captain Griffith, Mrs. Whiting quickly left the stew pot she had been stirring, Mr. Whiting put down his whittling, and they hurried to meet Meribah.

Mrs. Whiting took her husband's hand and began to speak. "We want you to know something, Meribah. We don't think it's right what you're doing with her—for your own sake, that is. And we don't think your pa should let you do it, or encourage it, as he seems to. But we guess you just feel you have to, you being her friend and all. We never did cotton to those folks, with all their airs. Well, even though we think it's all wrong and pray it doesn't do you harm, we still . . . we still . . . ." She began to cry softly.

"What Henrietta is trying to say is, we still like you and don't hold it against you, Meribah."

Meribah felt only confusion. She was both angry and touched. In their pinched minds they had found room for

124

both blame and pity, for disapproval and approval. It was an astonishing maneuver, like a buffalo trying to turn around in a pantry.

Will walked up just as the Whitings finished their speech. "What's happening?" he asked.

Dumbfounded, Meribah replied, "They say they still like me even though I walk with Serena."

"That's the gist of it," Henry said matter-of-factly.

Will looked equally stunned. "Oh!" was all that he could say, and he scratched his head. Meribah did not make biscuits that night.

A second unexpected occurrence happened the next afternoon. Meribah made her usual stop by the whist table, and as she and her father approached, she saw that Mr. Wickham was absent and his place had been taken by none other than Mr. Billings. She felt a slow flood of joy spread inside her. She realized that at last Mr. Wickham had invited Serena to resume their evening promenades, and in one glittering moment the world had been put to rights again. Everything began to swing back into sensible balance. She walked directly to the Billingses' wagon, eager to see an ecstatic Mrs. Billings and the two figures, those of Serena and Mr. Wickham, promenading near the white sandstone cliffs on their way toward the Heber Springs.

But Serena was waiting patiently in the wagon, hands folded, her pelerine wrapped around her shoulders and bonnet tied under her chin. The only figures against the white cliffs were those of the Boston Pack Mule Company following a cloud of dust kicked up by an oxen company in front of them. Everything was the same! Everything was as it had been! Mr. Wickham had not come for a promenade at all. Serena, pale and wounded, sat deathly still. Nothing had changed. Nothing, except one thing. Wrentham Billings was playing cards again. He was back at the whist table in Mr. Wickham's place.

Meribah did not know what to make of this. She stood barefoot in the chill waters of the lovely pool, absolutely confounded. Serena sat on the bank, which was fringed with marsh grass and wild cherry trees. It was an oasis of water and color after miles of baked, cracked earth. But Meribah, who only a few days before had thought she would never see enough color to quench her eyes or drink enough cool water to slake her thirst, was oblivious. She stood in the water and began to tremble, not with cold but with an anger so great that she thought her body could not hold it.

"Tell me again about the celery bouquets at Amish weddings, Meribah." Serena always wanted to know about Amish things now.

But Meribah turned away instead and fell down on her knees in the shallow part and beat her fists against a smooth stone. She struck the stone again and again, demanding in a choked voice, "Why? Why? Why?" until the word echoed meaninglessly. When she finally looked up, she saw Serena, now standing, her mouth twitching and her eyes wide and unreadable. "You're all wet, Meribah."

Mr. Wickham never did join them. He and Mr. Billings alternated at the whist table. When Mr. Billings was not playing, he sat around and joined the light conversation. He seemed to be his old affable self once more, full of grace and good cheer. The players were cordial, and he admitted with good humor that Mr. Thompson was a far better partner for Mr. Wickham than himself. Meribah gave up going by the table to ask Mr. Wickham. He would never agree to join them for a promenade, and now her stopping by was disturbing not just Mr. Wickham but the other men, including Mr. Billings. The late-afternoon outings with Serena continued. Meribah thought of them as "walks" however, not "promenades." They never took drawing materials. They never talked of poetry.

Once on another walk a few days after the one to Heber

Springs, Meribah and Serena were leaning against a steeply sloping knoll. Again they had placed the thin shoulder wrap over their faces, and this time they were looking skyward when Serena's father happened upon them. He obviously felt quite awkward encountering the two girls on the knoll.

"Well, my goodness! Whom do we have here? If it isn't Miss Meribah, the prettiest girl on the emigrant trail!" He spoke rapidly, quickly recovering his composure. "I dare say, is that a mosquito netting, Miss Meribah, or a bridal veil you wear?"

"We're both wearing it, Serena and I," Meribah responded somewhat coolly.

"So you are." He glanced perfunctorily at his daughter. "Perhaps a bridal veil for you, Meribah, and a mosquito netting for her." He turned on his heel, called cheerio, and walked away.

A small voice broke through Meribah's shock. "My father doesn't know that Amish girls don't wear bridal veils," Serena said, her gaze following her retreating father.

II

STAR SLOT

Toward the end of the North Platte the water became rank again. From the wagon seat, Meribah scanned the horizon for water signs—dwarf cedars, a rare grouping of willow or alders. But mostly there was sagebrush, low and dusty, growing where nothing else could. For two nights they had to camp near stinking alkali ponds. Oxen trains pushing on for good water passed them all night long. Mr. Moxley, who had ridden ahead, came back with the news that within a day there was a slew—Willow Spring, with good water and plenty of grass —and from there to the Sweetwater River was just another two days.

Meribah woke up one night and heard her father and Mr. Moxley talking just outside the wagon. Low and intense, Mr. Moxley's voice had lost its jolly timbre. Meribah listened quietly, her eyes focused on the star slot in the canvas tear overhead, her ears pricked.

"All men's bad traits are finely honed by the time they get to the rock," he said. "Their true character is revealed, Will, unvarnished, unfettered. I've seen things I'd never have believed, and I thought I was prepared, but some things I just can't accept."

"Like what?" Will's voice was low.

"I saw an old lady, dead just an hour. Thrown out on the trailside. She was in a clump of sagebrush. There was a fat old rattlesnake sleeping on her chest." His voice droned on in the night in an even and monotonous tone, as if he were trying to distance himself from the story. "She was from the Pitts-

128

burgh City company. I know it. I remember her from Fort Laramie. She'd been ailing there. Now, the Pittsburgh Company passed that spot half a day before and here she was, dead just an hour. So they must have thrown her out before she died. I spotted her easy. I saw her calico dress and white bonnet clear as Old Glory flying off Fort Laramie. I ask you, how many companies and independents in between must have seen her before she died?" His voice rose a little in intensity. "I know for a fact, Will, that the Springfield Company and the Boston Pack Mule Company passed there six hours before I did. And here in this company the Barkers and the Grays have been breakin' ahead. They must have seen her. I tell you, Will, I ride down this trail sometimes and think to myself, This is a story that I'm just not inside. You know what I mean?"

Meribah knew what Mr. Moxley meant. This was a story that she too did not feel inside. That afternoon she had been leaning against the right front wheel of their wagon as she watched Mr. Billings amble slowly back toward his Conestoga with the jug of milk she had just poured for him to take to Mrs. Billings and Serena. He had paused to speak first with Mrs. McSwat. From where Meribah stood, she could see the great mountain of a woman shake with laughter as Mr. Billings told her something that was apparently amusing. He opened the jug of milk and took a swig from it. He said something else, then throwing back his head, his chiseled profile lifted toward the sky, he took a long drink from the milk jug. He corked the jug again, made an elaborate bow to Mrs. McSwat, who blushed and giggled, and then he proceeded on his way. He stopped at the Browns' and chatted briefly with them, although long enough to uncork the jug and take another two drinks. Meribah judged that by then at least a quarter of the milk, perhaps even one-third, was gone. He did not bother to recork it for the short distance between the Browns' wagon and the Gentlemen's Wagons. The gentlemen were just setting up for whist. Mr. James and Mr. Thompson were erecting the awning to shade the players from the low-angle sun. Mr. Billings leaned his elegant frame against the larger of the two wagons and seemed to be offering suggestions regarding the placement of the awning in relation to the sun. Meribah could not hear him but he kept pointing toward the sun and then turning toward the half-raised awning. He drank at short intervals from the jug. He stayed there for ten minutes, maybe more, then he said good-bye.

There was no milk left by the time Mr. Billings arrived at his own Conestoga. Meribah could tell by the way he set the jug down that it was empty. But more telling was the expression on Serena's face as she watched her father set down the jug. Meribah had never seen such a look of profound pain and disbelief in anyone's eyes.

Later that evening Mr. Billings returned rather sheepishly to ask for more milk.

"It seems that I have been accused of stealing milk out of the mouths of babes! In my wife's eyes, this ranks with infanticide!" He spoke with a jovial charm. "I entirely forgot and drank it myself, I must confess. We would be eternally grateful if we might avail ourselves of a cup or two more of Simon-Whiting's bounty, and as a token of our appreciation I bring you some of our English tea biscuits."

"Oh, I think we can spare another cup for the ladies," Will said tersely. "And as far as tea biscuits, it's not necessary."

"I'll take the milk over," Meribah said. "I wanted to visit Serena anyway."

"So you too don't trust me, Miss Meribah!" He realized almost immediately that he had spoken too harshly, and with a light, quick laugh and a charming smile, he turned to Will, saying, "These women! The ideas they get about us menfolk! Eh, Will?"

"I don't know what thou means, sir. I only know that Meribah said she was planning to visit Serena."

"Aha! So you, too, are part of this!" Flickering in his eye was a dim light. "I'll tell you what," he declared. "Just fill up the jug halfway here and the two of you can accompany me back and make sure the old man doesn't sneak a sip, or I'll be in for a licking if I do, won't I?"

Meribah and her father were equally confounded by Mr. Billings's bizarre conduct. They both remained by their own campfire, but an uneasy silence enveloped them.

A few minutes later a high, slightly nasal voice came across the hollow square of wagons. "All safely delivered—every drop!" The announcement was followed by a tense, almost frightened-sounding, laugh.

Meribah had gone back to the campfire. Staring into it, she thought about the fears again—especially the nameless one, the one that was actually within but that people always felt was threatening from outside, the gnawing one that could massacre the spirit, the one she saw flickering in Mr. Billings's eyes.

Lying on her pallet that night, listening to Mr. Moxley talk with her father of real events that seemed like stories, Meribah reflected on what she had seen that afternoon, of Mr. Billings and the jug of milk. Sometimes it all seemed as distant as the stars in the slot of torn canvas above her pallet.

When Will turned in that night after his talk with Mr. Moxley, he found Meribah sitting bolt upright on her pallet. Her face was set, her eyes narrowed.

"I want to know!" Meribah said in a low, steady voice. "Thou need not give it a name. I know the name—rape."

"If thee wants to know why they did it, I cannot . . . It is impossible to understand them and their vileness. It's not even like rutting pigs."

Meribah blurted out, "I know that!"

Will made a gesture toward her. "I didn't mean it that way," he said. "I mean, it has nothing to do with regeneration. It's not life force. It's more to do with destruction, power—grinding power, a desire to destroy."

"Well, tell me this then: What is happening now? Why

does Mr. Billings drink all the milk for Serena and her mother? Why won't Mr. Wickham even speak her name? Why are the Whitings forgiving *me* for walking with *her*? Why is Serena 'her' or 'she' and Mr. Wickham still 'Mr. Wickham'? Why are the Timms never mentioned and Serena, the victim, is judged? Why? Why? Why?"

"Why is an old lady thrown out by the road to die? Why, Meribah? I don't know why. I just don't know." Will held his head between his hands, his face contorted. "Meribah," he said softly, "there are no answers. There are only questions. If thou wants easy answers, they are in Holly Springs!"

There was a long silence. Finally Meribah looked up, but not into her father's eyes, "Can one be angry with God?" she whispered.

"A good question."

July 24, 1849
Independence Rock, on the
Sweetwater River in central
Wyoming Territory

I2

THE WHALE'S EYE

Independence Rock swam up from the land like a whale—humped and large and blue—from a calm sea. It rose two hundred feet above the Sweetwater Valley, and below it ran the Sweetwater River, or Eau Sucrée. That was what Will said the French trappers had named it. The river was the last on the eastern side of the Rocky Mountains. They were now in what Will called the toes of the mountains, which were to the northwest.

The rock was painted and marked all over with names, dates, and initials of emigrants. Mr. Thompson and Mr. Billings proposed a hike up the eastern face to inscribe the names of their own company members, and were immediately joined by the Whitings, the McSwats, the Grays, and Dr. Forkert. Meribah and Serena, setting out to walk in another direction, followed a rill that ran off from the Sweetwater. At first the way was sandy, but as they followed the rill, the land hardened and became quite stony. The eroded slopes and banks had deep cuts that revealed a silvery gray rock underneath. Sometimes the silver rock, sandwiched between layers of a lighter beige rock, seemed to creep right out of the cracks.

Meribah, ahead twenty paces or more, had walked right by it, her eyes straight ahead, but Serena, who usually stared down as she walked, suddenly let out a small cry and dropped to her knees. Meribah spun around, fully expecting to see a striking rattlesnake. Instead, she saw Serena on her hands and

133

knees beside a smooth slab of rock tracing something with her fingers. Meribah walked back and saw, lying in a curl, as if napping, the perfect impression of a small animal in the stone. Its tiny hooves were still tucked and pointed back, its head turned upward. A curve of spine and several small ribs prints formed a perfect sweep.

"What is it?" Serena whispered.

"My pa showed me something like this once. I think he called it a fossil."

"What is a fossil?" she asked, touching the small bone prints.

"It's from a million years ago, when an animal died and somehow became printed into the earth forever."

"Forever?"

"Well, I guess. A million years sounds like forever."

"How odd," said Serena. "How perfectly odd and beautiful this little fellow is. What do you suppose he is, anyway?"

"He looks about the size of a dog."

"But he has hooves." Serena's fingers followed their outline. "But look, they aren't exactly hooves."

"No, there are three toes, it looks like." Meribah bent down closer to see. "Now what in the world has three toes?"

"Look at its head. It is similar to a calf's."

"No, no, slenderer I think. Closer to a deer's—perhaps it's a fawn or a doe." Meribah looked up at Serena. "Do you suppose it was nursing at the time?"

"At the time of what?" Serena looked hard at the small form.

"I don't know."

"You mean when it died?"

"Yes." Meribah hesitated. "I guess so."

"Well, I don't think it was nursing. Why do you say that?"

"Because of the way its head is turned, as if toward its mother's teat," Meribah said, remembering their calves back in Holly Springs.

"I've never seen a calf nursing, but I say that this one was not. No," Serena said, "it appears as if it is wrenching its head

134

up for air, nosing through this rock for one last breath."

"How terrible!"

"Yes. It looks as if it died confused and choking." Serena spoke with soft authority.

"Oh, no!"

"Oh, yes," said Serena evenly. "Dying was horrible, but death is not. Look, see how peacefully it sleeps in the stone now. And we can still imagine its beauty. The perfect curves of its back. Its hooves. I can almost imagine what it was. Can't you, Meribah, even though we don't know what to call it? It's been released in stone."

Meribah was perplexed. Serena's speech, bare now of its former curlicues, had become confounding, even mysterious to her. Her talk was full of twists. How is something released by locking it in stone? How can dying be horrible without death being horrible? Meribah had no idea what Serena was talking about.

The conversation around the campfire that evening was lively enough with its reports on the expedition to Independence Rock. Mrs. Whiting declared that there was more writing on it than in the *Springfield Courier*, and she had seen names she recognized from Illinois.

"There was barely room for our names. But we got 'em all up there!" she said triumphantly. "Everybody in the company's inscribed on that fool rock!" She laughed gaily.

"Some had to be just initials 'cause we started running out of space," Mrs. Thompson added. "But Henrietta's right, they're all up there."

"Mine up there?" Meribah asked quietly.

"Sure it is, child!" Henry Whiting replied.

"And mine," said Will.

"Did thou go, Pa?"

"Went up later to have a look, but Henry here had already pecked them in, both of ours."

"In full, I might add," Henry said. "One of the virtues of

135

having a short last name is that it got written out. Although for Meribah I think I put just M." He inscribed the letter in the air with his finger. "Yes, M-period-Simon. You see, if you had been named something short like Lil, or even Mary, we could have squeezed a little."

"Or Ribah!" she said. Will looked down suddenly. Instantly Meribah regretted her words.

"What's that?" asked Henrietta.

"Oh, just a nickname someone had for me back home. No, M-period-Simon is fine with me. Thank you, Mr. Whiting."

"Well," said Mrs. Thompson in her whiny voice, "we just got S.G.T. and E.R.T."

"Well now, Mrs. Thompson, don't you go complaining," her husband said. "Elizabeth and Stirling have to be the longest Christian names given. Not only was there not enough room, but you weren't the one doing the pecking, for once!" He laughed heartily at this.

"Really, Stirling! You mean thing." She made a nasty little face at her husband. Everyone else had managed politely to stifle their laughter.

As Will was pulling off his boots that night in the wagon before going to bed, he chuckled to himself. "That was durn funny what Mr. Thompson said about his wife. She is a chickeny sort of creature, isn't she?"

"Yes, she sure is."

"Here, can thou help me with my boot? This one's a sticker."

"Thou called me 'thou,' " said Meribah, tugging hard on the left boot.

"So I did. Thou is growing up."

"Hmm," Meribah said, and looked at her father closely, as if studying him.

"What does 'hmm' mean?" Will asked.

The boot popped off. Meribah fell back on her pallet. "Phew! Thy foot stinks!" she exclaimed. "Now that I am 'thou,' I guess that I can tell thee such things."

Will laughed. "When thou were 'thee,' thou would have told me, Meribah. I know thee well enough. Go get some of those sulphur powders for me. Thou is no sweet rose thyself, by the way. Thy boots could probably stand a shake."

"Pa," Meribah said suddenly, "was Serena's name up there on that rock?"

Will shifted uneasily on his pallet. "Got the powder?"

"Pa! Was it?"

"I'm not rightly sure, Meribah."

"Was Mrs. Billings's name there?"

"I . . . I don't know."

"Well, Mr. Billings's must have been because he was with the group."

"It must have been then," Will said tensely.

"But thou cannot remember about Serena and her mother."

"No, I can't recall. It could have been just initials and I could have missed it. We'd better turn in now, Meribah."

She waited until his breathing was regular. She could see the covers rise and fall rhythmically on his chest. When she was sure he was asleep, she got out of bed quietly, put on her dress over her night clothes, and knotted a heavy shawl around her shoulders. Once out of the wagon, she put on her shoes.

This was the night country, moon-bleached and stark. Every sagebrush stood out in prickly detail, and the ground lay naked, showing every clod and pebble in rounded clarity. The spine of the whale hoisted itself against the night. The distance was short, and Meribah was soon at its base. She picked up a rock with a sharp point and began to walk up the eastern face. She knew just about where the party had gone to inscribe their names. She followed a crack that seemed to go in that direction. The names became thicker. Painted in black and red, scratched, and pecked, they covered the rock. Then just at the whale's eye she saw it clear and bold and red—F. WRENTHAM BILLINGS. There was a cluster of other names around it. Dr. Forkert's was quite bold and beautifully pecked. The McSwats' names were scratched

137

with a wobbly grace. She found her name and her father's. The Barkers', the Whitings', and the Thompsons' were mostly in initials. The Grays' were written out in full. And there was Mr. Moxley's. He had already ridden ahead and was beyond Devil's Gate, so someone else must have pecked it in. But nowhere was there an S.B. or a B.B. Meribah found a small spot and began pecking. The moon sailed silver and cold above, lighting her work. Every tiny pit emerged white and perfectly round. She felt calm as she began to make the top curve of the *S*. She pecked each mark close to the other one to make a dense cluster. A pleasant numbness grew in her hand, allowing it to peck faster, almost as if it moved by itself, powered by something else that would never tire. She watched the top curve grow thick and bold in the moonlight. Yet even though it appeared to be a solid band, Meribah could still focus on the single pit, a silvery moon-limned dot. A wind began to blow. She had never remembered seeing so clearly. In this night of extraordinary perception, with her hand numbly riding a wave of rapid percussion, Meribah felt strangely removed from her own body. It was as if she were a shaft through which light poured, her hand a drum through which vibrations traveled, her body keen and strung for any wind to play.

13

A CLEFT IN SOUND

Two days after she had pecked Serena's initials in the rock, the tense, grumbling voices from outside came floating into the wagon. She did not need to be told what had happened. She was dressed and out of the wagon before her father. She stood there listening as Captain Griffith's voice sliced through the hysteria of Mrs. Billings, announcing that they would delay one day and one day only to search. Then with a grim rationality, the bad eye clenching in the sharp early light, he listed the reasons why it would be no use to delay any longer. Meribah saw Wrentham Billings nodding and bobbing his head in meaningless gestures. She heard others grumbling, some making plans to go ahead anyway, others saying they would give a morning for the search, rationing out their time like water in a desert. Others said nothing.

"When did she go?" Meribah had planted herself squarely in front of Captain Griffith.

"We're not sure. We think a short time after midnight."

"Which direction?"

"We don't know, child!" Captain Griffith said in exasperation, as if he had just realized that he was speaking to Meribah and not to her father.

"What are your plans?" she cried desperately.

He turned his back and walked away.

Meribah turned toward the others. Their faces were arranged in masks of sympathy. It was then she knew that she could kill. The masks under the blaze of Meribah's eyes began to blister and peel away like so many coats of paint, layer by layer. First, there was the confected sympathy, then the complacency, and finally the deadly twisting fear.

The company had camped near Bitter Cottonwood Creek. The land around the dried creek bed was mostly deep white sand, punctuated with small hills and odd-looking square towers of stones.

Directly to the north rose the rugged Rattlesnake Mountains. It was into this harsh, barren range that Will and Meribah felt sure Serena had fled. Two search parties, one composed of Will, Meribah, and Mr. Thompson, the other of Mr. Moxley, Henry Whiting, and the McSwats, began an ascent of the lower part of the range. Mr. Billings stayed behind to console Mrs. Billings. Captain Griffith led another group that fanned out in the area of the trail between Bitter Cottonwood Creek and the Sweetwater. Meribah felt this choice to be futile. It was well traveled and affording little hiding place; she was sure that Serena would not flee there. Always within shouting distance or eyesight of one another, Meribah, Will, and Mr. Thompson stayed within the lower part of the mountains. Not far above the river, this region was chinked with crevices and cavernous hollows, where it appeared bears had lived. Great masses of hard rock worn smooth as glass soared six hundred feet in perpendicular walls. Rattlesnakes abounded. Meribah had killed one, her father three, and Mr. Thompson two. But the snakes did not deter her from peeking into every crevice and cave and calling out her friend's name. Meribah turned down each blind canyon and gap as she hiked through the brutal mountains that day. Mr. Thompson declared himself too weary and lame after four hours and said he would join Captain Griffith's party in the sandy flats of the creek area. But Meribah pushed on, never saying a word, and Will stayed nearby, watching out of the corner of his eye each time his daughter disappeared into a hollow or leaned from a rock shelf to peer down a gorge. He would not stop until she did. Just before sunset, the heel tore off Meribah's boot and at the same time the seam gave. With no shoes, she knew that it was hopeless. They turned back toward camp.

That night there was an electrical storm. Sheets of lightning torn from the cracking sky laid bare the bones of trees and scorched clean the glassy mountains. The mountains' white feldspar veins became radiant in the crashing blackness. Inside the wagon, in the flinching white light of the storm, half-dreams of wake and sleep exploded in Meribah's head. Suddenly she was fully awake. Near the violent heart of the storm there was an astonishing silence, like a cleft in sound, a hollow in the night, that seemed to bend over her. In the absence of sound, Meribah listened hard and heard nothing. That was when she knew it was finished, but still she could see Serena. She would always see her in her dream eye.

A slow, sandy, streaming sound began, like something thick and choking running through a narrow space. Then there was a rush as it tore loose.

"Arroyo," Will said softly. "Not near here, up on the southwest side of the creek, near the mountains."

"What's an arroyo?"

"A dry gulch or creek. When a slew of mud runs off it, earth's often so dried out it can't hold the water. So it just kind of slides away."

"Takes everything with it, doesn't it?" she asked.

"Yes."

Sometimes what she saw in her dream eye was memory, and sometimes it was much more real. The images came with astonishing clarity—the small bone prints in a curve of sleep pressed into the earth clear as ciphers, the stone-pecking sound slightly mocking now. She could even feel the vibrations in her hand, the spreading numbness.

When they found Barbara Billings, her hand was clenching the ripped head of a rattlesnake. The company articles specified that no more than forty-eight hours could be spent searching for a missing person. When Captain Griffith announced they must move on, Mrs. Billings, though she hardly seemed resigned, had not protested and even appeared calmer than before. She had disappeared a day after the search had been called off. She had told her husband that she was going out for a short walk and would be back in time to help with the tent. She walked due east and then turned north into the mountains, and some said they heard her whispering, "I'm coming now, dear, *ma chérie*. Don't worry. Everything is going to be fine. Mama is coming."

For Meribah death had become imaginable.

August 1, 1849
South Pass, on the ridge that separates the
waters flowing to the Atlantic from those
flowing to the Pacific. The Wind River Mountains
are to the north, the Rocky Mountains,
to the south.

14

CONTINENTAL DIVIDE

"On this day, August 1. . . ." Mrs. Barker was writing in her journal and whispering the words as she wrote, "we are passing over the ridge that separates the waters flowing to the Atlantic from those that find their way to the Pacific. We have reached the summit, and I pray to God our team keeps working for the remainder of the journey and we do not have to cut the Conestoga in half!"

When Suzanne Barker finished writing the last word, she turned toward the three white stone knolls that designated the divide. A small group of men, including her husband, stood with a flag to the left of the trail by two of the stone knolls. A ceremony was about to begin. Mrs. Barker smoothed her skirts and stood up from the rock on which she had perched for her journal writing. Eliza Gray came to join her, and the two women linked arms and smiled at each other.

Meribah, who had been standing behind them, felt someone fidgeting with her cap.

"This is as close as you're going to get to church for a while, young lady," Mrs. Whiting chirped. "So let's have your cap on straight."

"And a smile on that pretty face," added Mrs. Thompson. "A pretty face without a smile is like a . . . uh . . . Oh, well! What do they say it's like, Henrietta?"

143

"I don't know. Apple pie without cheese is like a kiss without a squeeze." The two women exploded in giggles. Meribah drew her lips back slightly in an adequate semblance of a smile.

"Henrietta! I'm so excited about finally being here at this spot, and even though we can't see it, I feel as if I could just reach over that horizon and touch California!"

"Yes, we're finally here, and Henry has been practicing his speech all morning."

"So has Stirling, and I understand that Dr. Forkert has a few words to say."

So did Mr. Wickham and Mr. Billings. Meribah watched it all. She looked appropriately prayerful when Stirling Thompson thanked God in all His boundless mercy for their safe journey so far, "despite the loss of two"—who remained nameless. He prayed for strength of "man, wheel, and ox." He praised the glory of the mountains and the rivers. A banner was then unfurled to the wind, and it was Henry Whiting's turn now. In a quavering voice he spoke of this "great land" and the "glory of our attainment of this most glorious summit!" Meribah was mindful to smile and look proud while Mr. Whiting spoke, for Mrs. Whiting stood just beside him now and looked directly across to where Meribah, Will, and Mr. Moxley were standing.

Dr. Forkert gave a speech in which he compared the dividing ridge to a man's backbone. He pointed out all the anatomical parallels and enumerated all of the structural functions and miraculous capabilities of both. Then he veered from the backbone toward the circulatory system and talked about arteries and veins and rivers and creeks and oceans and blood and water and the Atlantic and the Pacific and back again to the ridge at South Pass, where they all stood. Meribah lifted her brows as if attending every syllable the learned man uttered.

Next, Mr. Wickham, his blond hair flying at the same angle as the banner flew, announced that he felt compelled to share a poem that he had recited many years before in the vale of

Chamonix in France while gazing upon the magnificence of Mont Blanc, and until this day "ne'er did I think I should see such a site of unparalleled grandeur as to inspire once more the recitation of Percy Bysshe Shelley's immortal lines written in the vale of Chamonix." He took a deep breath and began to speak the poet's lines.

"*The everlasting universe of things*
Flows through the mind and rolls its rapid waves,
Now dark, now glittering, now reflecting gloom,
Now lending splendor, where from secret springs
The source of human thought its tribute brings
Of waters—with a sound but half its own,
Such as a feeble brook will oft assume
In the wild woods, among the mountains alone,
Where waterfalls around it leap forever,
Where woods and winds contend, and a vast river
Over its rocks ceaselessly bursts and raves.

Thus thou, Ravine of Arve—dark, deep Ravine—
Thou many-colored, many-voicèd vale
Over whose pines, and crags, and caverns sail
Where power in likeness of the Arve comes down
From the ice-gulfs that gird his secret throne,
Bursting through these dark mountains like the flame
Of lightning through the tempest! thou dost lie—
Thy giant brood of pines around thee clinging,
Children of elder time, in whose devotion
The chainless winds still come and ever came
To drink their odors, and their mighty swinging
To hear—an old and solemn harmony."

Mr. Wickham stopped there. Meribah could not help but wonder what Alec Wickham knew of the "source of human thought," or for that matter, an "old and solemn harmony." But an exquisite expression bathed his face.

"Looks like he just heard the angels sing," Mr. Moxley

whispered in Meribah's ear, and a genuine smile broke across her face for the first time in weeks.

Mr. Billings strode over to Mr. Wickham and pumped his hand vigorously. "That was truly a magnificent recitation. I only wish," Mr. Billings turned toward the group, "that on my own grand tour of Europe, when I had the marvelous fortune to view Mont Blanc, Mr. Wickham had been in attendance to enhance my pleasure as he has today with this exquisite recitation. But that was so long ago, old boy, you were probably still in diapers!" There was a hearty laugh from the group at this cunning remark. "But if I may be serious for a moment." Meribah felt her heart beat faster. She waited tensely, completely alert now to Mr. Billings. Would he say something more than the cold prayers of burial? Would he speak of them as wife and daughter? Would he admit loss? "Mr. Wickham," he began, "to this wildness you have brought civility. To this grandeur you have brought elegance!"

Cowpiles! Meribah thought. Why do I always expect more? Why?

Mr. Billings continued. He spoke of "this ridge, this symbol of the Great West at hand! Within our grasp at last." His elegant hand did a ballet against the sky as he signaled the "crowning glory of our achievement. That attainment! The summit of humanity at the summit of the continent!"

Meribah looked about her. Every face, with the exception of Mr. Moxley's and Will's, seemed to shine with the golden prospect at hand, at the snowy mirage of achievement. These people seemed genuinely moved by Wrentham Billings's words. But it all seemed terribly cheap to Meribah. The more they talked about this dividing ridge, the more they trivialized it and promoted themselves. It was as if the people themselves felt they had somehow fashioned this ridge, these mountains, with their own hands. If the ridge did have any sacred dimensions, this place where the rivers divided, it was diminishing rapidly for Meribah. If she felt anything at all, it was a dividing within—self out of self.

146

"I have a word to speak." Mr. Moxley's voice was loud and clear.

"Be my guest, good scout." Mr. Billings had just finished his speech.

"It's brief. It's a poem."

"Aha! A poet-scout!"

"Well, I used to be a schoolteacher, so it's not uncommon for me to read occasionally!" He did not bother to look at Mr. Billings while he said this. "For almost a thousand miles now we have been traveling away from our homes, our country, our beginnings, away from one ocean, and now as we cross this dividing ridge, we pass another boundary and we begin to move toward another ocean. It is hard to know whether to think of this ridge as a beginning or an end. But before we head on, I want to remember what is behind. This is from a poem by John Keats. I dedicate it now to the memory of Serena Billings, and to her mother, who died trying to save her." He cleared his throat and began. Inside, Meribah felt herself grow still.

> *"And she forgot the stars, the moon and sun,*
> *And she forgot the blue above the trees,*
> *And she forgot the dells where waters run,*
> *And she forgot the chilly autumn breezes;*
> *She had no knowledge when the day was done,*
> *And the new moon she saw not."*

Meribah's eyes stung with tears, but within she felt a sense of release. Although things could not be changed, some things had been put in order. She silently thanked that decent man, Mr. Moxley. She knew now she could not look back, and so she turned west. There were no more choices for her.

Meribah marked the divide on her map in a way that she herself only half understood. She did not print the words. She did not stipple the ridge or crosshatch a mountain range. She made a few, very faint lines for the dividing rivers. But what she did mark on her map were the two oceans. In the wide margins of her paper she printed PACIFIC on the left and ATLANTIC on the right. In printing the names on her map, she reversed her usual mapmaking procedure, for she had never seen either ocean. But this did not bother her. She had marked what she had never seen, but could only believe to be.

15

LOST

Henrietta Whiting was seething mad. It was not yet eleven in the morning, and they had already tried three descents to reach the valley. One was too steep for the wagons, and the others were dead ends.

"Some shortcut! S'posed to save us five days, and here we've been two days just looking for a way down. And Henry's not feeling well at all. If it's really bad getting down, he just won't have the strength."

"Now, Henrietta," soothed Mrs. Thompson, who was walking beside her, "don't fret. Henry's going to be fine in a couple of days."

"Fine!" Mrs. Whiting's eyebrows flew up. "Fine! He's eaten hardly anything since we started this durned cutoff. Whatever he takes in goes right out. I've never seen such dysentery."

"You have him keep taking that medicine and he'll be good as new in two days. And I'll bet you anything we find a trail down by sunset. Don't you think so, Meribah?"

Meribah really did not know—nor had she thought about it—but she said yes anyway. Another voice seemed to take over for her more and more these days. Half the time she did not even know what the voice was saying, but it seemed to carry her through the endless hours of each day and through situations that might otherwise be unbearable.

Captain Griffith had decided to take Greenwood's—or Sublette's, as it had once been called—Cutoff. It struck out

149

due west from where the traveled road intersected Little Sandy Creek, and it ended at the Green River. The first part was desert for thirty miles or more. They were underway each morning by two o'clock so as to travel in the coolest part of the day. Each ox received one quart of water; each person, one cup. The road was generally level. Halfway through the third day, the road started to climb higher into the foothills of the Wind River Mountains. It was in this region that the old pack trail became sketchy and in parts was almost obliterated. Captain Griffith had led them too high, and finding a descent was proving difficult. Exhausted by the desert, the company had become short-tempered and irritable in the mountains. There was an undercurrent of angry mutterings concerning Captain Griffith, and some talked of appointing a new leader. Will called it the foolest idea he had ever heard, and he told Henry Whiting and Stirling Thompson just that.

Where others' strength ebbed, however, Meribah's surged. She possessed an uncommon energy. She helped drive the Whitings' wagon when Henry was too weak to drive and Mrs. Whiting too tired from nursing him. She mended clothes that had needed repair since Fort Childs. When at last they found water plentiful in the mountains after the desert stretch, she washed not only Will's and her clothes but the Whitings' and the Thompsons' in a clear stream, while the others complained about Captain Griffith and fretted over a way down from the mountains. She baked enough bread one afternoon to last them two weeks.

But the grumblings still continued, and there was no way they could not filter back to the captain, whose response was not to show anger or to apologize but to push on harder in his efforts to find a way out. With each day they were lost, the traveling time was extended longer and longer. At first the people were afraid to complain. But within two days they had been pushed to such a ragged edge of their own endurance that there was an angry explosion in the camp.

"I say we call him up right here and demand an explanation!" Mr. Billings sounded the first cry of protest.

Mr. Thompson pitched in, "For heaven's sake, armies have courts-martial. A wagon train should be entitled to a similar course of law."

"I'm with you!" said Dr. Forkert. "And I believe James and Wickham here are too!"

Meribah and her father leaned back in the night shadows of the wagons and watched the flash of tempers. They watched as Captain Griffith, who had overheard the entire exchange, strode into the center of the hollow square. The man stood massive, his big chunky hands not clenched but tense, waiting. His bad eye was clamped shut, but his good eye quickly darted over each person's face.

"Somebody have something to discuss here? I myself always prefer open discussions. Mr. Billings and Mr. Thompson, I believe your terminology is slightly askew: They don't call it court-martial, they call it mutiny." He paused. The eye darted in and out around the circle of faces again. "Now, let me explain one thing to you. I am your leader. In accordance with the bylaws of this company, if there is any breach of conduct by your leader—namely, drunkenness, obscene language, indecent behavior, undue punishment—you are within your rights to dismiss me with a two-thirds vote. I refer you to articles one through five of section one of the bylaws. It is my judgment that I am not guilty on any one of those counts. Now, there seems to be some consternation over...."

They watched. Captain Griffith was masterful in his presentation. His anger, never revealed, was more dreadful in check. His voice never rose. He carefully chose his words—big words, impressive words, words that one would not expect a rawboned wagon master to use, let alone know. Captain Griffith talked about "friable earth surfaces" that "precluded safe exists." He talked about "interbedded bands of shale and mudstone" that could "precipitate avalanches of wagons."

Then, with paternal assurance, he breathed air on any flicker of hope that was left by declaring that when he did find the "appropriate angle of declivity" where he could be "one hundred percent sure of every man, woman, and child's safety," then and only then would he permit a descent to begin. Until then they would continue to search, to hunt, to exhaust every possible turnout of these mountains. They would find one, but to do so required them to keep moving; therefore the long days. He ended his speech with a flourish that was a calculated turnaround of language: "Sittin' ducks get shot. And ain't nobody going to find a way out sittin' still. So we *move*!" This last pronouncement was delivered in a jocular tone despite the underlying deadly seriousness, and people actually chuckled, if somewhat nervously.

Each afternoon after the day's drive was over, after the mending chores and before supper, Meribah would set out for a walk, her drawing things in her satchel. Her drawing had changed, however. The perspective was different. No longer did she dare with chalk and pencil the edgeless world and the endless wind. She drew the close-up, finite things now—a sagebrush silvery with dust, a wheel hub, an interesting rock, a spindly tree growing straight out from a stone slope, a fish her father caught for supper. Close up and precise, it was not the perspective for which she had a natural inclination. It left no room where her mind could wander and little space where her fingers could work. But she did it anyway, cheerlessly, day after day, not permitting herself to use any color at all, only varying the shade and tone through stroke and pressure of her lead pencils. In a sense it was a relief from the voice that took over when she was around people and yet did not let her listen too closely to her own. If she was drawing a wheel hub or a rock, she would often become so focused on its texture, the grain of the wood, the striations of the rock, that she would come back to camp with no picture at all, just an inscrutable cluster of tiny lines or grainy dots. Meribah knew they weren't very good. She knew that there was a way to draw a wheel hub that showed how the wood had grown in the tree, or draw the pitted streaks of a layered rock that revealed how it had formed through time, through perhaps a million years of time. But something stopped her, stopped her hand, stopped her eye from letting the marks become a pattern and have meaning. She did not care much about meaning or pattern or design. Nothing made much sense to her now. She pecked at her paper in rather the same way she had pecked at that rock almost a month earlier, except then she had sought meaning and now she sought only the numbing vibrations.

The wound was a clean one. It had happened when Will was fixing a wheel on the Thompsons' wagon. It was a simple job. He had been prying off the hub band when his chisel slipped and gave him a nasty gash in his left hand. It was unusual for something like that to happen to Will. He didn't slip with tools. The only reason Meribah could imagine was that he had been tired from the desert trek. His hands were shaky and his mind lacking in concentration perhaps. "Stupid!" he had shouted when the chisel sliced into the flesh. Meribah had cried, "Ouch!" as the dark blood filled the curve of the hand between the thumb and forefinger. For a split second she remembered when her hands held the deep curves of blue prairie sky. Dr. Forkert said it was a "good" wound, meaning a clean one. When he dressed it that night, he showed Meribah how to change the bandage and clean it. That had been two nights ago. She recalled now what the doctor had said about good wounds as she unbandaged it after supper.

"Lucky this didn't happen in the dry stretch," she said.

"Why's that, Meribah?"

"No water there to clean it." She dabbed a fresh rag into the bowl of water.

"I suppose thou would have found it if thou really had to. I've never seen such energy in such heat."

"Can't find it if it's not there, Pa. But maybe off to the southeast where these buttes rose. I always . . . ."

She talked on about the lack of water, but her mind turned to thoughts of other wounds. She didn't mind cleaning this. It did not make her queasy.

"Moxley rode off that way," Will said.

"Not far enough. He had to go beyond those first buttes. I had hiked up high and I think I could see. . . ." Visible wounds, Meribah was thinking, were not the kind you had to worry about. It was the ones you couldn't see. No, this was an honest gash. She could see the little jagged edges if she looked very hard, just as she had looked at the wood grain that afternoon on a discarded wheel she had been drawing.

"Maybe it was a mirage thou saw?"

"What was?" Meribah had forgotten what the other voice had just said.

"The string of willows."

"No, I don't believe so." This wound still bled when she pressed it lightly, as Dr. Forkert had shown her. Wounds that never bled were scary. "Hey, Pa! I think it's started to mend. See, it doesn't bleed as much. It's starting to get tacky inside, like those little hooks of flesh have to lock together, just like the hooks on a single strand of carded wool.

The idea of carding combs and flesh was enough to make Will wince.

"Did I hurt thee?"

"Thy talk! Meribah! Keep thy carding combs and spinning wheel away from my gashed hand. I suppose thou shall be making a drawing of it next!" There was an edge in his voice.

"Thou doesn't like my drawings?" She knew it was not a fair question to ask when she didn't even like them herself, but she could not stop herself. Nor could she stop what she said next. "Thou is lucky thy wound can be seen to be drawn!"

In that moment they both knew what she had been talking

about. There was an odd gurgling sound deep in Meribah's throat. "I miss her, Pa!"

"Of course thou does!" With his good hand Will pulled Meribah close to him, then wrapped his arms around her.

"And Pa"—her voice was a low rasp—"I have such anger."

"I know."

16

THE VALLEY OF LA FONTENELLE

They broke out of the mountains after six days. The last two days they spent picking their way down over narrow crooked ridges of sandstone, and the final mile was made with the wheels double locked to prevent crashing down a stretch called Horn's Most Difficult Descent. But finally the jagged dark mountains let them free, and they caught their first glimpse of the Valley of La Fontenelle. A silver ribbon of swift creek ran through its very center.

"There it is—the tributary of the Green River!" Captain Griffith exclaimed with no small note of triumph in his voice. They were perched, double locked, on a high ridge of crumbling sandstone above the valley floor. Meribah should have been petrified. They were virtually hung up on the sheer cliff by some combination of locked gears, crossed fingers, and prayer. But she wasn't afraid. She did not think of the wagon's precarious position. She did not hear the tense conversations of the others. She did not feel the crumbly stone beneath her feet. Turning full face to the green cradle before her, Meribah arched and stiffened into a new wind that blew across the valley. She inhaled deeply and held the breath, not in fear but like a bird riding an updraft, lungs full and wings steady over the valley. A true valley, it was the most beautiful that she had ever seen, green with the wide, sinuous creek that coursed through it, sparkling and rapid. There were bright green grass and groves of willows along the banks of the stream. There were islands that dotted the silver like bright beads. There were stands of poplars and spruce.

156

They entered La Fontenelle a mile or more above a French traders' camp and set up their own camp adjacent to the traders' skin lodges. There was a mixture of white women and men, Indian women, and half-breed children. Some of the Indian women were deeply rouged with vermilion, and one Frenchman had several stripes painted across his nose and cheeks.

"Never in my born days have I seen anything the likes of this!" Henrietta Whiting exclaimed as the man with the striped cheeks passed.

"Makes that circus that came to Springfield last year look like church," Henry added.

Meribah was sitting on the ground with the Whitings and the Thompsons, watching feats of horsemanship by the French traders. The men rode full tilt on fat sleek ponies, then stopped, wheeled about, jumped off the ponies, remounted—backward, no less—and tore off at full speed while holding onto the ponies' tails. It was the most amazing and hilarious display. The traders were laughing and jabbering away in a mixture of French and Snake. Meribah had a hard time telling where one language ended and the other began. But she had heard the Frenchmen speaking to one another, and she thought it a most wonderful sounding language, nothing at all like the few words Serena and her mother had sometimes spoken. There was a deeper resonance, a rich tone, that made her think of Holly Springs and the sound that Briar Creek made where it disappeared underground, the loud babble quieting to a soft rumble.

Meribah wished her father had felt well enough that evening to see the Frenchmen on their ponies, but his hand had been bothering him and he was running a slight fever. He had turned in early—not, however, before negotiating with an Indian woman for a pair of beautiful beaver leggings for Meribah. She held the leggings now in her lap, stroking them, hardly able to believe that these beautifully stitched soft skins were hers—her first real non-Amish clothes. She could hardly wait until the weather was cold enough to wear them, but that wouldn't be until the Sierra Nevada—almost five hundred miles more.

Trading with the cutoff folks, as the emigrants who came into the valley by way of the Sublette Trail were called, was a thriving business for the French traders, and even Mrs. Whiting, who was most scornful of everything in the camp, from the "painted Frenchies" to their "fool prices," was impressed with the leggings.

"They'll keep you toasty as anything under your skirts, Meribah. I'd buy some myself 'cept they'd have to slaughter all the beavers in the valley to fit me," she joked.

Everyone laughed at this, and Meribah had to admit that in spite of all her truly annoying traits, Henrietta Whiting could, on occasion, have a sense of humor about herself. Since they had come out of the mountains, Mrs. Whiting's spirits had soared. She had even praised and thanked Captain Griffith —when they were lost, she had been so angry that she had stopped speaking to him. But even as she was laughing, Meribah noticed something odd about Henrietta Whiting. Thinking about it, she realized that this plump woman was much thinner, especially in her face. Henry Whiting had become rail-thin from his lengthy bout with dysentery. Henrietta had not been sick at all, but she nonetheless seemed gaunt and tired in much the same way as he. She no longer insisted on the good square hot meals each night. They ate cold food from the previous day, and she hadn't baked biscuits since they left South Pass. She even forgot to ask Meribah about rubbing down Simon-Whiting's "poor old udders" with the balm. This would have been unthinkable five hundred miles back. It was as if without experiencing the illness or the symptoms, Henrietta Whiting had been left with the sapping effects. Meribah was perplexed and slightly worried.

But mostly Meribah thought about the beautiful valley through which they were passing. Her thirst for certain colors and textures was finally being slaked. She could never take in enough of La Fontenelle.

For almost three days they wended their way through the valley. There were grouse and hares and deer and wild turkey. The stream leaped with salmon and trout, and the bushes were a riot of berries—raspberry, gooseberry, elderberry. Every day Meribah swam long, clean strokes in the stream. The creek bottom slid by below her, a shifting kaleidoscope of colored stones. Drying out on a mossy bank in the hot sun, she would close her eyes and see the ovals of color from the creek bottom floating before her. She began to draw again. She captured the warm tints of the valley's surrounding bluffs, with their strata of orange and blue rock, the deeper purples of the hills above them, and then the distant blue of the mountains. Mr. Moxley let Meribah ride his horse while he helped drive their wagon to give Will's hand relief. She had ridden only a little before but became quite comfortable on the horse and good at handling it. To be riding a horse in this valley was the next best thing to being a bird. It was the perfect level for seeing the life and color of the valley. Willows brushed her head, and narrow glens and vales off the wagon trail could be explored quickly on horseback. Riding allowed Meribah to break away from the group and come back with reports of wild geraniums as big as cacti and samples of vermilion flowers never before seen, of boxwood that crept like holly, and of strange markings incised on a face of sandstone. Meribah could imagine staying in the valley forever.

Three long blades of sunlight lay across her blanket. It was their third morning in the valley.

"Heavens, I've slept late!"

"So thou has." Will was rummaging through a keg of sundry stores with his good hand. "Must have been a good sleep."

"It was. Oh, Pa!" Meribah said suddenly, as if she were just remembering something, "I had the most wonderful dream."

"Now, what could that have been?"

159

"It was a dream of seeds."

Will looked up, slightly surprised, "Huh! That's funny. Just what I'm looking for now, some seeds I packed back in Holly Springs."

"Oh, my dream was wonderful. I can't quite remember it though. It was . . . well . . . ." She paused and scratched her head.

"Yes?" Will listened attentively. "Try and remember."

"I don't know whether I can."

"Try," Will urged.

"Well, it must have been a good dream because I feel so good inside."

"Yes?"

"I think . . . I think . . . Oh, it sounds so silly."

"No, no. Go on."

"Well, I think I dreamed that I was some sort of a seed princess. Isn't that silly?" Will leaned forward, eager to hear more. "I think that I was wearing—in my dream, or I have this memory—a crown of seeds. Only I'm not quite sure if I was wearing it or if it was a doll, like the ones thou carved for me back in Holly Springs. It's all mixed up. It's confused."

Will's expression was anything but confused. His eyes were clear. He turned back toward the keg. After a minute, he drew out a small burlap bag and placed it on Meribah's pallet. "Here are thy seeds, child. Don't forget them, no matter what. They're more precious than any gold and have more strength than an ox team."

"They are thy seeds too, Pa." Meribah said uneasily.

"So they are now. But they are all I have to give thee that's worth anything for the future."

"Don't talk that way, Pa."

"Just being practical. Come on, help me put them in those cotton bread sacks. I don't want them getting moldy."

August wore on. From the gentle Valley of La Fontenelle they passed into the dark rugged gorge of the Bear River.

160

On her map Meribah made her marks, sometimes a word printed, sometimes just a dense stippling of dots or a thicket of slanted lines to shadow a mountain range or suggest a valley. They followed the Bear River to the Green River and then into the valley of the Bear River. They passed springs called Soda and Beer, and one called Steamboat because its sound was so like that of steamboat paddles churning.

At Fort Hall, Meribah had her first night's sleep in a real bed since leaving Holly Springs almost five months earlier. The commander of the fort, a man by the name of Grant, was an old mountaineer from Canada. Will had joined Mr. Moxley and Captain Griffith to pay their respects to the commander, and Meribah was standing in the courtyard of the adobe-walled fort, waiting for them, when a figure in pure white deerskin strode across the quadrangular space directly toward her.

"My name is Mrs. Grant. Welcome!"

Meribah was startled by her directness. It was almost as if she had been expected. The woman, although not tall, gave the impression of height. She was dark, very dark for an Indian, and on either side of her center part were two streaks of silvery white in her otherwise black hair. A tracery of fine wrinkles swept out from the corners of her eyes toward her temples, and her slender waist was wrapped with a sash of exquisite beadwork.

"I am Meribah Simon." Meribah spoke in a barely audible whisper.

"Come with me, Meribah Simon. You look thirsty." The woman touched Meribah's elbow and motioned with her small, fine head toward the center stairs that led up to a balcony. Meribah followed.

Inside, Mrs. Grant settled her at the pine table. A young Indian serving girl came in and poured Meribah a glass.

"Lemonade!" Meribah exclaimed.

"Yes. You like it?"

"I do. Where does thou get lemons?"

161

"We trade." She laughed softly.

Meribah had heard Captain Griffith telling her father earlier how the Grants had become rich trading with Indians and emigrants. An "old Hudson's Bay man," he was known to be fair. The serving girl returned with a plate of sugar cookies and set them down on the table. Mrs. Grant spoke a few words to her and she left.

"Was that Snake thou spoke?"

"Yes," said Mrs. Grant. "Most white people cannot tell the difference between Snake, Panak, and Shoshone."

"Sometimes it sounds as if they speak them all at once." Meribah took a bite of her cookie.

"Sometimes they do—all living and trading in the same territory, so close to one another."

Shafts of sunlight fell in from the narrow vertical slot windows. It was a plain whitewashed room, with hard pine floors and a few heavy pieces of white pine furniture of a simple design. Against the white adobe walls were occasional pieces of brilliant beadwork—a turquoise banner with a radiating geometric design, a red and orange beaded pouch with rosettes, a pair of white deerskin moccasins with a filigree of black beading, hanging by a thong on a peg.

There was a beautiful simplicity and spareness to the room. There was not one extra thing, and yet Meribah felt that it was all complete. The spaces on the walls, the bare corners of the room, were as important as the table or the beadwork banner. Although there were only the two of them in the room, Meribah felt no need to talk. The spaces in the conversation were as natural as those in the room, and oddly enough, just as communicative as words. Meribah felt she did not have to speak with words for Mrs. Grant to know about her or their journey. And words would be of no use in trying to understand Mrs. Grant. Silence and pause became as intelligible as conversation.

"Meribah, I think, would like to spend the night with us, Mr. Simon, and take a real bath and sleep in a real bed,"

Mrs. Grant said when Commander Grant entered the room with Will and Mr. Moxley.

"Fine," said the commander. "But I want you to take a look at Mr. Simon's hand, my dear. He's had a nasty gash, and white man's medicine is not proving itself infallible."

"Certainly. Come with me, Mr. Simon." Will followed Mrs. Grant into another room.

When they returned, Meribah looked anxiously to the beautiful Indian woman for assurance.

"I have cleaned it again. You have been doing a good job, Meribah, but it needs more powerful medicines than you have had. I put some salve on it, but I want you to come with me now and I'll show you some important things to collect as you travel to help heal your father's hand and strengthen his resistance. You must learn what these plants and roots look like. I can give you some, but you'll need fresh ones."

They stood by a willow tree, and Mrs. Grant peeled off some bark with her small knife. "This willow bark you can never have too much of. It makes the best tea for easing pain and reducing swelling. It doesn't numb pain like the spiked plant that I showed you over there." She nodded her head toward the grove behind a knoll, where they had just been. "But it can ease it. A cup drunk in the morning will start drawing out the fluids no later than noon."

Meribah and Mrs. Grant had been walking for over an hour, following a creek branch of the Panak River. The basket that Meribah carried was almost filled now with a variety of barks, roots, and flowers that Mrs. Grant said were essential for helping Will's hand, as well as for other sicknesses or injuries that they might encounter. She explained the uses of each thing they collected, but there was no way that Meribah could remember it all. The words for the preparations were as confusing as the variety and classification of plants, and all swirled in her mind. There were infusions and decoctions; there were steeping and brewing processes. There were poultices that penetrated for warmth and stimulation of blood, as well as those that drew out the poison and reduced swelling. There was the spiky narcotic plant that was to be used sparingly and only for excruciating pain, and there was the one plant that Mrs. Grant pointed out to Meribah that caused the "deep-forever-sleep."

When they returned, Meribah was exhausted, and Mrs. Grant had the Indian serving girl prepare a bath for her. After her bath, Meribah fell asleep in the first real bed since Holly Springs. Will slept in the next room.

"You write too much, Meribah," Mrs. Grant admonished the next morning in the kitchen. The woman stood over a pot with her head bent down. The silver wings of her hair emerged like a bird in flight from the clouds of steam.

She was right. Mrs. Grant's method for packaging the medicines had proven to Meribah that there were more logical means than words, but they were still the only way Meribah knew to keep track of things. Certain classes of herbs were put into skin bladders, others into leather or deerskin pouches, and still others into small cloth or burlap bags. Each container preserved the material in a manner that simulated its original environment. Roots were kept in bladders, which allowed a minimum of light but maintained just enough moisture. Sagebrush leaves and dried flower petals and blossoms were kept in small cloth bags, which permitted free air circulation. If they became wet, they had to be dried out as soon as possible to prevent mold. Dried flowers already ground and mixed into powders were kept in leather or deerskin pouches. Meribah had made little tags with the name of each bag's contents, but she realized almost immediately that the type of bag itself was as good a label as the tag.

Meribah had been captivated by this quiet, peaceful woman. Ironically, it was her very quietness, the lack of words, the stillness of her body, and the economy of gestures that fascinated Meribah. For the first time Meribah was tempted to make a portrait, and she thought suddenly of Goodnough, wondering if even the portrait master of Indians could capture the supple grace of Mrs. Grant's walk as they had collected the herbs along the Panak the afternoon before. Following in her silent wake, Meribah had felt like an ox team pulling a Conestoga.

Just as it had been difficult for Meribah to leave the Valley of La Fontenelle, it was hard for her to leave Fort Hall. When she awoke before dawn on the second morning of their visit, the morning they were to leave, she found the tightly woven reed collecting basket packed with the pouches of herbal remedies, and on top of the pouches were the white deerskin moccasins with the stunning filigree of black beadwork.

Although Meribah had never mentioned Serena or even how she herself had come to leave Holly Springs, Meribah felt that in her way Mrs. Grant had come to understand her loss. It was not important that it had not been named or identified more specifically, and Meribah sensed that this Iroquois woman too had in some way sustained a deep loss. In the short space of two days, between the woman and girl a silent acknowledgment of each other had grown. There was no pity. There was only a profoundly human sensitivity and dignity. And although it was hard in many ways for Meribah to leave, she felt within herself a new kind of assurance and confidence as she walked out of the fort with her father toward the wagon.

At the beginning the road swung into a deep curve, allowing Meribah to look back easily over her shoulder at Fort Hall. In the narrow vertical window of the Grant's west-facing bedroom, Meribah could see the figure of Mrs. Grant leaning on the sill. When the road straightened, Meribah's view of the woman was obstructed by the cover of the wagon, so she scrambled inside to look directly out the rear opening. They were the last of the train, so now the view was clear. She could see the woman, and the woman could see her. They watched each other until the wagon became a dot and the fort a smudge.

Later that morning when Meribah, still sitting in the cool

shade of the moving wagon, was tracing the filigree of black beadwork on the moccasins, she knew as certainly as she had ever known anything in her life that at precisely the same moment Mrs. Grant was tracing lightly with her fingers the design Meribah had drawn on paper and left for her by the bedroom door. She could almost see the slender brown fingers following the outline of the silvery white wings that soared against the black background. She could imagine her eyes studying the renderings of plants in each corner. The bold but simple black-and-white design had a strange power, which Meribah felt as soon as she had begun to draw it. The design seemed to develop an energy quite independent of Meribah's skill. It was as if her hand had acquired a will of its own. At first glance the design seemed quite static, but before long, an enigmatic tension became apparent. The silver wings seemed at once in repose and in flight. Meribah's fingers continued to run over the beadwork of the moccasins as she thought of Mrs. Grant studying her drawing. Despite the distances, these strange magnetic traceries had pulled their two very different hearts and minds together.

17

ON THE RIM OF THE GREAT BASIN

Meribah awoke with pickets of ice in the ends of her hair that had sneaked out of her sleeping cap. Shivering, she hopped off the pallet and crawled to the rear opening. Everything was white with frost—and it was not yet September, she thought. There were patches of snow on the mountains that formed the northern boundary of the Great Basin. The company had been traveling the upper rim of the basin for the last few days. As Meribah looked at the frost, she felt a twinge of excitement at the possibility of wearing her beaver-skin leggings for the first time. At least, she thought, this frost should keep the dust down. A fine white dust blew up all day long from the massive bowl of the Great Basin. The dust was as annoying as it was insidious. Almost everyone in the company had developed tickling coughs. Wearing face masks helped a little, but Meribah could feel the dust in her throat all day, and she had been shocked to see the bloodstains on Mr. Whiting's mask at noon the day before, when they had stopped for lunch. She had never thought of the dust penetrating so deeply into the lungs, but Henry Whiting had indeed developed a lung-quaking cough.

Now as Meribah sat by the opening, she heard another racking cough coming from the Whitings' wagon. Mrs. Whiting lurched from the front opening and climbed down. Meribah jumped out the back end of their own wagon and raced barefoot across the frost covered ground.

"You've got it too?" she asked.

Mrs. Whiting closed her eyes in a gesture that said yes.

167

"Get back in the wagon. I'll bring you something."

"Yes. . . ." the woman answered hoarsely. "That yarrow tea did calm Henry's spasms."

"All right. I'll be over." Meribah suddenly wondered how much yarrow she had left. She had plenty of hyssop. Mrs. Grant said that hyssop was good for colds, but Meribah wasn't sure that it would work for dry coughs like these. Well, she would give Mrs. Whiting as much yarrow as she could and when that was used up try the hyssop.

Meribah looked uneasily around her, wondering if she could find more yarrow. Vegetation was not especially plentiful as far as she could tell. Indians who lived in the basin had come to be called Diggers because they lived mostly by digging roots. *Something* had to grow in this place. They had seen a few Indians with their digging sticks near the upper rim a few days ago. She supposed they would see more today as they started their descent into the huge bowl.

The tea seemed to work. The spasms that had shuddered through both Henry and Henrietta Whiting had subsided into shallow throat-clearing coughs. By ten, the frost had melted and Meribah was sweating profusely in her beaver-skin leggings. The dust was up again, and she could hear the scratchy coughs emanating from every wagon, including their own. Her father's cough was worse than hers. She had brewed up the remainder of the yarrow and had a skinful of the tea, perhaps a quart and a half all told. It would have to be shared out among her father and the Whitings. She didn't need any. Sucking on a sugar lump seemed to relieve the nagging itch in her own throat. In general, the younger people did not seem to suffer from the dust as much as the older ones did.

She wondered how the straggling bands of Digger Indians survived. Despite their emaciated condition, she never heard them coughing, and she never once saw one with a protective covering over his mouth or nose. They must have become accustomed to breathing the dust. Perhaps they would die without it, like fish out of water. Meribah mused upon this peculiarity as she saw a group digging away vigorously in the dusty earth.

When they stopped for lunch at noon, Mr. Billings came over, coughing fairly hard. Between gulps of air and coughs, he asked for some of the "magical brew that Miss Meribah has been distributing."

"There is not that much to distribute, sir, as I've used all the yarrow and Mr. and Mrs. Whiting are worse off than you."

"But we can spare some," Will broke in quickly.

"Yes, I suppose, half a cup." Meribah got up and walked over to the hook on the outside of the wagon where the skin bag of tea hung in the sun.

"Oh, that is indeed most generous of you, Meribah." A coughing fit seized him, and Meribah waited to hand him the cup until it passed. "You're . . ." He wheezed and started to cough again. "You're an angel! As I've always said, my dear—a veritable angel. I've always said it, haven't I?" The strange look in his eyes made Meribah turn away suddenly. "Well," he said quickly after a swallow, "that squaw lady of Grant's is as clever as she is stunning!"

When he turned to go back to his wagon, Meribah watched him. "I didn't like giving it to him. There's too little for . . . ." She didn't finish her sentence.

Will sighed. "Thou cannot judge who should or should not receive the yarrow, Méribah. Thou cannot refuse when asked. His cough's as bad as the others'."

Meribah was slowly beginning to realize that the basket of the healing herbs and her rudimentary knowledge of their powers might create as many problems for her as it solved.

The dust was left behind, but the coughs persisted as they entered the extraordinary valley called the City of Castles. It was a couple of miles long and perhaps a half-mile wide. Masses and masses of freestanding granite blocks had been buffeted by wind and rain and worn through the ages into intriguing forms. Travelers not content to leave them unmarked had felt compelled to label several in tar or paint with names that they thought were remarkably clever. One was called Napoleon's Castle, another City Hotel. Meribah failed to see the wit of any of these titles, and as she looked at one dabbed with GRANNY'S NEEDLE, Mrs. Grant's remark about writing too much suddenly came back to her. She forced herself to concentrate only on the strange formations that soared and mushroomed into a mythical kingdom of rock.

The next morning Meribah went to fetch some yarrow tea for her father.

"The tea is gone, Pa!"

"What does thou mean? Did it leak out?"

"No. I mean the whole skin is gone from its peg."

"Is thou sure thou left it on the peg last night?"

"Yes, I'm sure. It's gone."

All that morning Meribah was troubled by the disappearance of the tea. Coyotes were known to run off with things from campsites—Mr. Moxley had lost a pair of boots to a coyote—but Meribah doubted a coyote would have been interested enough in a skin of yarrow tea to jump that high and grab it from the peg, especially without either her or her father being awakened. No. It was impossible, and it was disturbing.

They were going through Pinnacle Pass, a very narrow outlet from the City of Castles. On either side there were high, jagged walls of granite with cedar brush protruding from the crevices. A tall rock appeared on the right side, marking the exit. Just after passing this final gate the train began to descend a steep hill. Suddenly there was a commotion ahead.

"*Double-lock!*"

"*Halt!*" The commands splintered the air.

"Quick, Meribah, down. You get the right front. I'll get the left rear."

Meribah slipped a stopping bar through the spokes. They

were not in imminent danger, as the steepest part of the hill was still a good distance ahead. Word came back that the Barkers' larger ox had slipped and broken its leg. A minute or two later a pistol shot cracked. From her seat on the wagon, Meribah could see Mr. McSwat, Johnny McSwat, and Mr. Gray drag the ox to the side of the trail. Mrs. Barker sat in a crumpled heap beside the empty yoke hoop.

A quarter-mile later, where the Salt Lake road joined the Oregon-California road, they cut the Barkers' big Conestoga in half. Mrs. Barker stared vacantly at the operation as Will supervised the carpentry. When the rear end of the front half was shored up with the last plank, Mr. Barker turned to his wife. "Well, Suzanne, what do we do with it?" he said, gesturing at the small mountain of dry goods by the side of the road.

A grim twist of a smile formed on her lips. "Eliza Gray!" Her voice suddenly sounded old and raspy. "You come here and take your pick!" But as she spoke, Mrs. Barker was not facing Eliza Gray. She was staring straight ahead at Wrentham Billings. "You pick good now. There's still some choice calicos left, a keg of rye flour." Her eyes did not move from their target. Mr. Billings turned his head and whistled softly. Eliza Gray stepped forward timidly and began to pick up a few articles.

"Miz McSwat!" Suzanne Barker called. "You come up here and pick something out for that baby girl of yours." Still she faced Mr. Billings, who had now started toward his wagon. "Meribah Simon! You get some of that nice cotton batting. It'll make good fresh bandages for your pa's hand, honey." Mrs. Barker, who had never offered a thing from their rolling storehouse of goods before and whose life on the trail had been so concentrated on managing the contents of the two wagons that she rarely had time for more than the tersest acknowledgment of people, was now giving it all away and addressing people by such endearing names as "honey" and "darling" and "old dear heart." One by one she called the people to come and take their pick, everyone except for Wrentham Billings, who had disappeared into his wagon.

"What do you want to do with the rest of this, Suzanne?" Mr. Barker asked. There was still a fair amount left.

"Burn it!" There was an ugly little curl in Suzanne Barker's voice. Her eyes bore into Mr. Billings's wagon with an intensity fierce enough to scorch the canvas.

"He could have offered the Barkers the white-face, couldn't he have, Pa?"

"Yes. But to tell the truth, I doubt if the white-face would have worked well with the one that's left. Still, that's no excuse. He should have offered the ox, but he wouldn't and didn't."

Meribah sighed. "It's so sad because it was as if the wagon and all the stuff in it, it was all they had—and not just for now but for the future, especially for Mrs. Barker. She put so much stock by it. She doesn't care about gold. She just wants to open a new store in California."

"Yes. She never has seemed too taken with the notion of gold."

"And they don't have any children . . . and the way she used to fret over keeping things in such perfect condition and sorting through them all the time. Remember when she got worried about the goose down getting moldy and nearly lost it all by trying to air it out on the Laramie Plains?"

"Yes." Will laughed.

"What will she do now? I mean, she took care of that stuff all the time, sorting it, drying it, wetting it down, greasing it up, picking weevils out of the flour, sending little gifts to Mrs. Gray. It was more trouble than a colicky baby."

"Well, now thou received a gift, at last!"

"Pa!" Meribah said with exasperation. Will was not following her thinking at all, but she could see that his hand was bothering him this morning. "Here, let me drive," Meribah said, and she took the reins from him.

18

THE BLACK ROCK DESERT

Captain Griffith had determined after almost a score of journeys between Missouri and California to take a more northerly route into California to avoid the bad water at the sink of the St. Mary River and the longer deserts. In addition, he had heard of a new route to the north in California called the Lassen Trail, discovered the previous year by a Mr. Lassen and a Mr. Myers, which led more directly to the mines and Sacramento. The Lassen Trail also promised an easier pass than either Truckee or Carson over the Sierra Nevada.

The rest of the company had been enthusiastic about the route change. The prospect of a more direct route to the mines, and the notion that few people knew about this shorter, easier trail excited them.

"Hard to believe," Mr. Moxley said to Meribah, "that a month ago they were ready to dump the captain."

"I don't think they were ever serious," Mr. Billings chimed in.

"You seemed fairly serious at the time."

"Oh, no!" Mr. Billings protested. "I beg to differ. I have always been one of the captain's staunchest supporters, sir!" Mr. Moxley raised an eyebrow, but Mr. Billings did not seem to notice. He was expounding enthusiastically on the route change. "Do you see what this new trail means? A desert run shorter by almost one hundred miles, less treacherous passes over the mountains, and we'll be in the fields quicker and in

173

better shape once we get there than any of those packhorse companies that have been clipping by us for the last two months. Mark my words!" Mr. Billings clapped his hands together in almost childish glee.

"Well, let's see what the captain has to say." Mr. Moxley turned toward their leader, who had just growled for order.

Captain Griffith rested his foot on a rock as he surveyed the gathering members of the company with his good eye. "I don't want to wait around for folks. We gotta keep moving," he said impatiently.

Moving! Moving! Meribah thought wearily. That's all he thinks about. He hardly stopped to bury Mrs. Billings, or for that matter, to look for Serena. The stay at Fort Hall had been too long, according to Captain Griffith. The man couldn't stand to stop.

"Meribah!" The voice sliced through her thoughts. "Where's your pa? Ailing?"

"Yes, sir. His hand is bothering him, but I can tell him whatever you have to say here."

"Tell him to be ready to move in an hour. What about the Whitings? They sick too?"

"A little." She wasn't imagining it. Captain Griffith was more intent on moving than ever before. She had seen his obsession with moving grow steadily since the City of Castles.

"A little? What do you mean, a little? Can one of them drive?"

"Oh, yes, sir!"

"Good! We gotta start moving, moving soon. We got a tough stretch ahead. My plan is for us to push hard when the sun is down and through the night on this desert drive."

"Didn't you say this way was easier?" Mr. Gray asked.

Captain Griffith shot him a dark look. "The passes over the Sierras are easier. Deserts are never easy—especially for fools. We go at night and we go hard!"

Meribah watched the captain. There was something unnerving about the way his good eye slid about, almost as if he were in a tight space looking for a way out. But here they were with nothing but sky and endless horizon—one coast thousands of miles behind them, the other hundreds away. And yet Captain Griffith was like a horse downwind in a burning field. The clouded left eye clenched tighter. She remembered her image back in St. Jo of the shuttle continuously weaving in and out of the land's warp. The piece is almost woven, she thought. Now what?

"So we keep moving. By my estimation, this desert is fifty-five miles to cross. Three days if we're lucky. This is *the bend*," he said with emphasis, "*the turnoff!* The desert begins up there at the forks. The grass here is poor. It'll be poor for the next three miles, then there'll be none—you can bet on it. The first ten miles will be marble-hard plain, and we can move across that fast. Then I imagine it all thickens up."

Meribah thought Captain Griffith enjoyed listing the dire conditions ahead and would be disappointed if there were good grass, drinkable water, and hard, smooth surface for the fifty-five miles to Boiling Springs. He would then be proven wrong, and being right now seemed for him nearly as important as keeping moving.

"If you think this is bad," he said with gravelly authority, "just try the desert to the south of here—and for a real treat, the Truckee Pass at the finish!" Captain Griffith's good eye glittered triumphantly in its vision.

I can't stand people who always think they're right, Meribah thought to herself. For the first time in months she thought of her smug self-righteous uncles back in Holly Springs, who, along with the other bishops, had led the battle against her father. The captain's righteousness was different—perhaps not as maddening but equally disturbing.

Captain Griffith was wrong. The marble-hard surface did not extend for ten miles. It lasted for only four miles. Then the parched, cracked earth loosened up into a pebbly surface that soon pulverized and thickened into endless miles of sand. Griffith pushed them later into the scorching afternoon sun than he had planned. It was apparent that they would not come close to the intended twenty-five-mile run he had hoped for. Meribah's thirst became a frightening thing. Her tongue felt like something else, unrecognizable. She could imagine it uncoiling and slithering out of her mouth, across the desert.

"Eliza Gray, you care for a wintergreen peppermint candy? Captain says we have to keep sucking on something to keep our saliva glands working."

Meribah pretended not to hear Mrs. Barker's question and sucked hard on the penny in her mouth. They had stopped temporarily, but were about to move on again, as Captain Griffith felt that they could find a better campsite three miles ahead.

When camp finally was made, it was not in the usual manner. The train merely halted in a straggly line. No fires were made. Suppers were eaten cold, and animals were given more water than people.

Barely had the sun gone down when the command came: "Chain up!"

"He must be crazy! We've been here only three hours."

"He wants to go while it's cool." Will spoke in a thick voice.

"Thou can't go, Pa. Thou can't stand another mile." Meribah looked at her father's hand. She had just taken the bandage off to let the dry air get to it. Red streaks radiated from the gash and were webbing the entire hand, both the back and palm. The wrist looked slightly puffy. "Thou cannot drive, that's for sure."

"Better I drive now than in the heat. Thou get thy rest for morning."

Meribah knew that her father was right. But it was the first time Will had ever given the hard piece of anything to anyone else and deliberately chosen the easier for himself.

"Why does Captain Griffith keep pushing everyone, Pa? Seems like he's pushing us harder than ever."

"I don't know, Meribah." Will sighed. "The man's got an unholy obsession with movement."

"Dying oxen, sick people, broken wagons—nothing stands in his way, does it, Pa?"

"No, nothing." Will paused. "Maybe he's frightened."

"About what?"

"I don't know—reaching the end, stopping." Will said suddenly, "Like the land's running out on him and he can't wait to turn around and begin again, get away from the edges. You know, I always loved to watch the stars cross the night sky. Sometimes Clayton Griffith reminds me of them except his motion seems less destined somehow."

The command came again: "Chain up!" Meribah watched the color drain from the red hills, then she turned to her father. Their eyes fastened on each other. Deep wordless feelings seemed to stir the air between them. Silently Meribah rebandaged his hand with some of the new cotton batting.

"Pa, thou drives till midnight, no longer. I'll take from midnight on. He'll surely not press on nearing noon."

"One never knows," Will said, attempting humor.

"If thou starts feeling queasy, like this afternoon, call me. Understand?"

Will nodded like an obedient child. They both sensed that in these extraordinary circumstances there was no time for their roles as father and daughter, that new identities had come of necessity.

Meribah did not sleep. For the first two hours she was so worried about her father that although she knew he would never call for help, she tried to listen for trouble. She lay in bed, tense and alert through the night. Sometimes she would doze for a few minutes, no more, but an odd creak or groan of a plank would wake her up immediately. She knew that outside the way was becoming thick with dead animals. The stench was unbearable. About an hour before midnight she heard a sudden choking and gagging from the driver's bench. The wagon stopped. By the time she was outside, Will was vomiting over the edge of the bench. A chill desert wind stirred her capless hair.

"Pa, get in the back," she said, mopping him up with her apron. "That camphor won't help. Take a swallow of the bark tea. It's in a skin by your pallet."

Meribah almost pushed him into the back of the wagon. Then she seized the reins and slapped the oxen's backs. They did not budge. "Damnation!" she exploded. She took the whip and whacked them. Still they did not move. Now she was really frightened. If they didn't move, they would be left. If they were left, they would die. A fury to survive began to swirl inside her. She jumped off the driver's bench and began to pull on the beasts' muzzles. Just as she was thinking that there was no way she could move the thousands of pounds of animal before her, she saw the water buckets hanging from the hooks on the wagon's sides. If not by force of her own muscle, she would move them by force of her own brain. She would cajole, persuade, trick, these beasts out of the desert. She put a bucket on each arm. "Come on, you old dears, come on now. I got some water for you, right here. Come on! Come on!" Josie started and Leander followed. "Come on, darlings! Come on! Water's coming. Right here! A few more steps." Meribah marveled at their brutishly simple brains. The symbol for water and the real object became so fused that the beasts lumbered ahead, allowing her to lead them across almost ten miles of desert.

That was how far Meribah had walked by first light. She saw the dawn because most of the time she had walked backward, coaxing the team, her arms aching with the weight of the water bucket. The black of the desert night faded to gray. Suddenly the horizon glinted with the bright sharpness of a razor's edge, and the sun rose slowly, dreadfully.

Meribah could hear Carrie McSwat crying fretfully. Surely the train would stop by nine o'clock. The Whitings had pulled to the side of the road already. Meribah could hear their hacking coughs. Mrs. Whiting looked out from the wagon. Her face had a chalky pallor.

"He got the flux again. We gotta stop here for a while."

"Can't you go on just a little?" Meribah had put down the buckets. The oxen stopped instantly. "Mr. Moxley's ridden ahead. He thinks there's a good spring just another eight miles."

"Just another eight miles! Meribah, we couldn't go another mile even if we knew for sure that there was water." Mrs. Whiting turned and disappeared into the black hole of the wagon.

Meribah did not want even to think what it was like inside that canvas tunnel of darkness, with its two husks of human beings, coughing and retching and fouled. The dark hoop opening of her own wagon beckoned like an immense and toothless smile with promises of cool sleep. Trust me! the black grinning mouth seemed to say. Meribah's head reeled. The white heat of the day rose, and blades of sunlight slashed the still air around her. The dark mouth invited, coaxed her toward its gaping hole, filled her brain. She walked unsteadily toward it. There was no sun, no heat, no dust, only blackness now. A horrid smell cut through her delirium. She shook her head violently as if to clear her brain. She was in her own wagon, though she had no recollection of getting into it. The last thing she remembered was talking sweetly to the team. Ah, yes! She had set down her buckets. Why? Because the Whitings. . . . Yes, the Whitings were sick and had stopped. Meribah was coupling thoughts together, one to another as a child might link the loops of a paper chain. They were stopped. They were not moving. They had to keep moving. Not to move meant. . . . That smell! That smell, what was it? A slow fear spread inside her. Her father was sleeping peacefully, but when she looked at his hand, she nearly cried out in horror. The bandage was soaked with a green stain. That was the smell! Then she noticed that his entire arm was

179

swollen. Oh, why hadn't she boiled up the pokeberry root last night and made a poultice? Meribah's mind raced. Maybe if she soaked the pokeberry leaves, scraped the inner bark of the willow, and mixed them with some vinegar, the combination might draw out the poison. After all, it helped loosen a cough. Wasn't the principle the same? She had to stimulate the blood to clean the wound. Meribah strained the little knowledge she had of herbs and remedies that Mrs. Grant had taught her. Reaching beyond that fund, she frantically tried to see the parallels between certain conditions and the connections between certain remedies. A congested chest was in some ways like an inflammation. Stuff had to be drawn out, loosened up.

When Meribah next looked out the wagon, it was high noon. The wagon train had disappeared. The Whitings' wagon, some fifty feet away, only increased her loneliness. She had dressed her father's hand. She wasn't sure if cleaning the wound had reduced the odor or if she had just become used to it. She was truly exhausted now. It would be crazy to try and catch up at this time of day. She looked out the back where Simon-Whiting was tethered. She might have to give her some water. But she couldn't give the team any. Not now. She would give them some just before they started up, to get them going, and then put the buckets back on her arms. But she would rest now. The others could not be that far ahead. What kind of pace could they keep in this heat? No, she would rest, regain a little strength, and catch up. She didn't think about the Whitings. She had only two thoughts: rest and catch up.

"Meribah! Meribah!" Her father was shaking her.

"What? What time is it?" The sun was at a low angle as it streamed in through the front opening.

"Must be about five o'clock."

"Oh, no!" Meribah looked at her father. He did look better, his color improved. "Let me see thy hand." The arm was still swollen, but the streaks seemed less red. She sniffed the bandage.

"What has thou put under there?" Will asked.

"Everything!" She looked up. "Does thou feel good enough to drive?"

"Yes. Don't worry. I can take a good spell now."

"Good, because the Whitings are real sick and I'll have to drive for them."

19

SKY WEAVER

"Mrs. Whiting! Mrs. Whiting! Are you asleep in there?" Meribah called into the wagon, thinking how stupid the question was, because of course if she were asleep, she would hardly answer yes to the question. "Mrs. Whiting!" She called again.

"Yes? What is it, dear?" Mrs. Whiting's voice sounded clear and composed. Perhaps things were better, Meribah thought, but she had no desire to crawl in through that dark hole and find out.

"Well, I just came over to say that I'll drive your wagon for you because Pa is much improved and can drive ours now that the sun's gone down. We're behind and should really move on."

"We're not movin' on!" The voice had a sudden scratchy stubbornness.

"What do you mean?" Meribah was confused.

"You come here. I want to tell you something, set things straight with you." There was an incredible harshness in her tone. It was almost as if another person were speaking. "You come here, young lady!" Meribah hung back like a child on her way to a scolding. "Quick now!" the voice barked from the black hoop. "You and your pa have to get on your way."

Meribah slowly climbed up through the dark hole. There was no bad smell inside. There were no fouled coverings or clothes. Everything was as neat as a bandbox. Clean cups hung on their hoops. Pallet covers were folded neatly. Tinware plates, pans, and washbowls were stacked in nests. Their food-stuffs—the flour, tea, coffee, sugar, dried fruit in canisters—

were arranged in orderly rows on the planks under sleeping benches. Everything had been swept and cleaned of desert dust. Meribah took it all in—the freshly wiped surfaces, the oiled ironware, the swept floor planks, the tidy pallets. Then she saw on a keg the small handgrip of a pistol under a hastily placed clean linen cloth. Next to it was a tin mug of water, untouched. She immediately averted her eyes.

Sunken-eyed and gray, Henry lay on his pallet. She breathed sharply as she saw his face. There was something terribly odd about it. His mouth looked like a picket fence. Then she realized that Henry's face had become so wasted that the outline of his teeth and gums showed right through the taut, thin skin. Her eyes slid back to the pistol, gleaming like a dark moon, next to the tin mug.

"I thought you and your pa would have gone by now. I wouldn't be put to this task if you had left. I guess it was foolish of me to think we could just stay behind without you or your pa takin' notice. So you're here...." The phrase hung in the air. Mrs. Whiting sighed deeply as if to gain strength for what came next. Meribah had always marveled at how strong the woman was, but Mrs. Whiting now seemed to possess a rare power. "We're not going on, Henry and me," she said flatly.

Henry groaned slightly. Meribah turned and looked at the wreckage of a man on the pallet. "We . . . ," he said in a whispery voice, "we have decided on another course . . . and . . . you must not worry 'bout us."

"What are you talking about?" Panic spread through Meribah like wildfire.

"See!" Mrs. Whiting said disdainfully as she turned to Henry. "I knew she wouldn't understand."

Suddenly Meribah was mad. "I don't like the way you talk to me!" She exploded. "You don't have to waste your precious breath on me, especially if it's to make me feel like a fool! I'm no fool! You're stopping. You know what that means? It means dying out here. I came over to drive for you."

"Calm yourself, child." The harshness had evaporated. Mrs.

Whiting now spoke with a gentle logic. "Henry is not going to make it. So why trouble?"

"Why trouble?" Meribah was astounded. "I told you that I'd drive for you!"

"Meribah, we don't want it to be that way. You can drive now, but your pa needs you too. There'll come a time when you'll have to choose him over us. That's the way it is."

"But that time isn't now."

"It'll come."

"But I can't leave you here now. That's like . . . murder—"

There was a sharp crack, like a board splitting, then Meribah felt the sting on her cheek.

"Don't you talk that way, young lady." Mrs. Whiting's eyes snapped as she spoke. "Now, we've had enough palavering. You take what you need here." She gestured at the neatly organized food stores. "Here's our water." She lugged a large bag out from under the sleeping bench. "Just saving one cool drink for Henry and me."

Meribah's eyes lighted on the tin mug. She felt the hair on the back of her neck stand up. For a moment all she could focus on were the motes of dust circulating in the dim light. Finally she made herself speak. "What about the oxen? Don't they need it?"

"Our oxen!" Mrs. Whiting almost hooted with laughter. "Heavens, no, child. They're almost dead as it is. They won't last through the night. I'd give it to Simon-Whiting before them." Then she was sober once more. She took Meribah by her shoulders and drew her face close to Meribah's, so close that Meribah could feel the tiny soft explosions of warm breath on her nose. "You listen to me, child. You save that water for yourself, not even for your pa! You know what I mean?"

"No!" Meribah said.

"Yes, you do, Meribah Simon! Me and Henry, we can stay out here together. It doesn't matter, 'cause it's kind of like we're one anyway. But you save that water for yourself."

She paused. Her eyes narrowed as she studied the young face. "And just remember, it's not the righteous who inherit the earth. It's the selfish!" With that, Henrietta Whiting turned Meribah's shoulders toward the front opening, which framed the setting sun, sliding below the horizon like a bloodied egg yolk.

Meribah dreaded explaining to her father about the Whitings. She didn't really think that she could explain. So she told a lie instead.

"They're going to catch up with us, Pa. They're feeling much better, but the wagon's a stinking mess from the flux. I helped them get started cleaning up, and they'll be coming along, but we're supposed to go on."

"What's that bag thou is holding?"

Meribah had forgotten that she was carrying the Whitings' water skin. "Oh," she said quickly, "it's some pickling vinegar she gave us."

"Pickling vinegar? What in the name of God can a person pickle out here except cactus?"

"Well, I think she was just trying to clear out stuff so she could clean up, and with their sickness, pickling vinegar was the last thing they felt like having around."

"Oh," said Will. But Meribah was quite sure he didn't believe a word she had said.

They had traveled barely a half-mile when the first shots rang out, the first two in quick succession. She almost thought she could hear the thud as the oxen fell. Will stopped the wagon and looked down. Meribah grabbed his hand. Another minute passed. Two more shots were fired. Will removed his hat. After several minutes, Meribah crawled back into the wagon and returned with the skin bag the Whitings had given her.

"Pa, would you like some water?"

"No, Meribah. Keep that for thyself." He slapped the reins on the team's back and they moved on.

The darkness fell softly around them, and the desert became still and cold like a great quiet secret in the night. Evening stars rose and began to inscribe their transit on the desert sky. A long time ago, Will had once explained to Meribah that the stars did not move separately but in concert. It was as though the sky itself turned around the earth. And the earth too was simply another star, one small part of the single sliding piece called the heavens. It was hard to imagine such a truth, but Meribah wanted to believe it. Especially tonight she wanted to believe that they were all part of this single piece—night sky, stars, air, sand, rattlesnake, cactus, seeds, ox, cow, father, daughter—were but parts of a whole. She imagined a sky weaver who wove the single great piece, and life and death were just strands of the piece, parts of the bigger design.

Will looked up at the sky and spoke softly. "There is one glory of the sun, and another of the moon, and another glory of the stars, for star differs from star in glory."

"Who said that?" Meribah asked.

"First Corinthians, chapter fifteen, verse forty-one."

"But we're all part of one glory, yes?"

"I think so," he whispered.

Just before daybreak they caught up with the rest of the train at the springs. Meribah was looking at the thin trickles percolating from the clay cliffs and wondering if they really deserved to be called springs when Mr. Moxley rushed up.

"Good Lord, child, I was worried about you and your pa. Is he all right?"

"He's doing tolerably. But we had to wait up. We just couldn't push in the heat."

"You're smarter than some I know." His eyes slid toward Captain Griffith. "I don't know what's seized that man, but he's hellbent on making his miles. Where are the Whitings?"

Meribah looked down. "They couldn't make it. They . . ."

She hesitated, then lifting her chin, she looked Mr. Moxley straight in the eye. "They chose to stay behind."

"I understand, Meribah. I understand. I'm sorry that you have to be the one to tell." Mr. Moxley swung around suddenly. "Hey, Billings and Thompson," he snapped, "get your teams out of there! They're crowding in and muddying up the water. Simon's team hasn't drunk yet. For crissake!" he muttered. "Unbelievable, Meribah! Unbelievable! Now, child, you can take your team to that basin and get them a drink, but for yourself, go up that rock slide no more than a hundred yards and you'll find several small springs of good clear water. I want to go visit with your pa."

Meribah unyoked the team and led them to the stone basin filled with coffee-colored water.

Mr. Billings looked up. "Lost one of my team, Meribah." Self-pity glazed his eyes.

"Sorry to hear that."

"Bet you are."

Meribah's head snapped up. "I am!" she said. Again she saw the dim flickering light in his eyes.

"You and the rest of these good people who urged me to give the Barkers my ox! Now where would I be? And if you must know, Lucille did not die of—how should I say— natural causes."

"You think someone poisoned her?" Meribah spoke tonelessly.

"Yes! But how did you know?"

"I didn't know. I just knew that you'd be thinking that. Come on, Josie. Come on, Leander!" She began leading the team to the other side of the basin. Mr. Billings looked after her, the light in his eyes growing stronger and flickering wildly. Meribah could almost feel it on her back, those shining points of fear.

The next spring, Rabbit Hole Springs, was seventeen miles away, according to Mr. Moxley, who had scouted ahead. The train was ready to move barely an hour after Will and

Meribah had arrived. Mr. Moxley insisted on driving their team for them. Meribah collapsed on the pallet across from her father. His hand didn't look good. It didn't smell good, but she was too tired to think about it. She never thought about anything any more—not Serena, not home, not even California—just water and dust and miles to go. The second desert stretch to come was longer than the first. She fell asleep finally and dreamed of rain—rain tracing silver paths on a windowpane, rain quilting the still water of a pond, rain drumming on the roof over her and Jeanette's bed, rain hammering the earth.

The heat woke her up, the heat and the smell of dead oxen. She guessed it was nearly ten o'clock in the morning.

"Be right up, Mr. Moxley!"

"Take your time. It's only called the gold rush by the folks back East. More accurate to call it an ooze."

How that man keeps his sense of humor, Meribah thought, is beyond me. When she came out onto the driver's bench, she nearly gagged from the stench. To the side of the trail she saw two wells, each filled with the swollen carcasses of dead oxen. Abandoned and broken wagons were everywhere.

They reached Rabbit Hole Springs by noon. The white clay land was beaten into a hard finish and scoured of everything except carcasses, discard, and wreckage. Animals were watered at the springs, bags filled, and Captain Griffith announced that people should be ready to move by four o'clock for the second desert stretch. Exhausted as she was, Meribah was forced to start up a fire and bake flour bread for the oxen and Simon-Whiting, as there had been no grass for them in days. The other women had done this before the desert stretch, but Meribah had been helping the Whitings and had never got to baking. By three o'clock, Meribah had baked ten large loaves of the bread. She fed the animals a small amount so as not to strain their stomachs, which were empty and not accustomed to digesting large quantities. She spread the remaining eight loaves on the driver's bench to cool and ducked into the wagon to catch a quick nap before Captain Griffith gave the chain-up order.

When she got up an hour later, she heard Will outside. "There's so much bread out here, how's a man to drive?"

"Hand it back, Pa. I'll put it away now."

The good hand reached through the front opening with a loaf. Five others followed. "All right, we're ready now."

"Aren't there more?" Meribah said.

"No, that's all."

"But there should be two more. I made ten in all."

"I don't see any more up here."

"Maybe some fell down."

"No, none on the ground that I can see," Will said.

Meribah sat perplexed in the back of the wagon. Was she going crazy? She had made ten, hadn't she?

"Chain up!"

Oh, be still! she thought wearily. Darn! What had happened to her other loaves? She suddenly remembered the disappearance of the yarrow tea miles and miles back at the City of Castles. The two disappearances were linked somehow in her mind. She didn't like the connection at all, but somehow her mind kept coupling the tea and the bread. As they traveled, the notion haunted her. The round-top mountains in the distance rose like loaves of baked bread.

They were crossing a narrow plain bleached white with alkaline encrustations, and even in the dark night this part of the trail went ahead like a white ribbon. The white ribbon continued through the night and into the next day.

Later in the following morning Will came out after a rest. "Bet this is a mud lake in the wet season."

"Wet season? Can there be a wet season out here?"

"There sure is."

And then as if the land had heard Will's words, it offered in the distance a long lagoon of light-blue water spilling over the hardened earth. Meribah caught her breath as she watched its edges become bordered with trees and small islands.

"Quick! Get cloth and cover the team's eyes!" Meribah knew exactly what might happen. Josie and Leander could stampede toward the mirage of water. It was all she could do to keep herself from stampeding.

Blinders in place, they began moving again toward the beautiful vision of water. Liquid and quivering, it tantalized Meribah, and she had to keep telling herself it was not real. But what was real any more? The heat. The dust.

However, an unexpected waterhole, small but with good clear water, was found soon after. People almost did stampede toward it, leading their animals and carrying every conceivable container for water to take them through the rest of the desert. Meribah again found herself standing next to Mr. Billings, who was watering the Thompsons' oxen along with his own, when Mrs. Thompson, loaded with bags and containers of every variety, joined them.

"Where did you get that skin bag?" Meribah exploded, nearly bowling the woman over.

"Which one? I'm holding about six," Mrs. Thompson answered with confusion.

"The one with the spots, in your left hand," Meribah replied.

"As a matter of fact, it's Mr. Billings's. I don't see why you're so het up."

"Well, it's our skin." As she spoke, Meribah wheeled around toward Mr. Billings. "How do you come to have it?" The dim light grew stronger in his eyes and began to dance with a sudden fury.

"I'll tell you, Miss Meribah," he said, lifting his chin high. "However, I do not like your tone. . . ." He paused as if waiting for an apology, but Meribah glared back in silence. He cleared his throat. "It came into my possession one morning when I found it crumpled and empty in the dust by my wagon."

Meribah narrowed her eyes. "I don't believe you."

"Meribah!" Mrs. Thompson exclaimed. "Your manners!"

"If you don't believe me, that is your problem, Meribah, not mine. I asked several people if it was theirs. I recall asking you, Mrs. Thompson, didn't I?" He turned toward her and leaned forward a bit in a gesture of utter charm and friendliness.

"Oh, yes! You surely did!" She nodded so furiously that Meribah thought the silly lady's head might topple off.

"You didn't ask me, and you should have known it was mine. After all, I poured you yarrow tea from it for your cough at City of Castles, if you recall."

"I do recall, Meribah, your sweet generosity and kind ministrations, but do forgive me for not being sufficiently familiar with the viscera of animals as to recognize one skin from another."

Mrs. Thompson nodded her head as if to say that any man who could speak such elegant, grand words to such a rude girl was a true gentleman.

"Now, Meribah," Mrs. Thompson said, "don't go getting yourself in an uproar over such a small thing. You're making a tempest in a teapot!"

"Or a tempest in a goat bladder!" Mr. Billings added.

"Oh, Mr. Billings, you are the funniest man!" giggled Mrs. Thompson.

"Well, now, if Meribah thinks she is the rightful owner of the skin bag," he said with mock gravity, "then by all means give it to her."

Meribah immediately held out her hand for the bag. As she took it from Mrs. Thompson, she looked Mr. Billings directly in the eye. "Would you care to explain what happened to the two flour bread loaves we are missing?"

"I'm quite sure I don't know what you're talking about, Meribah, and I certainly don't have to be taking this kind of behavior from you!"

"Certainly not!" Mrs. Thompson concurred. And they both turned their backs and walked away from her.

They came out of the desert late the following day at an encampment crowded with other parties near Boiling Springs. That night Simon-Whiting was stolen, and Meribah searched for her in vain. Early the next morning, as they were descending a canyon chute, a bolster split in the rear assembly of their wagon. The wagon slid one hundred feet or more, killing Josie, their stronger ox.

20

CAST OUT

"In the best interests of the company, I do not see how you and your father can continue."

The words were bouncing off Meribah like hailstones from a tin roof. She heard their din, she knew their meaning, but somehow she was not connecting them with herself. She was beyond feeling, beyond response. All she could think was that if Mr. Moxley were here, this would not be happening. The voice went on with crusty authority, a patient tone of logic. And that was what Meribah kept thinking as Captain Griffith spoke: This is supposed to sound reasonable. I keep listening for the reason but I can't find it. He says "best." I hear "worst." He says "sensible." I hear "insane." These people, our friends, are not going to let this happen. It was as unreal to her as the mirage back in the desert.

"We took a vote. This is the consensus of the company. Even if the wagon could be fixed, your second ox could not pull it by himself, and since your pa is really too ill to travel except on his back—"

"Who took the vote?" Meribah asked suddenly, raising her head.

"Why, Meribah, you were here when we took it. You know everyone said they'd be willing to take you in but didn't have space for a sick man."

"That's not so," she said. "They said they would take me in and our food and our ox and a good amount of our gear, but not my pa."

193

"That is correct," Captain Griffith answered.

"And I said I'd leave the food and the gear so there'd be room for my pa."

"But how would you eat, dear?" Mrs. Thompson asked.

Meribah stared at her, not relishing endearments from someone who was about to dump her from a wagon train in the foothills of the Sierra Nevada.

"Mrs. Thompson has a point, Meribah," Captain Griffith said. "These good folks"—Suddenly they were "good folks." It sickened Meribah—"cannot be expected to provide food as well as shelter for you."

"I'd hunt. I could find things."

"Now, now, dearie!" Captain Griffith laughed. "How's your aim?" He chuckled as if to indulge her momentarily in this little caprice of hers. "And anyway, you heard the vote."

"I don't care about the vote!"

"It's your choice to remain."

"There is no choice for me. The choice is yours. And you know this!"

Captain Griffith sighed deeply. "I don't think that this discussion can be of any further value to anyone here." One would have thought from his tone he was discussing the price of a bag of sugar. "I suggest we terminate it now." Meribah had noticed before that Captain Griffith used big words when he was uneasy, especially in situations where his leadership was challenged. It was an odd quirk that tended to obscure what was really going on.

Meribah found herself trembling. The people around her had begun to turn away.

Desperately she called after them, "Well, before you terminate this discussion, you should know what you are doing. You are not giving my pa and me a choice. You are not good folks. You are selfish folks, and you are murdering us. This is murder." But the people continued to walk toward their wagons while talking in quiet voices.

"Oh, yes, certainly!" Meribah could hear Mrs. Barker

saying. "That train we passed just at Boiling Springs had three or four big wagons with good healthy teams. And there is surely no way that we can accommodate the Simons in our chopped-up wagon—or in the other one, for that matter."

"No! No! There is no way you can," said Eliza Gray.

Only Captain Griffith remained. "Here are some extra cartridges for you," he said. Meribah silently stared at the captain. "Thought you might need them." He tossed them down at her feet from his horse.

Meribah raised her eyes to his. "I cannot believe you are doing this to us," she said in wonderment. "Are you really leaving —leaving us here." It was not a question. Stunned, Meribah was rehearsing an idea, trying to familiarize herself with a fact. "To die?"

The bad eye clenched, and Captain Griffith dug his spurs into his horse's flanks and began to move away.

"Captain Griffith," Meribah called after the broad back. "Where are you going? Do you know? The land will run out on you—murderer! Murderer!" She did not say it loudly, but she knew he had heard it. The word rolled through the silence like thunder before a coming storm.

Meribah watched them climb into their wagons, each wrapped in his own self-righteous logic and bitter dreams. She suddenly felt separate from them all, as if she were another species. She didn't want anything from them. She was angry that she had even begged.

Captain Griffith rode up on his horse and she turned away.

When she turned around again, Mrs. McSwat was standing there, quiet as a boulder.

"I don't want to hear your excuses," Meribah said.

"I didn't come to give any. I ain't proud of this, you know." She looked down at her feet as she spoke. "But I come to give you something. I got this parcel of meat here and this here bread and some fatback. It's all we got, and it's kind of green around the edges, but you can cut that off."

Meribah was sure this was the longest speech Mrs. McSwat had ever made. Mrs. McSwat shoved the package into Meribah's arms, turned, and lumbered off like a huge bear.

Meribah almost started when she saw Mr. Billings approach. Now what could he be coming for? she thought. Certainly not to give anything away.

"I have a proposal for you, Miss Meribah." He spoke cheerfully, with that easy grace that suggested an invitation to tea more than anything else.

"What's that?"

"Well, I must credit Mr. Wickham and Mr. Thompson with the authorship of this plan."

"What plan?"

"Well, seeing as the wheels of your wagon are still in relatively good condition despite the calamitous crash in the canyon and that it is your fractured axle and wagon tongue that prohibit your continuation, while my wheels, on the other hand, are on their last spokes, so to speak—spokes to speak!"—he chuckled at this clever bit of wordplay—"well, Mr. Thompson feels that we could in a relatively simple operation remove your wheels and put them on my wagon."

"And?" Meribah said, suddenly hopeful.

"And what? That is my proposal. No more."

Meribah grew livid. She turned her back to reach under the driver's bench of the wagon. When she faced Mr. Billings again, she was holding her father's Jake Hawkins single-barreled rifle.

Mr. Billings laughed nervously. "What's this all about?"

"It's about your simple operation. It's not going to be relatively simple. It's going to be relatively difficult. You'll have to kill me first."

21

"WHO ARE YOU?"

The sky was ragged with dark clouds. A chill wind blew down from the higher ridges of the Sierra range, bringing with it a light snow. The big wet flakes landed on Meribah's face as she sat on a stump staring in the direction where the train had gone. Her dismay was finished, her anger gone. She felt cold, she felt hungry, and she knew that she must get some tea and a little food, if only a biscuit, into her father. Some wet snow landed on her neck, making her shiver. I need to take care of myself first, she thought, if I am going to take care of my father. First a fire. She looked about. There was plenty of good kindling material. The problem was where to build the fire. Right there by the trail people would definitely see it, but it was too exposed to the wind. Better, she thought, if she could build it in a more protected place where the heat from it could collect. The night before, it had been miserably cold sleeping in the wagon, and as there was no way to warm the wagon, Meribah suddenly decided that it might be better to sleep out near a fire.

A hundred yards or more behind their wagon there was a small cliff in the woods with a rock overhang that formed a shallow cave. Meribah went to explore it. The floor was fairly clear of debris, and there did not seem to be any animals living in it. She could dig a small fire pit just like the ones she had seen back at the Pawnee village on the Platte. The overhang was lower than it appeared from the outside. A person had to hunch over in the space, but her father would be lying down anyway. Most important, it faced away from the mountain weather and wind. Good, Meribah decided. This would be their temporary home until.... She did not know. She would not let herself use that word. It was a tease. She would only think of *now*. And now she had things to do.

She went back to the wagon to fetch a broom and shovel. Her father woke up from his fitful sleep.

"Don't worry, Pa. I'm fixing up a nice place for us."

"I'm not worried, especially after what I heard thou say to Billings." He laughed weakly.

"Go back to sleep. Are thou hungry at all?"

"No, child, don't worry. Do what thou has to."

In a very short time Meribah had the shelter swept, a pit dug, and a fire going. She circled the pit with some smooth round stones that she had found in a nearby creek. Two of the stones she put directly into the coals of the fire to wrap up later and take to bed. She suddenly realized how wet and cold she felt, as it had begun to snow harder. She went back to the wagon and stripped off her wool dress and flannel under-things, then put on the beaver-skin leggings. What to wear for a top was the problem now. The shirt part of her wool dress was quite dry. It was just the skirt that was wet. She reached for a knife and soon had cut off the bodice of the dress, leaving enough from the skirt to tuck into the waist of the leggings. She put on a fresh white cap and a wool scarf. She was now dry down to her feet, but the leather shoes were soaked through, and it was senseless to put on dry stockings. She was staring at the empty skin bag, the one that had held the yarrow tea and then had so mysteriously shown up among Mr. Billings's belongings. Why not use it? she suddenly thought. She needed shoes, not water containers. If she cut the bag into strips, put on dry stockings, then wrapped the pieces around her feet, they should stay fairly dry. Carefully she cut out ovals for the soles. Then she cut narrow strips to wrap around the soles and tops of her feet. If the bag had been bigger, she could have fashioned a tongue to underlie the strips. There were a few gaps, but she took some straw that was poking out of the pallets and stuffed it in. There were plenty of leather thongs about for securing the footgear.

Now that she was dry, clothed, and shod, Meribah began to feel ravenously hungry. She thought of Mrs. McSwat's parcel of meat and fatback. She would use just a little to make a stew with their beans—something hot in the stomach to keep them warm through the night. When the stew was ready, Meribah moved Will from the wagon to the cave. She had made a bed for him near the fire. Things seemed better in the cave than in the wagon. It was warmer, for one thing. Her main concerns now were to get some food into her father, to keep him dry, and to make sure no animals trespassed their hearth. She was careful to keep the food tightly covered in tin containers and wooden boxes. She would sleep with the rifle beside her, but if she could keep the fire going, there should not be a problem with animals.

The overhang forming the shallow cave in the black volcanic rock was indeed a perfect trap for the fire's heat. Smoke curled up and blew out of the cave just at the lip of the overhang, but the heat was thrust back against the shallow curving walls. If a storm didn't come from the southeast, the direction the cave faced, they would be fine.

By the time she lay down to sleep that night, Meribah was exhausted. Her head, however, was still awhirl with thoughts. She must wake up in a few hours to stoke the fire. Tomorrow she would explore the other abandoned wagons and see what she could scavenge. She must also dig some more pokeweed roots and find a sheltered spot for Leander, whom she had guarded vigilantly until the others had left, near the cave. For a good while sleep escaped her, and Meribah stared into the licks of flame. She realized suddenly that she had not once thought of the people of the company since the train had disappeared from view. Her anger had been spent. She was through with them, and it felt good. Now she must think only of survival. She did not even permit herself the pleasurable memory of holding a quivering Billings in the sights of the rifle.

That first morning, after tending to her father, Meribah went down to the main part of the trail. She climbed fairly high up in a tree to have a longer view of the road and the incoming trains. She was surprised to see the remnants of the Pittsburgh Company coming around the last bend. When they had met back on the Platte, the Pittsburgh Company had been large, with a great amount of provisions. Now as they came straggling around the bend, Meribah could see that their numbers had been greatly reduced. They were a haggard and sullen-looking lot. Some had stopped a few hundred yards below the tree where Meribah was hidden. She watched one man from the company take a hammer and smash tools into useless fragments, tools that he could no longer carry and wanted to make sure that no one else would ever use. Meribah studied the other faces. Broken and anxious, the people filed by, their eyes glazed with self-need, brutalized spirits bearing mere traces of humanity. She hugged the trunk of her tree perch harder. Was this a mirror in front of her? Is this what she had become? Meribah began to tremble. There would be no help from the emigrants. The realization finally sank in. She must protect herself and her father from these straggling remnants of humanity. They would kill. They would steal. Hadn't Simon-Whiting been stolen just after they had crossed into California? She was glad that their cave was out of sight of the trail. She must strip down the wagon and cache things in and around the cave. They could not stay here forever, though. She must think of a way to get them to some settlement. She must figure out how to move them. Could she fix the wagon so that Leander could somehow pull it? She remembered the Mc-Swats sawing the Barkers' wagon in half. It had taken those two mammoth men all morning to turn the wagon into a cart. Perhaps there was some way she could do it. But then, there were also the wagon tongue and axle to be fixed. How could she ever do that by herself? Perhaps her father would be well enough to direct her as she did it. But she had never really worked with tools or wood. Scarfing! It was an overwhelming idea. How could she ever do such joinery work that would actually hold and endure through the steep ascents and descents of the rugged Sierra Nevada passes? She almost felt sick. Hot tears blurred the silent line of emigrants below. She held her hand over her mouth to muffle the small sobs in her throat. The night before she had been so full of plans. Those plans had not been real; deep inside she had always believed that someone would come to help them. She had been like a little girl playing house, playing at survival. It disgusted her. Now she knew the hard truth: They would live or die by what she could or could not do. She must do something with that wagon.

For the next several days, when she was not tending her father or minding the business of food and heat, Meribah was working on the wagon. In the warmest periods of the day, when the sun was the brightest, she would move her father on his pallet beside the wagon so he could supervise her work. The wagon was going to be a two-wheeled vehicle instead of a four-wheeled one. She sawed until she thought her arms would drop off, and when she could no longer saw, she would get out her drawing paper, sit down beside her father, and together they would talk through and sketch out the repairs on the axle and wagon tongue. The rear bolster, which ran between the wheels and held in position the two bars that swung out to form the coupling pole, was broken. The question now was whether a piece from the front axle assembly could be adapted for use in the rear. Also, the central branch of the coupling pole had to be shortened to fit the new halved dimensions of the wagon.

"I'm convinced," Will said, "that the bolster split before we slid down that canyon chute and not during it. I think that's why we did crash. So if thou does borrow any parts from the front assembly, we must make darn sure that there are no cracks in them."

Meribah listened carefully to Will. They discussed the alternatives of borrowing from one assembly or repairing the broken one. Directing Meribah in the reconstruction of the wagon seemed to give Will a new energy. He was eating more, resting better. His hand did not appear greatly improved, but his spirits definitely were. He watched with pride as his daughter grew in her skill with the adz and plane in preparing pieces for scarfing.

Morning, noon, and night they discussed wagon construction and carpentry. Although she was familiar with some of the language, much of it could have been Chinese that Meribah was listening to. Will talked about cross-bearing loads, pressure rotation, torque, alignment registration. It was like a science—opaque and complicated, something that Meribah thought she could never fathom. Will would send her out with a "shopping list" of pieces to pick off other wagons—bolts, nuts, U-clamps. One afternoon as Meribah was removing some hound plates from another wagon's coupling pole and thinking how their shape did indeed resemble a dog's muzzle, she suddenly thought of bishop's sleeves. Like dry leaves caught in an autumn gust, the old words fluttered brightly through her mind. Brandenbourg tasseling! Babet bonnets! Grenadines and ruchings! Crispins and mantels! Shirring and ruffling! The words were like strange sounds from some long-ago world.

It took Meribah five days to saw the wagon in half. Another week of work was required to make the repairs on the axle and tongue. Two weeks had passed since they had been abandoned. There were light snowfalls almost every day, but they kept warm under a heavy buffalo robe that Meribah had found tossed out on the trail. The wagon needed only some light forging work on the metal wheel cups that fitted over the ends of the axle upon which the wheel hub turned. Although Will said it was "light" forging, Meribah was not sure. A better word might be "delicate" forging, as the metal cup had to be slightly open so as to fit perfectly over the ends of the axle and allow the free rotation of the hub. For an experienced blacksmith it might be a simple task, but for a beginner, especially one who also had to hold the tongs and hammer, it seemed almost impossible. Will was still not strong enough to help her forge, and although he had devised a bracing system for the tongs for most of Meribah's forging, it would not be usable for this last and most delicate operation. Meribah was sure that she would smash the metal cup shut instead of opening it up. Snug under the buffalo robe, she thought about this as she stared into the fire, waiting for sleep. Her father was already asleep beside her. She had given him tea made with the spiked narcotic plant after dinner, for his whole arm and shoulder had been giving him a great deal of pain since noon. Just before he dozed off, when Meribah was talking about her fears of smashing the cup, he had whispered a groggy assurance, "Nothing to it!" Meribah was left alone to worry about the metal cup. She stared deeper into the fire and wondered what really would become of them.

"Who are you?"

She felt the words on the back of her neck, the breath speaking on her skin. Was it a dream? She tried to pull herself from sleep. It was like trying to swim up from a dive in a deep pond.

"What are you doing here? Who are you?"

She broke through the surface. Her eyes flew open and she sat bolt upright. The face! It was the face! The bluest, liveliest eyes ever. The hawk-lean face from the general store in St. Jo, two thousand miles back. Mr. Goodnough! Meribah sat in stunned silence, her cap askew, the buffalo robe held up to her chin.

"My God!" he exclaimed. "It's you! The girl who makes the wiggly lines and shadows! The fuzzy and uneven things of life!"

"True lines!" Meribah said. "The mapmaker. And the Indian painter?"

"Yes, but what are you doing here? Who's this man?" He nodded toward Will.

"My pa. He's sick." Meribah offered no further explanation. She just stared wide-eyed at Goodnough, not quite believing what she was seeing.

"But why are you here?"

"We were dumped out," Meribah said matter-of-factly. She could tell by the way Goodnough looked at her that he was incredulous but not really shocked. He had by now seen too many of the straggling, bitter emigrants to be shocked. "Our wagon broke. One ox died."

"Oh." He nodded as if this made sense.

"I know," Meribah said. "It is all very queer, isn't it?"

Goodnough nodded again. His mouth hardened.

"But it's all right," Meribah continued.

"What's all right?"

"Well, I've cut the wagon in half and rebuilt the tongue and got the axle fixed. There's just one little thing left. I have to forge some metal cups for the hub rods."

Goodnough's mouth dropped open. He stared in amazement as Meribah gave a running account of the wagon redesign she had executed in the past two weeks. "As soon as I finish the cups, we're ready to go."

"You did that all by yourself?" Goodnough said as they walked over to the wagon. He ran his hand along the wagon tongue. "And this scarfing too?"

"I did, and I'll tell thee it is the hardest thing I've ever done in my life. It would be easier to change a bull into a steer than a wagon into a cart!"

Meribah clapped her hands over her mouth as soon as the words were out. She was overcome with embarrassment. Goodnough held his chin in the cup of his hand and studied the girl before him. A grin began to crinkle in his eyes. Then he burst out laughing and slapped his leg.

Meribah turned around. "I have to get the fire going for the forging, and Pa needs something to eat. Is thou hungry? I can fix some coffee, and I baked some bread. We have a little dried fruit left."

"Oh, no. The coffee will be fine," Goodnough said.

Over their mugs, Goodnough and Meribah exchanged information about the last parts of their journeys from the Great Basin rim to where they were now, the beginning of the

Lassen Trail. Goodnough was fascinated by Meribah's map. It was detailed, but in a way totally original and not reliant on the usual cartographic symbols. Yet it spoke very directly about the shape of a journey. "You've done more than measure miles here, Meribah. It's . . . it's almost like a diary."

"Thou should see Meribah's drawings!" Will said proudly. "Pa!"

"Well, he should. She can make a person feel the wind. She sees colors ordinary eyes don't see, but thou knows they are there once thou sees them in Meribah's drawings."

"I'd like to see them. Tell me, why does your map stop in the Black Rock Desert?"

"Oh, I think I just got too tired to do any more on it. I kind of gave up there. Things were going so poorly—Pa so sick, and that crazy man, Captain Griffith, pushing us so hard."

"You stopped mapping at Rabbit Hole Springs."

"Oh, long before. I stopped mapping where the Whitings stopped . . ."—she paused—"stopped moving." Her voice had dropped to a whisper. "I don't know. I guess I just started to wonder where we were moving to."

"I see," said Goodnough, and she knew he did.

Goodnough was the leader of a packtrain—horses and mules, with a few wagons. He immediately made it clear that Will and Meribah should join his company with their half-wagon and ox. He could help Meribah drive, and he was sure that he could arrange space in one of the wagons where Will could stretch out and ride more comfortably than in the cart. The offer was generous but strangely untempting to Meribah. She liked Goodnough, but she did not like the idea of a company. There were too many people to get along with, to be accepted by, especially when her father was crippled by illness. They had been thrown out by one company. She was not eager for it to happen again.

Goodnough sensed her hesitation. "Look, Meribah, I understand your feelings about this, but you must understand two

205

things: First, there are some really rugged passes ahead. There is no way you are going to get your father and the cart down them alone. Second, you need not worry about the rest of the company. I'm the leader. I'll stand by you and your father. I give you my word on that one!"

On the morning of October ninth, Will and Meribah left with George Goodnough. They took their place in the line of the Washington Company in their own half-wagon, with Meribah on the driver's bench and Will Simon in the rear. Sick as Will was, he refused Goodnough's offer for more comfortable space in a larger wagon and insisted on riding in the cart that his daughter had rebuilt with her own hands. The cart fared well that first day, which was spent in ascending the Fandango Pass. The first quarter-mile of the ascent was gentle enough and brought them to a small meadow with good grass. Goodnough ordered a halt for grazing the animals and cutting some of the grass, an increasingly rare commodity, to take along. They had already seen entire fields purposely burned by emigrants who, in their incredible greed, wanted to make sure that those who followed would not share the bounty. The second rise, beyond the meadow, was much steeper. Dead oxen became numerous. There were more broken and abandoned wagons, more grim-faced stragglers on foot leading animals. Meribah saw one man leading a horse with a mattress across it and a man on top of it, dying of scurvy.

They descended the western side of the Fandango Pass late in the afternoon. A surface of sand and volcanic rock fragments hissed and crunched under the cart's wheels.

Goodnough rode up at the bottom of the descent. "Well, your cart made it, Meribah Simon! The first pass of the Sierras is behind you," he exclaimed. "You scarfed some good joints and forged some fine bonds. How's your father?"

"Pretty well, thank you."

"Still running a fever?"

"Yes. It seems to get higher this time of day."

"Well, we'll be making camp just a few miles down there, above Goose Lake."

Across from their camp that night, Meribah watched the distant fires of Indians on an elevated shelf of mountains.

"What Indians are those?" she asked Goodnough, who was smoking a pipe by their fire.

"They call them Diggers. They live all around the Pitt River region. They're supposed to be very hostile, murdering people, shooting up camps, stealing animals."

"'Supposed to be'? What does thou mean?" Meribah was not sure why, but since meeting Goodnough again she had slipped back into using "thee" and "thou" with him. She had ceased entirely to use these forms of address with anybody but her father. But it felt good now to address Goodnough this way.

"Well, that is the rumor. So far, I have seen no hostilities along this route coming from the Indian side, but I've seen an awful lot of murdering and thieving among the white folks. If they keep it up, there'll be no one left for the Indians to murder."

There was a long silence. Goodnough puffed on his pipe, and they both looked across at the mountain shelf that blazed with Indian campfires. Meribah watched the dark figures of men and women and children move slowly around the fires in their evening tasks. It was all reflected brightly in the lake below—the figures of people, the ring of fires. Meribah looked at the hundreds of emigrants who were camped near them: women sitting in clusters by their wagons, children playing about, people busy cutting whatever grass they could find, people tinkering with gear. This scene too was reflected in the lake, and except for the gear—the wagons, the horses, the tents—the reflections of the two scenes were the same. The Indian figures and the emigrants were as indistinguishable as the blazing fires.

"I'll still set a guard," Goodnough said. "People have to feel that there is something to fear out there."

The fear of fears. Meribah suddenly remembered. She had not thought of it in a long time. Goodnough was right. People did have to believe that there was something out there to fear, especially if the thing to be feared was within themselves.

The next day after they had left Goose Lake, at the ford of a creek, there was a board nailed to a tree with a neatly written card for emigrants:

> From here, to where the road leaves Pitt R. . . . 78 miles
> (To valley with water and grass ½ m. beyond)
> " Where the road crosses a brook 13
> " Spring of water, on right of road,) 12
> "   grass in wood close to   )
> " Valley, with springs and grass 14
> " Lake, a mile to left of road 11
> " Water & grass, 1 mi. East of road, ... 13
> " E. branch of Feather Riv: grass ½ m.
>   upstream 6
> " Next grass & water, very miry bad road, . . 6
> " Where there is grass & water, for 5
> " Butte Creek 6
> " To where there is grass & water, for 10
> " Last water on the road, ... 15
> " Crossing of Deer Ck. in Sacramento Valley . 36
> " Lassin's house 3
> From Lassin's to nearest Diggings 40
> "   "   "   Sutter's Fort 115
> " Sutter's Fort to Sacramento City 3
> " Sacramento City to San Francisco 100

But the distances were wrong by at least one hundred and fifty miles, and this mistake would cost the company time and bring them closer to the lacerating winter storms of the Sierras. The terrain after Goose Lake became increasingly rugged. It seemed to Meribah that it consisted mostly of long interior valleys and gorges that had to be ascended or descended by way of brambly ridges; and then there were the rivers and streams and creeks that broke from the mountains westerly toward the sea. Meribah had lost count of how many times they had forded the Pitt River. The weather became colder, and provisions dwindled.

But she had begun mapping again. Despite the difficulty of the terrain, despite the frustration over wrong information of mileage, despite the growing anxiety about winter's coming, she felt it made more sense than ever to map their way. Dog-tired by the end of a day of negotiating the cart bearing her father over this incredibly wild land, she nonetheless took out her pencils and chalks each night to map. She could feel the shape of this land in the bruised arches of her feet, the steepness of the endless ridges in the hamstrings of her calves. It was as if every contour of this land were being pressed into her skin, her muscle, her entire body. Goodnough led them with patience, clarity of vision, and good humor. And Meribah mapped their way with a new energy, a new sense of direction.

"It's starting to look like a great gathering of sleeping dinosaurs," Goodnough said as he looked at the ridges in the distance.

"Well, let's hope they don't wake up while we're around," Meribah said.

"I like that frizzled line you've been using with the pink smear over it for the brush."

"Oh, thou understands that it is for the chaparral?" Meribah brightened. She was pleased that her frizzled line, as Goodnough called it, was so easily read.

"It was a good choice. Much better than simple cross-hatching."

"Well, it does appear rather prickly, doesn't it?"

"That it does."

"I have to make up new symbols to show the shape and feel of things out here. Does thou know that sometimes, no matter how real I know this land is and however long it has been here,

209

I sometimes feel as if I am reinventing it as I move through it?" Goodnough was looking at her with amazement, and Meribah suddenly became flustered. "I didn't mean it the way it sounded!" she apologized. "I make it sound like I'm God or something. I . . . thou must think that I am the most stuck-up girl in the world!"

"No!" Goodnough protested. "It has nothing to do with being stuck-up. It has to do with being a mapmaker. You are a true mapmaker. Indeed, you map more than you think, Meribah Simon!"

A week later than Goodnough had intended they ascended the eastern side of a long stony hill. At the summit Meribah double-locked the wheels and looked across at the summits of Mount St. Joseph and, to the south, Mount Tschastes. Snow-capped peaks flashed against the bluest of skies, and below, long silvery clouds streamed through the narrow valleys like fish. It was breathtaking. This is beautiful, Meribah told herself, but she could not think about mountain peaks. She could only think of the gnawing pit in her stomach and how she had foolishly eaten all the fatback a few weeks before without thinking to reserve some for later.

"How are you doing?" Goodnough had walked back to check on her.

"Hungry!"

October 20, 1849
Lassen Foothills in the
northernmost part of the Sierra Nevada,
between the Mill and Deer creeks

22

BETWEEN TWO CREEKS

They were hungrier a week later on the thickly forested ridge that divided Mill Creek from Deer Creek. Hunger was not the only problem that plagued them. Some mules had died, as well as Leander, who had traveled with them over two thousand miles. Will had taken a turn for the worse. Goodnough himself had injured his back, and the rest of the company was growing cantankerous. That night Goodnough sat in his large tent, which he now shared with Meribah and Will, smoking his pipe. He had hardly said a word during supper. Earlier Meribah had noticed him carefully studying the other men of his company, listening to their talk of the murderous Mill Creek Indians or the thieving white men from the valley, known as shinglemen. The shinglemen were supposedly engaged in cutting timber for pine shingles, but their favored occupation seemed to be stealing animals and goods from newly arrived wagons. Mostly, however, the men of Goodnough's company talked about the settlements, the mining villages just fifty miles away over the most rugged trails they would yet encounter, trails that were often so steep and narrow that only a mule could pass. Now as he sat smoking, he studied no one, but seemed lost in his own thoughts. The hawkish lines of his face were oddly relaxed.

"Meribah," he said suddenly, "I've made a decision." Will stirred on his pallet.

"What's that?" she asked.

211

"I'm sending the men on without me. I'm resigning as leader."

"What is thou talking about?"

"Let me finish. Your pa is too sick to travel. The way down the gorge is too rugged for any cart or wagon, and he certainly can't make it on foot."

"But thou can," Will said thickly. "I won't hear of it."

"Let me finish, Will. Our two wagons can't go down that gorge into the valley either. No wagon can. Why do you think the shinglemen are having such a high time of it here? People abandon their wagons to make it to the settlements in the valley. The shinglemen advise them to leave their wagons and then they haul off the goods. My plan is to pack our two wagons with the company's provisions and everything except what they will need to go down. I'll stay here to guard the wagons until the men can send back help and food for us. I think we could get you down, Will, if we had another mule and a sledge. The men here are growing more hotheaded each day about getting to the settlements. I have brought them to this point in better shape than any other company in this entire migration."

"That thou has," Will said.

"I owe it to them to get them there. If they can travel light, with only the barest necessities, they can make it. I'll give them my horse to take, too. They in turn will send somebody back with food and help for us. If they go tomorrow, they should be able to send someone with a sledge and food within two weeks at the most—before the big snows come."

The decision was made and accepted enthusiastically by the company. Edgar Perkins, a close friend of Goodnough's and second in command, had agreed to return with help and provisions for them. No one had volunteered for this job, even with the promise of good pay per mile from the company treasury and Goodnough's own pocket. So lots were drawn, and Perkins pulled the shortest. He was cheerful enough, however, and the following morning at their departure came to the tent to bid his friend good-bye.

"How 'bout a parting smoke before we leave, George?"

"Absolutely! And do you care to share the last drops of this brandy?" Goodnough reached for a bottle from a stash of supplies and equipment in the corner of the tent.

"Certainly," Perkins said, glancing over as Goodnough rummaged through the pile. "And it won't be your last. I shall bring some back with me next week. My God, George, you're a veritable pack rat with that heap over there. What's holding up the tent? The pole or the pile of junk around the pole? What a jumble!" His eyes set on the heap. "Are they asleep?" He nodded his head toward Meribah and Will.

"Most likely."

Meribah then stirred.

"You asleep, Meribah?" Goodnough asked softly.

"Trying," she answered from under the buffalo robe.

"Sorry," Perkins added cheerfully. "That the company's?" she heard him ask.

"No. It's Meribah's," Goodnough answered. "She found that robe way back before Fandango."

"Nice find. Well, aren't you going to come outside and wish me luck and all that, old boy?"

"Sure." Goodnough said and got up to walk out with his friend.

Minutes later Perkins reappeared in the tent. "Back so soon, you say?" Perkins winked at Meribah. "Forgot my pack! Sleep on, dear. See you in a week." He bent over, gathered up his pack and left again.

The camp felt empty without them. In much the same way eyes cling to color long after it has disappeared, the tall pine woods seemed to hold the jubilant din of Goodnough's men as they began their quick, light descent to the mines.

"Wish you were going to the fields, Meribah?" Goodnough asked almost apologetically.

"Heavens, no!" she said. "I mean, I wish for food and feather mattresses with sheets."

"And fresh milk!" Goodnough added, brightening.

"And clean clothes!"

"And books!"

"Oh, yes, books! Millions, jillions, of them!"

"And people who have read books!" Goodnough laughed.

"Oh, yes! Yes! And people who have slept in warm houses and played with babies and told stories, real stories, and dreamed real dreams, not just gold dreams, and planned a field of crops through a growing season, and drawn a picture, and made a poem!"

"And," Goodnough offered, "people who might ask you a question about things other than food, routes, campsites, and prices."

"Yes," Meribah sighed.

"Civilization!" Goodnough said it, and finally the word made sense to Meribah.

Through those first few days after the company's departure, Goodnough and Meribah fed their spirits more than their bodies on remembered moments from other times. Fragmentary and elusive, these moments could be rekindled by a mere word, a glint in the eye, a sharp intake of breath, as some long-forgotten memory was stirred. The cold frosty air of the tent would suddenly seem warm and dappled with the glittering moments from past lives. One day just as she and Goodnough were entering the tent, Meribah looked out the tent flap and saw the shape of a hawk's wings printed against the sky. The image was like a precise reversal of the silver wings in the jet-black hair, and Meribah began to describe in spellbinding detail to Goodnough the quiet grace of the Iroquois woman at Fort Hall with whom she had walked through the woods gathering plants.

That evening Goodnough took out the tin tubes in which his drawings and paintings were rolled up. For hours Meribah pored over George Goodnough's amazing documentation, made during the last ten years, of Indians and their way of life. Some of the drawings, especially the earlier ones, were meticulously detailed studies, formal portraits of plains warriors with shaved heads, painted bodies, elaborate feather headdresses. These were very similar to the painting Meribah had seen in St. Louis. But Goodnough's work of the past two years was entirely different. There were fewer formal portraits and many more quick sketches that included background details and the smaller incidentals of everyday life—Shoshone women drying meat and packing parfleche bags, Indians weaving baskets and cultivating corn, Indian children playing around the earth lodges of the Pawnee. The sketches were quicker, with fewer lines, but the impact was bolder.

"What's happening here?" Meribah asked. There was a hastily drawn landscape with a splash of Indian figures chasing buffalo. The action she understood, but there seemed to be something else in the picture, a desperation that Meribah could sense but not quite comprehend. "What's happening here?" She asked again.

"What do you mean?" Goodnough watched her closely.

"It's as if they are about to melt away, just vanish, and thou is trying to rescue them."

"Not just them, not just their lives or race. They are doomed. I can't reverse that, but I can help people remember their way of life, their physical beauty, their manners, their civilization, before ours destroys it. My palette is not going to leave these people harassed and chased, bleeding and dying—and forgotten!"

Goodnough and Meribah rolled up the drawings and paintings without saying a word and put them back into the tin tubes.

One morning Goodnough looked out of the tent. The ground was silvered with hoarfrost and morning light.

"The week of the fig tree!"

"What?" Meribah asked, turning to him. In spite of the chill and her hunger, she felt a warm twinge of excitement.

"My father had the only fig tree in the county. It had come from Italy with his mother." Meribah knew that figs were fruit, but she was not sure what kind. It didn't seem to matter. She was set to enjoy this story. There was no breakfast. This would be it. "And," Goodnough continued, "we would bury it every fall."

"Bury it!" Will said. "Prop me up, Meribah. I want to hear this one."

"Sure, you have to bury a fig tree for the winter—to protect it from the cold. And just like clockwork, within the week after it was buried, there would be a frost like this one."

"Goodness! What a bother, to bury a tree!" Meribah said.

"You wouldn't say that if you had ever tasted a fig. We'd have a big celebration every year when we buried the tree. It sounds odd, but it was almost like a funeral and a birthday all at once. We were sad to see it vanish for the winter. No more shade, no more sweet figs fresh from the limb. But there was the promise of next summer and the long winter of anticipation to sharpen our taste."

"What was the celebration? How did thou celebrate?" Meribah asked.

Goodnough's eyes became even livelier as he described in vivid detail the two celebrations in winter and spring for burying and digging up the tree—the dancing, the songs, the bread and ham spread thickly with the preserves from the previous summer's figs, the sweet fig tarts, the wine. "It was the only time of the year, other than Christmas, that the children got to drink wine."

"I would never have taken thee for Italian, George," Will said.

"Just one-quarter."

"I'll call thee Goodnoli from now on," Will joked. He paused and looked at Goodnough with new seriousness. "Tell me something, does thou remember any of those songs or dances? I've heard of an Italian one called a tarantula or something?"

"A tarantella." Goodnough laughed. "I might recall a few steps."

216

"Well, come show us!"

"Oh, yes, do!" cried Meribah.

"All right!" Because of his height he had to slouch a bit in the tent. He began to hum a lively fast tune. His legs, stiff from the cold, quickly limbered up, and soon he was spinning about the tent, and everything seemed caught in the whirl of Goodnough's energy. "Come on, Meribah, dance with me!" The swirling eddies of the dance lapped at her feet.

"Go on! Thou can do it! Dance! Dance!" her father urged.

There was no hesitation this time. For a split second she remembered the little girl on the prairie, so long ago, astonished by the shape of a song on her lips but no sound, as she had watched the Whitings dance. Now she hitched up her beaver leggings. As Goodnough surged by, she was swept into the wild current. Will's fever-bright eyes shone with a new kind of warmth and peace. For a few bright swirling moments, the desperately sick man seemed radiant with a sense of well-being. His eyes had no questions, and at last there was no hunger, no fear, no pain. There was only a dance and these two mad beings flying about the tent. He caught Meribah's hat with his good hand as it came sailing off her head. Her blond hair, loosed from the knot, flew like licks of pale fire about her head.

November 11, 1849
The camp between the Mill
and Deer creeks

23

THE DAY OF THE SQUIRREL

Edgar Perkins never came back. By the end of that first week the little meat that they had was gone, and meals were reduced to boiled bones and tea. Goodnough hunted for the few small animals that remained at this time of year, but winter game was scarce. Their situation grew clearly more desperate with each passing day. They ceased to talk of when Perkins might return, and no one said "if." They were reluctant even to think that Perkins could have abandoned them. Meribah and Will felt that they could not raise the subject because Perkins had been Goodnough's close friend from Washington. For them to raise questions about Perkins was to speculate on the worth of a friendship. It would be unfitting for Meribah and Will to share such speculation with Goodnough. Meribah knew this. Will knew it, and Goodnough knew it. So for many days the name Edgar Perkins was never mentioned. There was a tacit acknowledgment that it was Goodnough's place to speak first about his friend. He did on the twenty-first day after Perkins's departure.

"They're gone," he said. His eyes had turned icy blue, and around his mouth there were harsh lines that Meribah had never seen before. An unspeakable fear began to spread like poison in the air of the tent.

"What's gone?" Meribah whispered.

"My heavy boots."

"What do you mean?" she asked, although she knew the answer.

"Perkins stole them. He stole them the morning he left. When he came in here to say good-bye. When he asked about the buffalo robe, remember?"

"Yes, but you were here. How could he have?"

"Yes, and remember, I walked out with him. But he came back in. Do you remember that, Meribah? He said he had left his pack—which he had."

"Yes." Meribah gave up concealing the tremble in her voice.

"He also left with my boots. They were stashed in that pile there." Goodnough pointed a shaking finger at the heap of equipment piled around the corner tent stake.

She did not remember the boots being there, but every other detail of that morning came back with clarity. It was as if each moment was a framed picture illuminated now by the harsh facts of their fate: Perkins entering the first time, talking jovially with Goodnough while his eyes swept the tent, the eyes suddenly fastening on the pile of equipment by the pole as if trying to sort out the jumbled heap, then almost self-consciously shifting his focus to her and her father. "Are they asleep?" "Most likely. You asleep, Meribah?" The words, the scene, flooded her mind. Crystalline and precise, the images rose—every gesture, every inflection. She saw Perkins leave, reenter, quip about being back so soon. "Sleep on!" he had said as he bent over to get his pack, open it, rummage through it, take something out, put something in. She saw it all now as if in a dream.

There was no more guessing or silent speculation. Edgar Perkins had abandoned them to starve. As if to seal their fate, a first winter blizzard swept in that evening. By the next morning there would be nearly four feet of snow. They would be cut off, locked in and starving in the glistening whiteness of the mountains.

The last of the emigrants had straggled through almost a week before the blizzard. They had shared the last of their flour and jerked meat with the threesome. Nothing moved now in the mountains. It was a trackless world, white and silent. In a mirror of starvation, they watched one another's faces become thinner. Pieces of hide were cut into strips, toasted, scraped, and boiled to the consistency of glue. Marrowless bones, already boiled and scraped, were roasted and eaten. Leather tying thongs were boiled too and chewed endlessly. They ate the sperm candles, and both Meribah and Goodnough nearly knocked each other down when they pounced on two field mice that had crept into the tent.

A sunbeam stole through a slit in the tent and onto Meribah's lap. She played with it for a few minutes to distract herself from the gnawing in her stomach. Goodnough was outside probing through the snow for animal carcasses when she heard the rifle crack. She jumped up, spilling the beam from her lap. Had he found game? "Pa!" she whispered, more to herself than Will. Then there was a whoop of joy. Goodnough came jackknifing through the heavy white blanket outside, sending up tiny soft explosions of snow. Bright drops of blood stained the snow as he held aloft a fat old winter squirrel!

24

AFTER THE SQUIRREL

He refused to take the reserve parcel of squirrel meat. They had not said good-bye. There had been no parting smoke or draining of brandy bottles. An hour and a half after he had left, Meribah lifted the tent flap and looked at the snowshoe tracks that disappeared into the woods, and she knew she was alone again with her father.

Goodnough had decided to break out of the mountains for help. They had arrived at the decision the morning after the squirrel dinner. In Meribah's mind, everything that happened was either before the squirrel or after the squirrel. There could not be a before-Goodnough and an after-Goodnough in time. It was unthinkable. Fortified by the squirrel meat, Goodnough had raised the possibility of his going for help. He thought he could make it. The weather promised to be clear for at least two days. He thought that he could get below the heavy snow line by then. That had been four days ago, five days since the squirrel. She chewed a little piece now from the parcel and looked at her father. What had happened? He had been so good the day after the squirrel. He really had shown improvement. But then the smell had come back. With its sweet rotting pungency, it had awakened her. She watched. His breath came in a low rasp like wind through a distant canyon. His chest heaved. She had given him a triple-strength dose of the narcotic tea. Earlier he had whispered something about seeds and dancing, but now he slept in some thick, dreamless world. As Meribah watched him, she tried to think how to shore herself against

221

this coming loss. This man and she, they had shared so much. They had left their family, a family that had shattered and lay behind them in their memory like shards of broken crockery. They had gathered together what fragments remained of their own lives, of themselves, and set out, not exactly to mend, but to see if a part in itself could have a wholeness, could become complete in some way. They had traveled across a continent, away from their safe valley of April to these snow-locked mountains of November. She had parted with so much already. Whatever had been left to them had been wrung out by deserts and canyons and mountains. The land ate at their wagon, sucked life from their animals, twisted those around them into wreckages of human spirit. She had had a sister who made the stillest part of the night a warm and cozy place to be. She had made a friend who was so different that their friendship was as unlikely as corn and violets growing side by side in a field.

She moved closer to her father's pallet, where he lay festering, his breathing a thin whistle. She rested her cheek lightly against his shoulder. This was her father, who had been shunned and berated and told not to father or farm. This was her father, who had been the sky in low-ceilinged rooms, the flicker in the long Amish night, the cloud in its harshest light, the mountain just beyond the valley. This father had dissolved her fears in the immensity of the prairie, stayed her on the sides of mountains, spelled her in the desert, and helped her to walk the hollow square to a friend. Now he lay dying. What had become imaginable for Meribah four months earlier in the Rattlesnake Mountains was now familiar. There was no slyness or design. Death was a patient host in the tent.

There were no gestures of farewell, no cries or complaints. Indeed, there seemed to be a consent between Will Simon and death. He left cleanly. Hours earlier he had spoken of seeds and tarantellas, and those were his last words.

"Dying was horrible, but death is not"—Meribah understood Serena's words now. She sat beside the body of her father through the night. She had washed his hand. There was no more festering. The smell had vanished. The lines of pain graven in his face had dissolved. He became young looking again, and Meribah, sitting quietly by his side, tried to imagine him as she could never have known him, when he was a small boy. She could imagine that there was little that was solemn about him then. She could picture him charging joyfully about the small farm of his parents, full of mischief, full of purpose as he tended the special growing plots that were only his. She could see him kneeling to plant a row of seedlings, stirring and tamping the earth. She could imagine him climbing high up a ladder to wind the green bean tendrils through the lattice—easing creation.

Bleak with her loss, she found the sun insulting in the morning, invading the privacy of her sorrow, challenging her claim on grief. How dare the dawn break! Insolent and blaring pink, it was an affront to everything she felt. She remembered when her grandmother had died. What a hubbub there had been in the house that day: the comings and goings of people, the baking, the setting out of foods, the clearing out of things. None of that busyness that came with death made its way into Meribah's snow-locked world.

She sat still and silent through another day and a night. She did not eat or cry. She felt emptiness but no hunger. Late into the second night she finally fell asleep. She dreamed the dream of small bone prints pressed into the earth in a curve of sleep. Cleft by grief, she awoke with a start. In a rage of clarity she realized how alone she truly was.

By morning Meribah had built a sledge from scraps of wagons. She set out, pulling her father's body over the snow, to find a place for him.

25

TO SURVIVE

Three weeks had passed since her father had died. It had seemed longer, she thought, as she snowshoed back. She had to stop every few minutes to adjust her load—the hindquarter of a doe's carcass slung across her back. She had just wrested it from the scavenging birds by practically breaking one of the bird's wings with the butt end of the rifle. I am a rotten shot but have a good swing, she thought grimly. The wraps on her feet had loosened, and snow pushed in around her toes. That was all she needed—frostbite! She was so anxious to get back to the tent and eat the new meat that even if her toes dropped off, she would not stop for it. The thought struck her as funny, and she laughed out loud. As she did, the rifle wobbled and caught in a snowbank, throwing her off balance into the snow. She was fuming as she pulled herself, the rifle, and the doe quarter out of the bank. "Idiot!" she muttered. Probably wind up shooting myself, she thought. How convenient for the birds! Picking up the rifle, she pushed on.

Back in the tent, Meribah relit the fire. Over it she hung a pot half-filled with snow and put in some pieces hacked from the doe. She sat down in front of the fire to wait for the soup and to think. She had to calculate how long she could survive on the pot of soup if she stayed quiet and did not use the energy. Or should she not stay quiet and instead use the energy to hunt? There had been no new snow in the last week. The days had been warm. A bit of a winter thaw had set in before the next storms. She might be able to find some game. The question was, could she shoot it? The rifle and she were an unnatural pairing. She had come to realize that. But whether she could shoot was not the real question. The one she resisted asking with every fiber of her will for the last few weeks was if Goodnough would come back, especially now that things were melting. This was his chance—the thaw, the slot in the Sierra winter between storms. Now Meribah cupped her chin in her hand and succumbed to thinking about the question. Just then she heard outside a crunching noise coming nearer. There was a cough, the tent flap tore open. Meribah screamed.

A savage face was framed in the opening. The black grin of a toothless mouth slowly spread across the face. A shingleman! Meribah thought as he lurched through the opening. He spoke one word. "Alone?" She did not answer. "Alone?" He snarled. She said nothing. He laughed and muttered something. His eyes slid languidly over her. "Pretty uppity for such a scrawny thing."

She knew what was coming next. She saw the glint of the knife. Was this the way it had been for Serena? Fear stole away. A dim rage began to well inside her, and with it came a fierce clarity of thought. Like a razor's edge her anger was honed. There was no sudden movement. She took the rifle in a smooth, almost gentle, gesture. He started for her. Point-blank. Blood exploded before her face. Like sheets of lightning limning a landscape, splattering blood reddened the tent. For a moment everything seemed washed in it. Blood blotted out every object, every sensation. It was after the explosion that sensation returned to her in small pieces. She felt the noise in her ears and heard the crack and then the rumble, as if the sound were fleeing the tent. She felt the small curve of the trigger still pressing into her finger. She put down the gun. There was a bloody mass at her feet, a face half torn away. Bloody scraps were scattered everywhere—the floor, the canvas tent sides. She looked at the stewpot. "Thank God, I put the lid on it," she said softly.

She was in the tent and then she was outside with her

sledge. It didn't take her long to pack the sledge. She tucked
the buffalo robe around the stewpot. She packed the thin tubes
of Goodnough's paintings and her own bag of drawing tools.
She packed what few clothes she had and the coffeepot. She
packed some pieces of hide and Mrs. Grant's herb basket. She
packed her father's tools and the rifle. She packed a knife
and the seeds and a tin of matches. And then she left. She
walked away from the tent and never looked back. She walked
along the silvery rim of the gorge, in and out of the howls of
wolves. She walked until the graying light before dawn, when
she found a small south-facing cave. There she stopped.

January 1, 1850
The cave on the gorge
between the Deer and
Mill creeks

26

MIRACLES

The sun filtered through the snow hole at the top of the cave
entrance. Meribah had been careful to keep it open during
the days of the blizzard to let fresh air in. Bright beams of
sunlight played over her face now. She yawned and rubbed
her eyes. Her first thought was that she had slept late, but a
second thought rushed up and crowded out the first. The
snow had stopped! Two blizzards back to back had blocked
in the cave and Meribah for a week. There could not be a
third one—not so soon, at least. Meribah took her knife and
poked open the snow hole a bit wider in order to see out
better. In the morning sun the white world sparkled like an
immense jewel. To the south and west, bare windswept ridges
rose like ranks of ever breaking waves. The mountain forest
was sheathed in snow and morning light. Pine trees bristled
with a million icy needles. The oak's branching limbs, blazing
in the sunshine, appeared like ice lace in the winter stillness.
The sharp whiteness of the air pierced Meribah's nostrils and
stung her cheeks. She was eager to be out. There was much
to do.

But first the mark. Meribah took a flake of obsidian she had
found near the cave and scratched a line on the wall. It had
been three weeks, not since Goodnough had left—that had
been seven—not since her father had died—that had been
six—but three weeks since she had left the blood-splattered
tent and found this cave. It must be the first of January

according to Meribah's calculations. The first of January, she thought. I'm fifteen. How much longer until a real thaw? Until the last of the storms? She rekindled the fire. There was still some doe soup from the hindquarter she had wrested from the birds. In the few days of grace after she had left the tent and before the blizzards, Meribah had found a cache of acorns hidden in a tree hollow in a tightly woven basket. Meribah would never have thought of eating acorns, but the fact that they were in a basket suggested that someone had thought of them as food. Also in the basket were some camass and tiger lily roots—something else she had never thought of eating.

She experimented carefully in eating these new things. She remembered that Mrs. Grant had told her that many things were poisonous when eaten raw but not when boiled slowly. So after a long cooking time, Meribah would take little bites of the new food. If it tasted all right, she would eat a little more, attentive to any effects. Acorns became her favorite. In the week of captivity she had devised different methods for cooking them. They were very good roasted and eaten whole, which was the quickest and easiest way. But their flavor was best when she simmered them slowly, then ground them into a paste and added some of the sweet birch bark from Mrs. Grant's basket. The inner bark was especially sweet, and this took the edge off the slight bitterness of the acorns.

If acorns tasted so good, she reasoned, there might be other nuts and perhaps even seeds that she could enjoy. So she was eager to get out this morning and look. Besides, she felt odd about taking from the basket. It was so clearly somebody else's supply, and the idea of gathering nuts was more appealing than probing the snow for oxen or mule carcasses from wagon trains. It was as if on that bloody night when she had walked out of the tent, taking only what she needed on the sledge, she had left behind a fundamental way of living. The former resources seemed as fragile and unsustaining as the old dreams. It was all fool's gold. Since she had been eating

228

the acorns and boiled roots, she had felt much less hungry than in the days back in the tent when she had been eating squirrel and mouse. Not once since being in the cave had she experienced that peculiar sensation of feeling her skull become paper thin, almost transparent, as if the cavity were bright with too much light. Indeed, Meribah had often felt as though she were outside her body and peering into her own skull. She had not felt that way in days.

In a grove of oaks she dug down under the snow for the acorns. Some were rotten from the dampness, but she found a number of good ones. Nearby she also found hazelnuts and buckeyes. Spotting a small winter bird pecking at a pine cone for its nuts, she decided to try some of these also. Although autumn was the time for gathering nuts and many of Meribah's appeared rotten, she had found ways of peeling away the bad parts, drying them slowly in the heat of warm ashes, and then roasting them, to make them palatable. She headed now on her snowshoes for a grove of birch trees that she remembered.

The snow was becoming softer and more difficult to walk on. She stopped on a bare crest of hill to take off the hood that she had made from the pelt of the squirrel that Goodnough had shot. The snow had never been able to gather on the windswept crest, but an ice lip had formed on its edge. Meribah looked at the glistening rim of ice. Ice burn, she thought as she saw the patches of scorched grass beneath the ice. She had seen this before on the ridges of the gorge, which were often swept bare of snow by the wind. The ice acted as a magnifying glass to scorch whatever grew beneath it. The nurturing warmth of the sun was turned into a fire by the ice. What was supposed to nourish instead consumed. It was an odd act of nature that fascinated Meribah.

As she stared down at the icy crest, something caught her eye. Bright and red as jewels, they sparkled under the ice on a cushion of scorched grass. "Raspberries!" she cried, and dropped to her knees. She took out her knife and chipped through the ice. Raspberries for her birthday. The berries were plump and ripe. In another hour they would have been burned. There were perhaps three handfuls, which she ate right there. They were not meant to be saved. They were meant to be eaten there, straddling that thin silver rim of ice at the top of a new world. With the sweet juice of a miracle in her mouth, Meribah looked out toward the march of snowy peaks.

That night by her fire she thought about the raspberries. She could still taste their sweetness. No summer berry would ever taste as sweet. She would always have the taste of these, clinging and more real than a memory. She began to think about things that cling. Her father, he was gone, but yet she lived with him, seeing his face, hearing his voice. It was as if he were still there with her, a presence streaming through the minutes of her life like a current in a river. Miracles, Meribah decided, were not meant to be pondered too hard or studied too deeply. They just happened, and one felt blessed by them.

The next morning the sun poured into the cave, and Meribah, feeling warm and still blessed, looked over at her substantial cache of nuts. She decided that perhaps she should replenish the woven basket in the tree hollow. She set out immediately after her breakfast of acorn mush sprinkled with pine nuts, a new flavor that she liked as much as the acorns.

The snow nearly reached the lower edge of the tree hollow, but the basket was still there. Meribah had not realized before how lovely the basket was. Not only was it tightly woven but beautifully shaped into an almost perfect oval with elaborate designs. When she reached into it to put in her acorns, she gasped. The basket had been refilled, and this time there were more camass roots and dried apples! This was meant to be pondered.

There had been evidence of Indians everywhere between Mill Creek and Deer Creek. Especially since she had left the tent to come to the cave, Meribah had seen many signs—obsidian chips from toolmaking, heavy flat stones used for grinding. She had even taken one such stone back to the cave to grind her own acorns. She was surprised not that there were Indians but that a sign had been made to her. As little as Meribah had seen earlier of the California Indians, just after they had crossed Fandango Pass, she realized that these Indians were different from the ones of the plains. She and Goodnough had talked about these differences. The Pitt River Indians, which included the Mill Creeks of this region and those to the north and east where the Pitt River originated, were neither painted nor befeathered. They seemed to blend in with the forests and rugged terrain in which they lived. Unlike the Plains Indians, they sought no contact with the emigrants for either trade or confrontation. Withdrawal seemed to be their pattern. Very rarely was a Mill Creek ever seen by a white person, and yet they seemed to have the run of the gorges, the hills, and the forests between the Mill and Deer creeks. Meribah was stunned now as she stood holding the dried apples and camass roots in her hands. A clear sign had been given, a contact of sorts had been made. What did it mean?

Each day the basket was replenished in a small way—a root, a piece of dried deer meat or salmon, some nuts. Meribah continued to look for her own food sources. She did not feel it right to take everything from the basket or to become reliant solely on her secret benefactor. The notion of total reliance on anyone except herself was becoming an alien one to Meribah. But she did continue to visit the tree hollow almost daily—never, however, catching a glimpse of the basket's replenisher. Between the basket and Meribah's own successes in finding nuts, food was not the problem that it had been several weeks before.

There were, however, two other problems. The first was that of making fire. Meribah had fifteen matches left for starting her fire. She tried hard to keep the coals going, but when she was out gathering, they often died. Meribah knew no other way to start a fire than by striking a match. She had heard that Indians rubbed sticks together until they smoked or sparks flew, but to Meribah this seemed like a magic reserved for Indians alone.

The second problem was loneliness. As Meribah's hunger diminished, her sense of loneliness increased. Questions of survival had occupied most of Meribah's time. As she grew more proficient at the tasks of survival and more a master of her cave-forest world, she had more time to think about things other than keeping her stomach full, her body warm, and the cave safe from predators. Meribah came to realize that simply to survive was not enough for her. There were periods of loneliness, of need for human conversation, that were as acute as hunger pangs. She missed her father, and she missed Goodnough. Their conversations had blazed as warmly as any fire. She yearned to share a thought, a word, a sunset, with another person, not just any person, but one who could respond in kind.

To Meribah's mind, the first problem was more solvable. There had to be another way to start a fire, and she was determined to do it one mid-January morning as she looked out the cave and saw a light drizzle veiling the forest and gorge, for she was sure it would take more than a single match to start her fire. She really had to give the Indian method a try. There was all to gain and no matches to lose. Perhaps it was not so magical. Meribah began rubbing some dry kindling sticks together. After five minutes she had a small pile of finely shredded wood. After ten minutes she had two broken sticks, and she was considerably irritated. What would she do! There had to be a way of starting a fire without matches. She picked up two more sticks. She would change her rhythm and the length of her strokes. She had not rubbed ten strokes before the sticks snapped. "Darn!" she muttered. She looked up out of the cave and grimaced.

It might have been a full fifteen seconds that Meribah

stared out the cave pondering the problem when she realized suddenly that there was another human being staring back. Her first problem was unsolved; her second one, the incredible loneliness that gnawed like hunger, might be over.

The young woman seemed to have grown out of the trees, which she stood among so noiselessly. Her copper skin, her skirt of shredded bark, the dark fur cape, all made her indistinguishable from the textures and colors of the forest. Meribah hardly breathed as she looked upon the Indian woman. She was human, yet she seemed to be of another order. The woman was at the cave opening. Her damp woody fragrance washed over Meribah, and Meribah felt her own heart beat wildly. At last she was not alone! Meribah savored that human face, the first she had seen in almost two months, as a starving person would savor food. The Indian woman's face was bathed in Meribah's joyous gaze.

The woman looked about the cave. Her eyes settled on a flat piece of wood. She picked it up. Then sorting through Meribah's kindling, she picked out a straight stick of cedar. She dropped to her knees by the fire pit and motioned for Meribah to sit beside her. From a small fur pouch the woman took an obsidian knife with a pointed end. She quickly gouged out a socket a quarter of an inch deep in the flat piece of wood. She notched the edge of the socket and cut a shallow channel between it and the edge of the flat piece of wood. Meribah watched with rapt attention as the woman deftly chiseled and refashioned the wood. When she finally finished, she looked up and smiled.

"*Muehli*," she said, pointing to the wood piece. It was the first word that Meribah had heard spoken by another human being since the last day at the tent. The sound was exquisite in her ears—a soft, honeyed oval of a sound. She wished that the woman would say it again. She leaned toward the Indian and tried to repeat it. "*Moo—*"

"*Muehli*," the woman said once more, and tapped the wood.

"*Muehli?*" said Meribah.

The woman smiled and nodded vigorously. Meribah wondered what the word meant. Was it "wood," or did it mean the gouge in the wood? Meribah touched another cedar stick. "*Muehli?*" she asked.

"*K'ui, k'ui.*" The woman shook her head. "*Ishi! Ishi!*" she said, holding the stick.

"*Ishi?*" Meribah was confused.

The woman took the flat piece in her left hand and the stick in her right hand. "*Muehli.*" She spoke the word and held out her left hand toward Meribah. "*Ishi,*" she said, putting the other hand forward. One was called *miehli* and the other was called *ishi*, but they were both wood. Was she referring to the shape of the wood or the kind?

The woman was now tapping her chest lightly and saying the word *muehli* again. She pointed toward Meribah and said the word.

Meribah was still befuddled. Was this the woman's name? Was she supposed to say her name too. "Meribah!" she said, pointing to herself.

The woman now looked perplexed. "*K'ui, k'ui.*" She shook her head again as if to say that this wasn't Meribah's name. "*Muehli!*" She pointed to Meribah. "*Muehli!*" She pointed to herself. Suddenly Meribah understood. "Woman!" she exclaimed. "Yes! You're woman! I'm woman!"

The Indian woman nodded excitedly and now repeated the English word fairly closely and held up the flat piece of wood.

"And *ishi!* Man!" Meribah grasped the stick.

The woman nodded again. Then she put the two pieces together. "*Siwini,*" she said. She pointed to the other pieces of wood in Meribah's kindling pile.

"Wood!" Meribah whispered, and then repeated the woman's word for it: "*Siwini.*"

The woman again nodded and directed Meribah to watch. She took some pine needles from a pouch and then crumbled some bark from a log and placed it in the notch and along the channel of the flat piece as well as on the ground near the channel's runoff. Squatting, she held both ends of the flat piece of wood steady against the ground with her feet. Then she placed the cedar stick upright, the larger end in the socket. Holding the stick between her palms, she began to rub them together back and forth in opposite directions. With each motion the stick rotated to the right and then the left. Her hands bore down, pressing the twirling stick into the socket. Small bits of wood were ground off the sides of the socket, making a wood powder. Meribah's eyes widened as she saw the powder turn brown and begin to smoke. The woman twirled the stick faster, coaxing the smoke from the powder. The powder turned darker and darker, and more smoke came. The accumulating wood powder began to seep down the channel to the edge of the flat piece of wood. The woman worked even faster, keeping the stick in a twirling fury until a tiny spark glowed in the powdered wood. The spark formed just at the notch of the socket, where it traveled down the channel to the tinder at its end on the ground.

"*Auna!*" the woman exclaimed as the first lick of flame consumed the pine needles. She added some more and blew gently on the newborn fire.

It had taken the woman less than ten minutes to make the fire. But Meribah felt as if she had been in some dream world, witnessing a most extraordinary fantasy, for the last half-hour. It had been barely that long since she had looked up from her own pathetic efforts at firemaking and spotted the woman. Since that moment it seemed to Meribah that the entire world had changed. Fire had been made. New words had been spoken. And, most extraordinary of all, she was no longer alone.

27

SALTU

Muehli. The word was smooth as a river stone on Meribah's tongue. She had whispered it softly to herself as she followed the woman through the forest to Wowunupo Mu Tetna. At least that was what Meribah thought the woman had said. She had repeated the name for her slowly four times until the syllables became a series of clear if not understood sounds. Meribah presumed that the woman was taking her to her own settlement and that this was its name: Wowunupo Mu Tetna. The woman, however, had not told Meribah her own name. Meribah had tapped her own chest lightly and said "Meribah," but the Indian woman had only smiled awkwardly and nodded. She had understood, Meribah was sure, that this was her name but had not offered to reveal her own. Perhaps it was not customary to tell one's name to a stranger. However, as she followed the woman in and out of the shafts of sunlight that filtered through the tall pines, the word *muehli* played softly on her tongue, and soon Meribah began to think of the woman as *muehli* and then Meli. The word became a song in her head, a feeling on her lips, a name.

They were at least five hundred feet above the creek on a narrow ledge screened by thick stands of the tallest trees Meribah had yet seen in the forest. They had been walking through the trees for several minutes before Meribah suddenly realized that the ground was clear of snow and that a faintly worn path was underfoot. She looked up and saw that she was in a village. It had appeared as quietly as Meli had first appeared to Meribah—seeming to emerge out of the forest. Until they were almost in the middle of the village, it had remained camouflaged. Meribah stood between two tall trees just by a square pit that was packed with snow. An Indian woman was filling a basket from this reservoir. As Meribah looked to her left, she realized that what she thought had been a tree was actually a small house with a framework of lashed poles and thatched with boughs of bay. Meli did not hurry Meribah but let her study and try to comprehend the village on the shelf.

Except for the woman at the snow pit, Meribah had thought that there was no one else. Soon, however, she became aware of other figures moving down the narrow connecting paths, emerging from buildings that she had first thought to be brush or trees. A smoky mist rose from a low thicket of brush to her right. Meribah at first thought it to be an old fire extinguished by the morning drizzle. When a woman carrying a child walked out of a doorway, she realized that it was a house sunk in a slight hollow, covered over with a brush roof. The roof not only provided weather protection but diffused the smoke so there were no telltale blue curls to rise and mark the settlement. Even in the village proper, trees remained, and space was not entirely cleared or level for structures. There was no discernible pattern to the settlement's layout. Trees and houses intermingled, with only the dimmest of paths connecting them. She followed Meli along a meandering trail past a larger substantial building that was an *A*-shaped bark-lashed structure, its top thatched with laurel. Two men had just walked out. Just beyond this building, by a sprawling oak tree, was another smaller structure made entirely of driftwood from the creek and covered with an old wagon canvas that appeared scorched. Meribah stopped to look. It was a fascinating scramble of twisted, odd-shaped pieces of wood that were stacked and packed higgledy-piggledy into a curious shape of a house.

"*Charqui,*" Meli said.

But Meribah did not understand. From another small house an old man came who was twirling what appeared to be a newly shafted arrow. Meribah had begun to recognize a conical structure banked with dirt as being most common, and guessed that these were single-family dwellings. Meli now stopped in front of one and motioned for Meribah to wait. She then disappeared into the bark-sheathed house. A minute later she emerged with a young man and a small boy perhaps three years old. The man did not bow, shake her hand, or even look at her directly, yet Meribah felt acknowledged. "*Saltu.*" That was what she thought Meli said when she presented Meribah to her husband and boy. Inside there was an old man and an old woman. The woman stroked a sleeping child on a mat next to her. The word again: "*Saltu.*" It could not be the young husband's name, or the child's. The word could only name one person, Meribah realized suddenly —herself! But why *Saltu?* She had told Meli her name. She knew the woman had understood her, but she had chosen to call her something else. Was it a name, though, or was it a word for a category of things? Meribah wondered. It did not matter for long, for whenever Meli spoke the word, she said it with a quiet respect that Meribah could not help but respond to. It felt so good to be called again, even if it was not by her true name.

So Meribah became Saltu, and the woman who found her was Meli. They had named each other, and Meli seemed to accept her new name as much as Meribah did Saltu. It was not long before Meribah realized that these Indians rarely used names as a form of address anyhow. Names seemed to remain an inner part of one's identity, private and inviolate. One never spoke one's own name, as Meribah had done that first day with Meli.

Most likely, Meribah guessed, Saltu meant "different." From the very beginning she had heard others refer to her that way. Perhaps it meant white or white woman. But there was nothing derogatory implied as there had been in the past when people like the woman so long ago in St. Louis had called her "pee-culiar" and stared right at her. Nobody stared here or stole a glance, at least as far as Meribah could tell. She saw that men and women never looked directly at one another unless they were married to each other. This applied to brothers and sisters, once they were grown, as well as to fathers-in-law and daughters-in-law and to mothers-in-law and sons-in-law. Meli never looked at her husband's father.

They took Meribah in. They shared their hearth, their bark lodge, the last of their winter provisions, which were stored in the beautifully woven baskets. For Meribah those first minutes in the conical lodge became linked in some odd warp of time and space to other minutes in another time and dwelling. The damp wood smells of the fire filled the bark lodge, and once again Meribah felt suddenly at rest. There was repose. There was balance. The conical bark dwelling wrapped the people in its woody pungency, encircling them but never enclosing them.

In the middle of the lodge was a circular pit three or four feet deep and ten or twelve feet across. Inside the pit was the fireplace. Along the pit walls stood the exquisite baskets of various shapes and sizes. There were also ladles and stirrers and paddles and tongs, fashioned from wood and bone, hanging on the walls. It was within the pit that the rest of the family was sitting when Meribah first entered. The floor of the pit was lined with tule mats, as were its walls. A stone ledge encircled the pit. More baskets, fur clothing and blankets, tools, and hunting gear were hung on the walls or were stored on top of the ledge. Beyond the ledge, at ground level, was a low entryway, but inside the pit there was another passageway. A notched ladder post went from the pit and out through the smoke hole at the top. This was the way Meli had entered the lodge and come out again with her husband. This was the way that Meribah had first entered the lodge, and she had first heard herself called Saltu while one foot was still on the ladder and the other just touching the pit floor.

Several weeks after Meribah arrived in Wowunupo Mu Tetna, it began to snow—the last blizzard of the Sierra winter. Although it was the last strike of winter, it was the most savage. For six days they were confined to the lodge, and for six days Meribah observed in these close quarters as the family cooked, repaired baskets, wove ropes from milkweed fiber, sewed quivers and clothes, knapped flint into arrows and spear points. They told stories during the long nights. The old man, who could sit motionless for hours on end, was also capable of recounting an animal adventure with a few words and fluid hand gestures that were as vivid as pictures. Although by now Meribah understood a few of the words, she could barely follow the story. But soon, within the context of the old man's gestures, facial expressions, and intonations, more words acquired meaning for her. One was *tetna*, which Meribah came to learn meant "grizzly bear." As Meribah listened to the family speak during the long six days and as her ear grew even more attuned to the sounds, she also began to realize that a man's pronunciation of certain words differed from a woman's. It was almost as if there were two languages—one for men and one for women. The word for grizzly bear, when spoken by the old man, was pronounced *t'en'na*. After hearing Meli say, "*t'et*," and point to the fur pelt on which she and her children were sitting, Meribah realized that this word too meant "grizzly bear." It was confounding, but not as disturbing as Meribah once might have thought. Mrs. Grant had been right—words were not the only means of communicating, and by observing Meli's family carefully, a new comprehension of these people's ways began to open up for Meribah.

When the old man or Meli's husband chipped away at their pieces of obsidian and flint, the flakes were contained on a small grass work cloth. When Meli and her mother-in-law ground acorns or made gruel or mush cakes, the task was accomplished with a minimum of mess and utensils in the smallest amount of space. Similarly, when they worked with skins and hides, sewing them or preparing them to be sewn, the bone needles, awls, and scrapers, along with the sinew and gut string, were unrolled from their neat little packet. Each tool, no matter how briefly used, was restored to its original position so that the scraping, boring, and sewing were carried out in an almost rhythmic sequence. It was not mere orderliness, however—Meribah had come from the most stringently ordered household imaginable. This was different. There was a kind of pleasure in the arrangement of things in this Indian lodge. It was not order for the sake of order but order in service to a beauty that was a part of living.

In the small bundle that Meribah had carried with her from the cave, she had packed a few drawing materials. During the blizzard she began to draw pictures of the tools contained within the lodge. The perspective was close up, but she did not attempt the precise rendering of every dot and grain of texture as she had in those oddly lifeless drawings made when they were lost in the Wind River Mountains. These showed shape and volume. If she drew a bone scraper, the sharpness was there, understood and existing in tension against the buckskin hide on which it lay. The drawing of a grinding stone, with acorns set atop it, suggested the gritty sound about to happen. In still another drawing, the pressure of hands twirling the fire drill was felt, and the spark, although not yet aglow, was expected. Meli and her family were delighted with Meribah's drawings, and she could have done them no greater honor than to draw for them the tools of their lives—their instruments for living. Portraits, like revealed names, would have been unthinkable.

The storm finally stopped. The storage baskets in the bark lodge were nearly empty, the dried salmon meat gone, the dried deer meat almost finished. Meribah and Meli, her husband, boys, and in-laws climbed out of the lodge into the pale light of a March afternoon. Other families began to emerge from their conical lodges. Although she had been there just a few weeks before the blizzard started, Meribah thought that the Indians—the *Yana* was Meli's word—appeared much thinner than before the blizzard. They had a winter-lean look about them. Meribah had noticed the very first day in Wowunupo that their faces had more rounded contours than the Plains Indians', with their craggy, aquiline profiles. On this particular afternoon Meribah saw hollows in their cheeks and new angles in their jaws. It had, however, been the last blizzard. Meli told Meribah in words and signs that winter was finished, that a new time was coming. She made lovely motions with her hands. They became fish streaming up a creek. The light danced in Meli's eyes. Her little boys ran in quiet merriment around her skirt, ducking in and out of its folds, like minnows in a brook.

The snow from the blizzard melted so fast that one would have thought the sun had shone all night. One morning, there was an excitement in the bark lodge earlier than usual, long before dawn, as the first of the big winds blew down from the mountains, announcing the end of the snow moons and a new beginning. The smell of renewal seeped through the bark of the lodge and filled the air inside. The next day the warm rains began. Almost overnight there was a miraculous greening of everything. New clover covered the hills and meadows and rocks. The winter-bound earth had finally unlocked. The streams and creeks swelled with the rush of spring water. From the sea came the salmon. In silver leaps they made their way upstream. The men speared and netted the fish. Meli and Meribah and the other woman gathered basketfuls of new clover. The deer ran again, and there was fresh meat for stews and soups afloat with spring greens. There were bulbs and fiddlehead ferns and tender shoots to eat. Meli and Meribah and the boys often sat down on the ground to eat the early sprouts and greens that grew up around them.

Meribah did not spend all of her time in the village with Meli's family. Some nights and days she stayed at the old cave by herself, drawing, experimenting in toolmaking, being alone —but not necessarily lonely. Meli understood, and Meribah realized that the gentle Yana would never be alarmed by another's need to be alone. And this was at times a need for Meribah. Besides, she liked the cave. It had sheltered her during days of incredible anguish and hunger. In a way she felt that some part, some essence, of the cave had become a part of her and that she in turn had given something to the cave. They shared a spirit.

Most of the time, however, Meribah stayed at Wowunupo. Spring was a festive, social time in the village. There were feasts of thanksgiving, with dancing and singing long into the night to celebrate the release from hunger, from winter. There were wonderful new foods—puddings made from pounded salmon bones and spring greens, whole baked salmon, tender vegetable stews of wild asparagus, mushrooms, onions, salads of dandelion leaves and wild chives. Roasted roots like anise and tiger lily were served up with deer meat. Even the mosses that grew in the gorge found their way into the stews and soups.

Meribah sat cradling Meli's younger son, Yuno, in her arms and watched the dancing while rocking back and forth to the cadences of the singing and chanting. She was Saltu, she thought—"other," "different." But even apart, she did not feel estranged. And though she was not Yana and never could be, the Yana rhythms, their cadences, their ordered beauty, had touched her deeply, touched some core within her. Core—it was an odd word. Some core within her. She remembered so long ago, back in St. Jo, her agonies over the "particles of doubt" within her, the ones that had bitten like grains of sand. They seemed quite opposite—core and sand grains. If one imagined a drawing of one's insides, she mused, could there be both at the same time—a core and doubts? It must be so. She still had her doubts. They just were not the same ones—at least, the old ones no longer dug at her. What difference did it make if one were Amish? Or what was it

that the Billingses were—Episcopalians? Or Meribah? Or
Saltu? Or Yana? She only knew that no matter what her
name was, these people had touched her, touched something
that was so much a part of her it needed no name. She looked
down at the child in her arms. The little copper moon of a face
was tilted up toward her own. A lullaby came to her.

> "Hush, little baby, don't say a word
> Mama's going to buy you a mockingbird.
> And if that mockingbird don't sing
> Mama's going to make you a little birch swing. . . ."

Within the thrumming cadences of the spring dance, Meribah's body rocked to her own rhythm. Sometimes she stopped
her singing and let the Yana rhythms lap over her and swirl
about her like eddies of the Deer Creek.

Strong in the water, Meribah swam long, powerful strokes upstream. She stopped at Hand Rock, a rock she had so named
because a million years of rushing water had worn a perfect
curve in it for her hand and she could rest and feel the lively
swirling waters around her. Meribah loved this lively, mad,
raucous creek. Letting go of the rock, she caught the surge
again, joined the current. She felt it stream under her. It was
almost as though she were another strand in it. She felt the
silvery brush of salmon swimming between her legs. She
felt! She felt! Meribah! Saltu! Ribah! Felt! The crystalline
gray eyes! The meaning burst upon her like an exploding
star. Stunned, she swam out of the current and reached for an
overhanging alder branch. That had been the color that had
tantalized her in the bleached earth of the North Platte country. The crystalline gray, the clear early gray of the world
just before dawn, just before lighting when the sun is
trusted—that gray she could not name. "Mother," she whispered. And holding the low arch of alder, Meribah remembered a time long ago and far back, a time of warmth, of

244

fullness, of holding and calm and trust and light, of a voice singing "Ribah" like the softest lullaby. All this she remembered in the chill swirling waters of Deer Creek. She held tight to the branch as the current pulled.

28

TO LIVE

The figures blended so well with the rock wall that he had not even noticed them at first. He was looking across from the other side of the canyon and began to perceive a light scaling motion on the rock surface. The figures twirled and slid and paused in a silent dance suspended against the sheer wall. He became fascinated by the filigree of motion being inscribed on the canyon face as the two figures, one deeply copper, the other much lighter, lowered themselves by ropes down the perpendicular face of the canyon toward the creek.

The light figure—it was Meribah! He knew it was she as soon as her feet touched the ground. Watching them descend the rock face, he had become so involved with the intertwinings of the dark and light figures that he had not really perceived them as people. They were as inseparable as the fibers of spun wool. Somewhere deep inside he might have had a glimmering that it could be her, but he dared not believe it after what he had seen at the tent.

Now as Goodnough lurched down the back side of the gorge on his crutch, his entire body seemed to shake with the wild pumping of his heart. The chaparral was dense and scratchy. He cut through it with his knife and swatted at it with the crutch. Small rocks slid in noisy cascades, and wood crackled like fire as he plunged and tore his way toward the creek. When at last he did arrive, there was no sign of her. He stared across the creek to the very spot where she had touched ground just minutes before. His body sagged on the crutch as he looked across at the rock wall. The memory of the dark and light against its face washed away like watercolors.

"Goodnough?"

He spun around. His eyes widened in disbelief. She had simply appeared out of the screen of alders. It was as if she had materialized from the very bark of the trees. She wore a tunic of shirred bark and grass. She had turned honey-colored with a band of dark freckles across her nose. Her hair was wet and plastered to her finely shaped head. A wet alder leaf lay in the hollow of her collarbone.

Back in the cave, she listened quietly to Goodnough. He had arrived at the Davis Ranch "chopped and frozen" in his own words. He had lost all the toes on his left foot and two on his right. They wanted to amputate more of his foot, but he wouldn't let them. "But I still have all my fingers!" he said cheerfully, spreading both hands in the gold light that filled the cave.

"And I still have your drawings, all of them!" Meribah got up from the buffalo robe and fetched the tubes.

"Good Lord, Meribah! How did you ever think to take them after that night at the tent?"

"It seemed important," Meribah said quietly.

Goodnough looked at her a long time. "You never doubted, did you, that I'd come back."

"I don't think so. No, I guess I never did. I figured something must have happened."

"Well, you certainly survived." He noticed a slight knot form between her brows as he spoke. "Well, you did survive!" he said again.

"Yes, I did. But it was not just surviving."

"What do you mean?"

"I don't know myself." Meribah laughed gently. "It's something I've been thinking about a lot. It's difficult to explain. It has to do with a way of living, not just living."

"It has to do with the Mill Creeks?" Goodnough was quick to realize that.

"Yes, but don't call them Mill Creeks. They're all called Yana, and this group in this part is called Yahi."

"I won't pretend to understand all this, but I won't pretend either to think that it can be explained."

Meribah nodded appreciatively.

On the third day after Goodnough's arrival, he was desperate to understand something Meribah was saying. "What?" he asked incredulously.

"I'm not going down to the Davis Ranch with you. Not the Davis Ranch or the valley."

Goodnough had just asked Meribah if she had brought his mapping instruments from the tent, as he intended to triangulate the distance between where they were now and the Davis Ranch on their way out.

"Well, what are you planning to do?"

Meribah bit her lip and looked down.

"Are you planning on staying here with the Yahi forever? I mean, that is just . . . just foolishness!"

"It is not foolishness," Meribah said firmly. "But I'm not planning on staying here."

"Well, where are you going if you're not staying here and not going into the valley? The choices seem rather limited."

"Oh, no, they're not!" Meribah's eyes were bright with excitement.

"Then are you going home, Meribah?"

"No. Not exactly. Not to Holly Springs. I'm . . . I'm going to a place . . . It's very difficult to explain all this, Goodnough!" Meribah stammered.

"Well, try!" Goodnough was beside himself with agitation.

Meribah took a deep breath and began again. "It is a place that I've been to, and it is a place that I know is really my home. Its name is the Valley of La Fontenelle. It is a place where I can grow things, where I can put something in the ground and make something grow out of it."

"It's your place," Goodnough said with a trace of frustration.

248

"No! No! Not my place at all! Just a place where I can be."
He looked down at his foot.

Meribah sighed. "You can't walk much on it, can you? Does it hurt all the time?"

"It's not my foot, Meribah. Yes, it hurts, but that is not why I can't go with you." He looked up at her, his eyes steady, true. "I cannot go with you *now*," he added softly.

"And now is when I must go."

"I know that."

They were silent. The tension and frustration of the past few days melted. Goodnough and Meribah understood each other at last.

"But can you survive?" Goodnough asked.

"Can I survive?" Meribah said, smiling. "I can do better than that. I can live!"

29

ANOTHER VALLEY

He stood on a bare crest of hill and watched her descend the
east slope. He noticed the muscled grace of her movement as
she quickly traversed the steep slope with her backpack. She
walked with an easy balance, a confidence in her reflexes.
Meli's family had said good-bye to her on the edge of the Mill
Creek canyon, but Goodnough felt compelled to hobble up to
this last ridge. He knelt down to rest his maimed feet on the
seared grass, which had never greened. He took a telescope
from a pouch that contained his mapping instruments and held
the diminishing figure in the sights. When he could no longer
hold her steady in the crosshairs, he put the telescope down
and lightly touched the two pieces of paper folded and safe
in his back pocket. One contained the compass bearings for a
glen deep in the Valley of La Fontenelle, and the other was a
sealed letter addressed to Constance Simon, Holly Springs,
Pennsylvania.

Goodnough looked in the direction where Meribah was head-
ing. He could barely see her now. He slid the scope into his
pouch. His hands touched the dividers and the compass. His
tools suddenly felt heavy in the pouch. He had worked for the
government for ten years mapping and surveying, reducing
the land, its mountains, its rivers, to the conceivable, the meas-
urable. He was a cartographer—one of the best, they said. He
had been educated and trained as one. He knew trigonometry,
calculus. He knew how to triangulate his way across a country, around a globe, and yet in these last few weeks with Meribah, he had begun to doubt it all. In her extraordinary pres-

250

ence, as he explained to her how to take compass bearings and do certain calculations, he had felt smart but not wise. He knew many things, but she knew something else. As a cartographer he knew the land, but she knew nature. He drew boundaries. She didn't. He measured. She invented.

On that burned crest, Goodnough realized that Meribah Simon had mapped something besides the land. She had mapped herself. He ran his hand over the dry stubble of grass. There were some bare patches where the grass would never grow and just below some scorched berry vines. He stared at it for a minute, thinking about this odd paradox of nature. Then he thought about another paradox—the surveying tools in his pouch. They would be little help to him now, not with the distance he had to map, he thought. He ran his hands over the bare ground once more. "Ice burn!" He spoke the words clearly, got up, and turned toward the other valley, the safer one.

A few short months after Meribah Simon walked out of the
Lassen Foothills, the first series of raids on the Yana began. By
1865, all of the Yana except the small Yahi tribelet had been
eliminated by the white settlers in the valley. In August of
1865, Robert A. Anderson opened fire on a Yahi village. As
some of the Yahi tried to escape, they became targets for his
friend Hiram Good's gun. A final massacre of Yahi was
carried out by four men—J. J. Bogart, Jim Baker, Scott Wil-
liams, and Norman Kingsley—at a site known as the Kingsley
cave. In the blood-soaked years between 1850 and 1872, there
were only twenty recorded deaths of white people killed by
Indians, or one white person for every thirty to fifty Indians
killed. By the early 1900s, there remained only one Yahi—a
man called Ishi. Theodora Kroeber has written a biography of
his life entitled *Ishi: The Last of His Tribe,* and much of the
information concerning Meribah's days with the Yahi is based
on Mrs. Kroeber's knowledge of these people and her persis-
tence in recording their heroic efforts to endure.

The idea of doing a book about the Old West and the Gold Rush had hovered in my mind for years. I was reluctant to begin, however, because I knew I had watched too many television programs and movies in which images of the West blurred together into one handsome cowboy—Hopalong Cassidy, Roy Rogers, and Matt Dillon. From this image I saw that all Western women wore long skirts and sunbonnets, and cooked vittles for the "menfolks," or else they wore riding skirts and brimmed hats like Dale Evans's and rode alongside their husbands. Bad guys rustled cattle, robbed banks, and scowled a lot. The good guys rounded up the bad guys and protected their womenfolk and children. I had no other images than these, and little confidence in my own imagination.

One day I picked up a book by Theodora Kroeber about a man named Ishi, who was the last free Indian in North America. In the beginning of her book, Mrs. Kroeber writes extensively about the Gold Rush and the stream of emigrants that poured into northern California, where Ishi and his people had been living. Ishi was a member of a lost tribe that had been killed off by the white settlers over the years. Mrs. Kroeber's story was the first true Western tale I had ever read. This was not the West of television, nor was the Gold Rush the one written about in my schoolbooks. The bad guys were worse than I had ever imagined, and the greed for gold was pernicious and deadly to the human spirit. People did not just rob, they killed, and on occasion massacred. The conditions of survival were the most arduous imaginable, but there was one emigrant whose spirit was left miraculously intact.

J. Goldsborough Bruff was a draftsman in the Bureau of Topographic Engineers in Washington, D.C. He took a leave from his job to go on the Gold Rush, and led a party of sixty-six men to California. In Mrs. Kroeber's words, "No man was ever less brutalized by his experiences than Bruff." This single observation excited me tremendously. This would be the germ of my story—the challenge of survival, not just of the body, but survival of the spirit as well.

Mrs. Kroeber mentioned that Bruff had kept extensive records and journals which eventually were published in a limited edition. My next task was to find these journals. This was not all that easy, for I live in Boston and the primary source material about the Gold Rush would be more available in California than in Massachusetts. I spent three days calling every rare-book shop I could

253

find, and finally did locate a copy in downtown Boston. "Don't sell it before I get there!" I told the man. The book was almost eight hundred pages long, but it proved to be a gold mine for me, in terms of information and detail. There were other books and materials I discovered later and used, but Bruff's was the most complete. And Bruff himself became a model for George Goodnough.

I had become so fascinated by Bruff that when my husband went on a filmmaking trip to California in the summer of 1978, I accompanied him with our infant son, and insisted that we try to find the site of Bruff's camp. It supposedly had been marked in the country between the Deer and Mill creeks. We were traveling in a camper and soon discovered, to our amazement, that the region between these two creeks was every bit as wild and rugged as it had been in 1849. The only roads were logging ones, rutted and thick with mud and rocks. The forest was so dense that one's sense of direction was hard to maintain. We became lost, stuck, unstuck and confused.

For five hours we bounced over the roughest terrain I had ever encountered. We were totally unprepared for this experience, and when the sun passed the noon mark, I became really fearful of what the night might bring. If it had been just my husband and myself, that would have been one thing, but to be doing this with a 7-month-old baby was terrifying. I was ready to turn back but we didn't know which way to go, and there was no Hopalong Cassidy to point the way. Then suddenly we came to a small clearing—there was a marker indicating that this indeed was the site of Bruff's camp. We had come a long way and yet for me this was just the beginning.

I had bought my copy of Bruff's journals in 1972, but I did not start writing *Beyond the Divide* until 1978. I got stuck in 1979 and put the book away for the rest of that year, and most of 1980, while I wrote *The Night Journey*. I began working on *Beyond the Divide* again toward the end of 1980, finishing it in 1982. I must thank my husband, Christopher Knight, not only for his skillful driving over impassable "roads," but also for his forbearance with me and his cheerful help with the children as I pursued my own version of this Western dream.

—K.L.

TWILIGHT™

WHERE DARKNESS BEGINS...

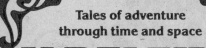

YOUNG Love®
IS A VERY SPECIAL FEELING